MW00697934

Shield of Destiny

(BOOK 1)

Quest for Elderstone

Written by

Charles Carpenter & Ski-ter Jones

Quest for Eldestone

Book One
from the Shield of Destiny series
is a work of fiction. All related names, characters, places and
indicia are trademarks of and
© Charles Carpenter & Ski-ter Jones.

"I know that much can change in a year. I know that not many actually return to the Glass Tower after their Testing," Terridous taunted. "Bringing you out here, fate has a funny way of showing you it cares, boys. Callings never test you when you are ready. And you hardly seem ready, do you?"

"I am moments away from coming back there!" Wren warned.

"You come back, and I'll bend you over my knee for playing at being a soldier," Terridous laughed hysterically. "Imagine if I claimed to be a Magus when I was your age. Ha! I would have been laughed out of every school of the magics that exists. We Magi spend a lifetime learning the magical arts…and more time still perfecting them. You two you pups barely have hair on your loins! Soldiers…ha!"

With that, Terridous sat back in the center of the wagon. His thick gray beard barely stopped wagging in speech the entire time.

Since Wren and Corwyn were heading to their childhood homes in the northland, they were tasked with escorting the old Battle Magus on the final leg of his journey from the southern city of Longshire to the prison camp in the northern city of Tanner's Landing.

Their portion of the journey had them traveling with him for the past few weeks. They were prepared to battle man and beast alike to ensure the old spellcaster's arrival at the prison. Little did they know that their greatest battle would lie in trying to keep the old man's mouth from driving them insane. Corwyn knew that Terridous was just trying to goad them into verbal confrontations. However, the old man's words had merit.

Corwyn was young, to be sure. It was also true that most of what he knew of the world did come from books and lectures. He was well-studied, and he was among the top

10

are. Besides, I would rather have you here than Daneth. Her hair smells like apricots, and her bosoms are plump and ripe. It is very distracting." Wren smiled at Corwyn.

"I like apricots," said Terridous.

"I grow tired of you, old man," Wren fired back.

"My only point," Corwyn said, as he leaned forward and lowered his voice, trying in vain to keep his words from the eavesdropping Terridous, "is that there are other cadets far more capable than I. I just think—"

"Corwyn, you think too much. That's your problem. Your instincts are strong if you would only allow yourself to trust them."

"I was just wondering," Corwyn whispered.

"I still hear you," Terridous called out. "You can whisper all you bloody well want. It's just the birds and us out here. What else do I have to listen to?"

"Can you please just sit in your strongbox and rot?" Corwyn requested.

Terridous moved closer to the bars. "You can't let yourself get all worked up. Life is too short. Ah, but what do boys of 17 winters know of life anyway? All you know is in books and training halls."

"We are 21 winters," Wren replied. "And I have lived far more life than just in the training halls."

"Pardon me," Terridous gave a partial, mocking bow. "I take it all back. At 21 winters, you are virtually ready to retire. Let me guess, Mr. Twenty-one winters, this is the first time you and your jumpy friend here have gone out of the Glass Tower, is it not?" Terridous could see Wren and Corwyn both stiffen their backs slightly at that remark. "Yes, that is it, then. You both are on your Testing. A year away from the Glass Tower to see whether you are cut out for the demands of an Olsyn's life. Isn't that right?"

Wren chuckled. "You know nothing, old man."

moments.

"No," Terridous said, finally. "I don't think I will. You think that just because you young pups carry swords that you can intimidate me? Hah! You are not Oslyn ... yet." That last comment sent Terridous into a fit of mocking laughter that broke down into a wheezing cough.

Wren put a steadying hand on Corwyn's arm. Where Wren was tall, athletic and muscular, Corwyn was slightly shorter, his frame leaner. Both had spent the last five winters in the Glass Tower, training to be Oslyn, the mystical warriors that served to protect all the kingdoms. Each of them had been trained well, honing their bodies and minds through the most intense training subjected to any warrior. Despite their extensive training, Terridous was still able to aggravate and annoy them.

"Relax, Corwyn. He means only to antagonize you."

"Yes, Corwyn," Terridous mocked. "Relax."

Both Wren and Corwyn sat wishing that the old man's mouth had been as firmly bound as were his hands. For although they attempted to ride in silence, Terridous did not.

"Remember our training," Wren said. "We are well-prepared for what has been tasked to us."

"That is easy for you to say," Corwyn was quick to comment. "You are the top cadet in our class. Master Benjen always holds the rest of us to your standard."

"Master Benjen will say anything he deems necessary. He tells me I should be more like Serra Daneth ... a bloody woman! Believe that, if you will."

"I believe it," Corwyn responded. "She is a great fighter. I wonder if it should be she, not I, accompanying you on this charge?" He nodded his head back in reference to Terridous.

"Probably," Wren spoke plainly. "And yet, here you

1: Deadly Reception

Corwyn's chest grew tight with anticipation as he became more alert. He grimaced upon feeling a pull directly on his Heart's Eye.

"What is it, Corwyn?" Wren asked.

"I don't know. I've never felt this before."

"It is the walking dead that lurk in the shadows," Terridous the Bold, the haggard prisoner of the northland, said with a sneer. "They're here to claim their prize." A mocking grin found its way onto his face. Corwyn let out a nervous laugh at the thought of being stalked by supernatural spirits made flesh.

"Well, let them come. They will find no joy in our reception," Wren replied.

The light rain that had recently fallen made the air dense with fog as they traveled deep through the Nortgard Forest. The Nortgard was a beautiful place, vast, majestic, and ancient. Travelers needed to be prepared when moving through the mighty forest. Stories abounded of the hapless losing their way and being claimed by the shadows in the Nortgard, stories that held more truth than fiction. Only the hearty and the wise survived the Nortgard.

"Boys, let me loose. When they come, I can help you," Terridous whispered in an eerie tone.

"Would you please be quiet?" Corwyn asked, as he turned around in the wagon's high front seat to look back into the cage at Terridous.

Shackled to the prison wagon by a heavy chain around his neck, Terridous had his hands bound together firmly with a silver cord. That was to insure that the old Battle Magus did not make any foolish attempts at casting a spell. He looked at Corwyn with mild distain for several long

Fortelling of the Oracle Gywendolyn

She dances through the clouds, the messenger is she
A vision most pure, of thought and deed
She glides on the sky, swift and high
She laughs on the wind, the rain bears her cry
To her terrible goodness, the darkness must hide
And in doing will rouse the Mystical Pride
---- Foretelling of the Oracle Gwendolyn ----
62 F. A. (First Age)

third of his class in terms of skill behind Wren. But he often doubted his own abilities. He knew that all the skill in the world meant very little without experience.

Corwyn felt another unexpected pull through his Heart's Eye. He sat up, reaching out even further with his senses. Again, he felt a strange sensation, almost like his soul was being yanked off to the north, deeper within the forest.

"Wren," Corwyn began. "Did you feel that?"

"What?"

"Your Heart's Eye? Did you feel that … that tug?"

"Here now," Terridous said. "What are we feeling up there?"

Corwyn gestured for Terridous to be silent and turned his attention back to Wren. Wren reached through his Heart's Eye and out into the surroundings.

"I feel nothing," he said. "Why? What's wrong?"

Wren knew better than to dismiss Corwyn's concerns. The Heart's Eye was the place of deepest concentration and focus within a warrior's soul. Being able to tap into it is perhaps the greatest skill the Oslyn possess. It allowed an Oslyn to sense more fully the environment around him, to become one with his surroundings. Doing so sharpened the senses and quickened reactions to a point that could almost be considered magical. It was not magic, of course. Rather, a state of union in which all five senses were heightened to create a virtual sixth sense, a battle sense that turned the Oslyn into a weapon.

Corwyn was reasonably effective at focusing his concentration through his Heart's Eye. He reached out once more for some time longer, but the pull had vanished. "It's no longer there. It was strange. It was as if something was calling to me."

"Sounds like you are getting the bush willies," Terridous said. "Happens on extended treks through the deep

11

woods. And you don't get much deeper woods than the great Nortgard, now do you, boys? Of course, I'm sure you have probably read all about that," Terridous's comment was dripping with sarcasm.

"Well … I am feeling a tug," Terridous said. "I think it's time I be about my business, if you catch my meaning? Nature and all that."

"Your business will have to wait," Wren called, turning his gray-eyed gaze to Terridous. Terridous merely smiled in return, his bushy, gray brows concealing any emotion his eyes might display.

"Suit yourself," Terridous continued. "But we all remember what happened the last time you decided to make me wait."

Corwyn quickly pulled up the reins of the large packhorses.

"This looks like as good a spot as any," he said, as he bolted the wagon's wheel lock in place and leapt to the ground.

"Now, there is a man of action," Terridous laughed. "Let's get on with it, boy."

Corwyn unlocked the heavy padlock attached to the rear door and entered the back of the wagon. Riding on the raised bench at the fore of the wagon, he forgot how badly the old man smelled. Corwyn released the iron sleeve that encased Terridous's hands. It was the silver cord that neutralized any link between Terridous and the magic inherent in the surroundings; the sleeve was just an added measure.

Wren was waiting at the rear of the wagon by the time Corwyn got Terridous to the open cage door. Wren grabbed the old man roughly and yanked him to the ground.

"Come on," Wren said, as he dragged the old man to a thicket just off the roadside, some 20 feet from the wagon.

"Be about it, then. And don't think we will clean anything you decide to get on yourself. Foul old bird."

"Too bad," Terridous called, as he squatted low. "I cooked this one up special for you. Hah!"

Wren backed away and approached Corwyn who was near the side of the wagon. Each stood facing in opposite directions, surveying their prisoner and the forest. Their intense gazes swept through the trees, just as they had been trained to do.

"Another few days at this pace, and we will reach Tanner's Landing," Corwyn projected.

"Good, then we can part ways with this foul little pimple of a man. How I long to be rid of him. Hurry it along, old man!"

Terridous answered back with a gravelly laugh … along with loud flatulence.

"Give him another few moments," Corwyn laughed. "I would rather he leave it all in the forest."

"True."

"So," Wren continued, changing the subject. "Do you really mean to stay in that tiny, nothing, little border town of Silverton?"

"I grew up here in the Nortgard. That little, 'nothing' town is my home. And yes, it is there that I plan to stay."

"Was your home. You have not seen it for five winters."

"The Tower is where I reside," Corwyn stated. "Silverton will always be my home. I long to return." Silverton was where he spent 16 winters of his youth. It gave him the skillsets that had been enhanced at the Glass Tower. Silverton was also where he felt the sting of loss. He lost his mother and father there. He wondered what it truly meant to be home. "I did not have so lavish a sendoff as you did from your home, my friend."

13

"True enough," Wren laughed. "My family could not wait to see me go."

"At least you have a family," Corwyn said softly. "My brother was all I had left."

"Why was he not brought to the tower also?"

"I asked that of Master Benjen," Corwyn stated. "He said Alek had a Heart's Eye that could only see inward, that the tower would distort his fate."

"Ha!" Wren bellowed. "More cryptic nonsense, spoken like a true training master. I say fate is what you make it."

Corwyn smiled. "I thought you might say something like that."

"You see, there's your problem again. Thinking too much."

"That does not seem to be a problem from which you suffer at all then."

Wren laughed loudly. Corwyn could not help but chuckle as well.

"Nicely done, which is the only reason I am leaving your head on your shoulders."

"My head and shoulders, thank you."

After a few moments of laughter, Wren turned to Corwyn.

"What makes you think your brother is still there?"

"Hope," Corwyn replied. "Hope."

"Well, I hope my parents have the hearth fires warm and the ale cold," Wren said. "Then it is off to the east and the Kyldsong Mountains."

"The Great Rift. You really mean to go there?"

"To the place where the magic of the world and the very fabric of time itself were ripped apart? Absolutely!" Wren stated. "That is where we will find adventure. There are creatures unlike any in the Known Kingdoms that constantly emerge from the Rift. That is where an Oslyn can find the best use of his sword, my friend. That is where we will become legend." Wren went off to get Terridous. "Let's move, stinkpot. The light is fading, and I wish to be rid of you as soon as possible."

Corwyn continued to survey the area as Wren threw Terridous back into the wagon and shackled him to the interior.

A sudden jolt shook Corwyn to his core. He doubled over and brought his hands to his knees, steadying himself. Something powerful swept over him. It was that tugging sensation once more. This time, though, it was intense and carried with it something greater. He felt a surge of emotions racing at him through his Heart's Eye, emotions of panic and fear. He could also feel anger buried deep beneath the fright.

"Corwyn!" Wren yelled as he ran over to him, drawing his long sword and taking a protective, defensive stance next to his friend.

"It is that tug. It is calling to me again," Corwyn said. The pull was growing steadily stronger. "Do you not feel it?"

Wren searched out into the forest with his Heart's Eye. "I feel nothing."

Corwyn looked around beyond the road, past the wagon, and deeper into the forest. "There," he pointed, rising to his feet. "I feel it there. Someone needs help."

"How do you know that?" Wren asked.

"I feel it through my Heart's Eye."

"That is impossible." Wren stated. "It does not work that way. Sensing the feelings of others, that is left to the Magi, not the Oslyn."

"You are not an Oslyn yet!" Terridous shouted from the wagon.

"Shut up, old man! Damn you and your ears!" Wren shouted back.

15

Corwyn looked directly in the direction to which he was being pulled. He pointed it out to Wren again. "I do not know how it is I know, Wren. I am being pulled."

"Being pulled—" Terridous began.

"Silence, Terridous!" Wren roared. Amazingly, Terridous grew silent. Wren looked at Corwyn. "Are we Oslyn not taught to follow our Heart's Eye?"

Giving it thought, Corwyn knew he could not dispute Wren's point.

"And what of him?" Corwyn asked, pointing to the wretched old Terridous.

"I will hold fast to him."

"I will return to you as quickly as I can!" Corwyn shouted as he ran off into the forest. The sun was quickly descending in the western sky. The huge trees cast their long shadows across the countryside like dark, spectral fingers.

Within a short while of solid running, Corwyn came across a small path. It was a skinners road. That explained why it was so remote. It was meant for smugglers and other such types to move through the forest quickly and as unseen as possible. Now that he had found a road, it offered him good, level footing. His focus stretched far. He felt a sense of urgency, as if someone desperately needed his assistance.

The road curved with the valley for about a mile before it turned in on itself and ascended in a snakelike manner. The trees, growing thick, were beginning to take back the road here. He left the clear path of the road for the shadowy camouflage of the trees. These people, whoever they were, had used their weapons recently, causing the forest to grow more active. The wind became intense and took on a new scent. It carried to Corwyn's nostrils the smell of blood.

Approaching cautiously, Corwyn drew near a covered wagon. He saw a long object, wrapped in dirty blankets, just to the wagon's side. From his vantage point, he could see two men milling about. Each wore their long, dark hair in braids down their backs and sported padded leather armor. Corwyn was quick to note that each was armed, the larger one with a sword on his hip, the smaller with an axe strapped to his back. He paused for a moment where he would be unseen as something was suddenly thrown out of the back of the wagon.

"Aw, bloody damn! Where is Gall with that water?" Corwyn heard the larger of the men call. "We lost another one."

"It's not the Lyndrian, is it?" the shorter, skinnier framed of the two men asked.

"No," a man called back from within the wagon. "The Lyndrian still lives."

Corwyn winced at seeing a dead body thrown to the ground, limbs extending in a grotesque manner. He took a deep, calming breath as he looked on.

"You see, Merril?" the shorter one asked. "It's not all bad."

"Wrong, Jevin," Merril stated flatly. "It is bad."

"They still pay us for the corpses." Jevin said, rubbing his dirty beard. "We can't be blamed for the hardship of the road. People die."

A third man emerged from the wagon, dragging out a person covered in a coarse, gray cloak. He yanked the thick chain shackled to the wrists to bring the person to the ground. Falling heavily, the person grunted in pain. It was a woman. The third man wrapped the chain around a cargo peg that extended from the wagon's side.

After seeing the cloaked woman, the pull Corwyn had felt intensified. She suddenly looked up in Corwyn's direction. He knew she could not see him in the darkness and shadows of the night, and yet, she stared straight at him. As

17

the third man neared, she quickly lowered her eyes to the ground.

"Don't go thinking you're going to have your way with this one also, Kellis," Merril stated. "That's probably what led to the other two wenches' demise."

The three men had a bawdy laugh at that.

"It's the fever what got them," Kellis said, looking the corpses over. "They enjoyed my attentions just fine; you can be sure of that." He laughed as he looked back at the woman, now the focus of Corwyn's attention. "I'd sooner rip out this one's throat. She nearly scratched my eyes out when I tried to get her out of the wagon. Didn't you, wench?" He drove a boot into the fallen woman's side, knocking out all breath from her. She curled into a ball from the pain.

At that same moment, being led by his Heart's Eye, Corwyn's anger rose as he drew his hand-and-a-half sword, Taryn, from its sheath on his back. The hilt was set with a single stone at its base, a round garnet of deep red, with what seemed like tiny tendrils of white smoke spread throughout. The long, straight edges of the blade could taste blood this night.

Corwyn's increased senses felt someone stealthy approaching. He turned, preparing to engage someone who must be the fourth member of this company. About to pounce, he saw Wren approach with his sword drawn. Wren came to a sudden halt upon seeing Corwyn facing him, sword in hand. Corwyn lowered Taryn to his side as Wren made his way silently next to Corwyn.

"What are you doing here?" Corwyn whispered.

"I could not just leave you to go at it alone, now could I?" Wren replied, as if it were the most logical thing in the world.

"What about Terridous?"

"That smelly old codger is shackled tightly within his

cell," Wren stated. "He's not going anywhere. If the walking dead are out there, let them have him, so far as I am concerned."

Corwyn was about to express his gratitude when another grunt from the woman brought their attention back to the situation at hand. Corwyn and Wren turned to see that the one called Kellis had kicked the woman again.

"They harm women, do they?"

"We have to move now," Corwyn whispered. "Lest that brute kill her."

"Adventure at last," Wren said with a hint of a smile. "It is time they met with the justice of the Oslyn."

They both moved stealthily nearer to the men and the wagon.

"Leave that one be, Kellis," Merril stated. "We need at least one alive, especially the Lyndrian."

Kellis spat on her, rubbing at the scratch marks near his left eye. "She'll live. This one's tough as old leather. Aren't you, sow?" With that last insult, he grabbed the chain and yanked her to her feet, preparing to give her a backhanded slap.

Seeing this, Wren burst out onto the path in front of the men, his sword at mid-guard. Corwyn was at his side in an instant.

"Strike her again, and you will have to answer to me, wretch!" Wren called out.

In an instant, the three men had their weapons drawn. Kellis let the woman fall back to the ground.

"If you put down your weapons and surrender yourself to the Oslyn True, we shall sheath our blades and no harm will befall you as is contracted by spirit," Corwyn announced. That was the Oslyn's ritual verbal guarantee. As a recognized 'order of lawful intent' by most sovereign countries, Oslyn could assist in matters of civil unrest.

Speaking that oath magically bound Corwyn and Wren to its words.

There was a moment of silence as the three men stared down Corwyn and Wren. The men's sudden, uproarious laughter broke the moment. Despite the laughter, Corwyn and Wren were still at the ready.

"He said—" Wren began.

"We heard what he said," Merril chucked.

"We just can't believe he said it," Jevin stated through a grin that was missing several teeth.

"Oslyn, are you?" Kellis continued to laugh, as he and the other two began moving slowly forward. "What would two mighty Oslyn be doing out here in the deep woods?"

"And without a stitch of armor, other than bracers," Jevin chided, referring to Corwyn. "At least your partner there has the good sense to be wearing some padded leather."

"Not that it will help you any," Merril said.

Corwyn unconsciously ran his left hand along the bracer that covered his right forearm. They were only visible because his beige shirt was cut at the elbow. Wren, for his part, was adorned in the padded leather armor his wealthy father gifted him.

"Boy's got some muscle on him. At least that's something," Kellis stated, looking Corwyn up and down. "Too bad. You two are in it now."

The men were steadily approaching. Corwyn's senses were riled.

Wren, shifting his balance from foot to foot, bounced slightly. He seemed to be spoiling for a fight.

"We do not want to hurt you," Corwyn said. "But we will if we must. Just give us the woman, and we will be on our way."

"The thing about Oslyn, boy," Merril said, swinging

his sword in slow arcs, "is that they don't make that pledge before the fighting starts." He smiled, his evil intent evident.

Corwyn cringed in spite of himself. Fool. He had magically bound both Wren and himself from harming these wretched men. Wren looked over at Corwyn with shock. Apparently, he did not realize what had happened either.

"You won't raise your weapons?" Jevin snickered. "Means we get the first shot, nice and clean."

The three were almost upon them. Corwyn could feel the magic of the ritual agreement, staying his sword. They could not raise their weapons until the attackers struck first. That was the only way the ritual compact could be nullified. Unfortunately, that first strike was all these killers would need.

Corwyn and Wren slowly backed away. Quickly reaching under his shirt, Wren removed several small, shiny gray pellets from a little compartment at the front of the leather belt he wore. He threw them to the ground in front of him, just as Kellis loosed his killing stroke. The pellets exploded with a bright flash and produced thick, grey smoke.

Corwyn ducked, just avoiding having Kellis's blade slice off his head. Temporarily blinded, Kellis yelled in shock as he covered his eyes. Corwyn ran into him, lowering his shoulder and slamming it into Kellis's side, knocking him to the ground.

Wren rushed around to the other side of the men as Jevin and Merril swung wildly. Corwyn and Wren reached the fallen woman quickly. They only had a few moments. The effects of the flash pellets would wear off in seconds.

Corwyn unhooked the thick chain from the cargo peg, and Wren tried to help her to her feet. The woman lashed out suddenly, launching a well-placed kick that caught Wren solidly in the abdomen, knocking him off balance.

"Wren!" Corwyn called, as the three assailants

21

emerged from the smoke. The broken cloud cover had cleared substantially, and the moonlight illuminated the night.

"That one's mine!" Kellis yelled, pointing at Corwyn. The three men charged. In an instant, the fight was upon them.

Corwyn and Wren met the attackers' fury head on, their training and instincts taking over. Corwyn intercepted the powerful downward strike of Kellis and shifted swiftly to counter. Kellis, a well-seasoned survivor of hundreds of skirmishes, dodged the blow and struck again. Corwyn countered and nimbly moved to Kellis's side, putting himself close to both the wagon and Jevin's swinging axe. In an instant, Corwyn now had to fend off two attackers.

Wren had his hands full with Merril. The large man was raining down slash after slash, putting Wren completely on the defensive. Every time Wren thought he had an advantage, the killer shifted his body, changing the angle of attack, and kept Wren at bay.

Corwyn continued to fight off both men though one of Kellis's strikes had cut a small slash into his arm just above his bracer. The men seemed surprised that he was as quick and able as he was with a sword.

Corwyn suddenly dropped low beneath a wild, high swing of Jevin's axe and angled to Jevin's side. Corwyn fired a low side kick at Jevin's knee and buckled the short man, placing him temporarily between Corwyn and the highly skilled attacks of Kellis.

"No!" Jevin yelled, as he clutched at his severely damaged knee. For all intents and purposes, he was out of the fight.

Corwyn dove under the wagon just as Kellis brought his blade around to bear, cleaving a downward strike that just missed. Coming out the other side, Corwyn felt the pull of his Heart's Eye yet again. In the heat of the fight, he had not noticed that the woman had run off into the forest.

Wren, forced to back up to the front edge of the wagon, had his hands full with Merril. With the wheel locks on, the upset horse could not move the wagon forward. Wren took advantage of the distracting horse to gain some distance on Merril, but the big man moved steadily ahead, unconcerned about the animal.

Merril raised his sword high just as Corwyn came around the far end of the wagon. Wren blocked the blow as Corwyn turned the corner. Corwyn's presence took Merril's concentration away just enough for Wren to drive a knee into the large man's midsection. As he doubled over, Corwyn fired a kick that caught him in the temple and knocked him unconscious.

"Well met," Wren said.

"And you," Corwyn responded as Kellis came upon them.

With his advantage lost, Kellis began to back away.

"The woman has fled," Corwyn said.

"You sensed her," Wren countered. "Get her before she goes too far. There are more dangers in the Nortgard than just these louts." Wren smiled. "Go."

"No, we finish this."

"Go after her!" Wren shouted.

"Yes," Kellis said to Corwyn. "Bring my prize back to me."

"Quiet, filth!" Wren warned Kellis. "Corwyn, I will take care of this one and join you shortly. Won't take long."

With a small nod of acknowledgment, Corwyn ran off after the woman.

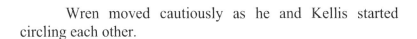

Wren moved cautiously as he and Kellis started circling each other.

"Come, let's end this," Kellis said.

"By all means," Wren snarled.

They engaged each other. Each parried the other's strikes. Jevin was trying to get up to no avail, his knee having been too badly injured. As such, he was able to do nothing but hurl insult after insult at Wren.

Wren knew he had to end the fight soon before the large one regained consciousness. Wren moved quickly, striking again and again. "I have you now, swine," he said as he positioned Kellis with his back to the wagon.

"Do you now?"

Wren sensed his mistake too late. He was struck on the back of the head and fell down the steep grade off the far side of the path, his body rolling to a stop some 50 feet down the embankment.

"Well done, Gall," Kellis smirked.

"What happened?" Gall asked.

"The Lyndrian got away."

"And my leg got broke!" Jevin yelled.

Neither Kellis nor Gall paid Jevin any attention. Merril rubbed his temple and got up to his feet.

"Well, let's go get her back," Kellis said.

Gall looked down at Wren. "What about that one?"

"If he didn't die from the hit, the forest will claim him soon enough," Kellis said. "He's too far down to be of concern now. Merril, let's go. Jevin, get the wagon down to the lower bend, where the ground flattens out. We will meet you there."

"What about my leg?" Jevin yelled in agony.

"If we don't get the girl, you will wish your leg was all you had to worry about." He turned to Merril and Gall. "Let's go."

They set a quick pace and went in the direction of

Corwyn and the woman, Jevin's hurled insults fading away in the distance.

Corwyn had caught up to the woman in short order. She had not gotten too far before collapsing. He found her lying on the forest floor, completely unconscious.

Corwyn moved swiftly and knelt by the woman. Beneath the woman's coarse, gray cloak was nothing more than a collection of ripped tatters, barely concealing her femininity. Laying his hands on her, he reached through his Heart's Eye and delved into her energy. He could sense various injuries. He could also sense strength in this woman's soul as he released his concentration from his Heart's Eye. Oslyn were not healers, but they could sense well enough the physical states of others. She was hurt but could survive with quick attention to her wounds.

Pulling the hood from her face, Corwyn could see she had been punished. The bruising stood out in striking contrast against her ivory skin. When he rolled her head gently to the side, her exposed hair further increased his shock.

Long, totally straight and black as pitch, her hair was fashioned into a long braid on the right side of her head. The braid looped back in on itself and was tied at its point of inception near her scalp. The left half of her head was shaved completely bald. The loop in her hair, half-bald cut, and pale skin marked her as a Lyndrian of the eastern nomadic tribes that hunted on the steppes and plains beyond the Great Rift. It also marked her as a slave.

Corwyn set her head gently down and turned away in anger. He could think of no worse fate than being held as the property of another. Corwyn's senses alerted him to danger. He lifted up the battered woman easily in his arms and took off. He almost wanted to stop and turn around, feeling a pang of guilt at leaving Wren to his fate. That, though, would have defeated the entire purpose of the rescue. He had an unconscious woman in his arms who was being hunted. Like it or not, he had to keep moving.

Even though fatigued, Corwyn set as fast a pace as he could with the weight of the Lyndrian woman upon him. The radiance of the bright moon lit up the valley spread before him in a haunting iridescence. The shrubs and meandering streams of the valley floor would make for quick movement but offered little in the way of protective cover. In the distance, he saw the soft glow of faint torchlight. He did not need sharpened senses to tell him those were his pursuers or that they were gaining on him. Fatigue replaced with the empowering rush of adrenaline, he sprinted across the valley floor. He needed to find a defensible position, and he needed to find it soon.

Having reached the far end of the valley and the relative safety of the thick copses of birch and cedar, Corwyn set the woman down and leaned against a low, under slung branch to catch his breath. Sweat drenching his frame, he looked like he was smoking in the chill air of the mountainous forest. An idea came to him.

"The Weaver's Hut!"

Reaching down, he picked up the woman and set off again. "Let us hope she is still there."

Corwyn carried the woman further up in elevation. The uneven ground became more gravelly, soon turning into a landscape of huge fir trees surrounded by jagged outcroppings of granite. In the shadows of night, Corwyn counted on his keen senses to stay sure-footed.

Through the trees, he saw the flickering of torches. "They're too close." Had he been alone, he would have made his stand long ago. However, the Lyndrian forced him into a protracted escape.

Being led strictly by memory and no small measure of luck, Corwyn took them through a small rift set between two granite formations. Through the rocks, they emerged into a small granite gully and quickly reached the floor. It was perhaps 200 feet in length and 50 or 60 feet wide at its widest point. The granite walls stretched some 40 feet into the sky, completely enclosing the area. Several hardy oak trees had gained purchase in the tough land, their knotted roots extending like swollen veins along the ground.

There, at the far end of the gully was the sight that caused Corwyn's heart to leap. It was still there. The Weaver's Hut, home to one of the Nortgard's most colorful residents—whether she still lived was another matter entirely—and still looked to be in satisfactory condition. A long structure, it wound with the far wall of the gully, having been built to butt up against the granite. Here, he could make his stand.

"Mama Weaver!" Corwyn called as he ran toward the ramshackle hut. It was more a collection of loose crossbeams, stout elk, caribou bones, and leather canvas stretched thereabout than hut. "Mama Weaver, are you there?"

There was no answer. He reached the entrance, which itself was nothing more than a loose tent flap.

Probably for the best that you are not here, Corwyn thought. He pulled back the hut's flap, laid the unconscious woman down inside, and pulled the flap closed. Catching sight of a faint shadow on the granite wall, he immediately dove to one side. A crossbow bolt tore a hole through the hut's leather covering in the very spot he stood only a moment before. He sprang to his feet and drew his sword, Taryn. His attackers barely made a sound as they entered, their torchlight casting dancing shadows along the walls.

Kellis and Merril dropped their torches and drew

their swords.

"You have something that belongs to me," Kellis called out. Corwyn was surprised that he could hear them so clearly at this distance. The granite walls made the acoustics amazing in the gully. Breathing deeply, Corwyn worked at steadying his nerves, seeking the calm focus of his Heart's Eye.

"The woman is not your property," Corwyn responded. Needing cover, Corwyn made his way toward one of the oak trees nearest him.

"She was a slave when we took her!" Merril yelled. "She's less than that now!"

Gall, seeing that Corwyn was trying to get to cover, took aim and fired. The bolt fired true, but Corwyn's quick, snapping blade intercepted it. The bolt shattered with the impact and fell to pieces onto the ground. Corwyn sprinted for cover behind the tree.

"You see," Kellis cautioned Gall, who was already refitting his next bolt. "I told you he was quick."

"Only a moment separates the quick and the dead," Gall replied.

To deflect a bolt was an impressive feat, but to do so at night was astounding. Kellis moved to the left wall, silently signaling for Gall to move up the center.

"I'll get to the girl," Merril whispered softly.

Kellis nodded in confirmation and took the left flank. "Impressive, boy!" Kellis shouted. He closed the distance to Corwyn's covered position. "Or lucky. How many of our bolts do you think you can block? Gall is a very good shot."

Corwyn's blood pumped furiously, his heart close to beating out of his chest. Chancing a quick look from behind the thick trunk, Corwyn saw the men moving out, flanking him on either side. As they got farther from the fallen torches, they melded with the shadows. Even in the moonlight, their positions were well-hidden. To stay where he was would be suicide. He had to take the fight to them. He reached into a small pouch on his belt and pulled out flash pellets.

Corwyn saw Merril quickly trying to make his way to the hut. If Corwyn had any chance to intercept him before he reached the woman, he had to do so now. He launched the pellets to the ground, sprang out from behind the tree, and headed left toward Merril's large form. The smoke filled the gully quickly.

"Argggh!" Gall yelled, clutching his eyes. That would buy Corwyn some time at least.

Corwyn crossed the distance between himself and Merril in three immeasurable bounds, bringing his sword down on Merril with tremendous strength. Along with the momentum of his run, his attack proved overpowering and drove Merril back to slam into the wall with a violent impact.

Corwyn spun away immediately. With Merril temporarily dazed, Corwyn focused his next attack on Gall. If he could disable the crossbow, he might then be able to use the shadows without fear of an aerial attack.

Corwyn launched himself at Gall whose vision was only just clearing. He looked up in time to see Corwyn's foot a moment before it crashed into his nose. The well-placed kick found its mark, shattering his nose and sending Gall crashing to the ground. He dropped his crossbow and tried to stem the blood pouring from his crushed nose.

Kellis, though, had closed the distance to Gall more quickly than Corwyn had anticipated. He came through the smoke and swung his sword just as Corwyn's feet touched the ground. It was all Corwyn could do to block the powerful slash, which sent him reeling backwards. Corwyn tripped over the large roots of the nearby tree and fell on his back. Kellis was on him in an instant, bringing his blade slicing down. Corwyn, right hand on his sword's hilt, left palm on the flat of his blade, deflected the blow wide, kicking at Kellis's midsection as he did so.

The force of the kick, which allowed Corwyn to stagger quickly to his feet, pushed Kellis back. Merril, highly angered at having been hit so hard moments before, immediately set upon Corwyn.

"Time to die, boy!" Merril yelled and slashed at him several times. Corwyn dodged the initial high attacks and sidestepped the lower ones. Moving back, he spun and brought his blade up. Merril took the bait, bringing his sword up to block, but Corwyn shifted his momentum and instead brought his sword slashing down across Merril's exposed abdomen, ripping through the leather armor and tearing deeply into flesh.

Merril howled in agony as he clutched his stomach and fell to the ground, blood streaming through his fingers. Corwyn barely registered what had happened when he suddenly sensed Kellis at his side. He turned, bringing up his sword, and managed to deflect the brunt of Kellis's strike. It was not enough to stop the blade completely, though, and it cut into his lower back. Corwyn fell forward, fiery pain racing through his body. Kellis struck again, this time, slashing at his head.

Injured as he was, Corwyn instinctively blocked, bringing his blade in an arc at Kellis's waist. Kellis sidestepped the attack, but the movement gave Corwyn time to back away.

The smoke was steadily clearing, which did not favor Corwyn. Remembering his training, Corwyn opted for attacking full force. His lower back burned from the slash; running was not an option. If he died, it would be in the defense of the woman, not while running away.

"Come on!" Corwyn yelled, charging back toward

Kellis.

His sudden surge took Kellis off guard for a moment. Corwyn deflected Kellis's sword and spun into very close range, using his whipping momentum to smack Kellis in the head with a powerful spinning back fist. Kellis fell to the ground as Corwyn came out of his spin. While reorienting himself, a powerful blow to the ribs sent Corwyn buckling. He drew his sword in, clutching his side, and staggered backwards. Gall had reentered the fight, a one-handed hammer in his grip.

Gall pressed the attack forward. Corwyn used Taryn to effectively block Gall's incoming attack. However, with his injured ribs causing scorching pain with each breath and his lower back torn open, his single armed defense did not last long. The effort he exerted dazed him, and he could not properly defend Gall's next swing. The hammer itself Corwyn blocked with both his sword and bracer, but the force of it sent him completely off balance to the ground. Suddenly, a kick to the side of his head caused an explosion of pain that clouded his vision.

Trying desperately to regain focus, Corwyn strained and saw that it was Kellis who had kicked him. Kellis had pure fury in his eyes.

"You fight well, boy. I'll give you that," Kellis spat.

Corwyn saw the two men looming above him. He tried to lash out with all of his might, swiping Taryn for all he was worth. The sword hit nothing and was summarily kicked out from his hand by Kellis.

"Now," Kellis said, drawing a wicked dagger and leaning down to Corwyn. "Let's see how well you die."

2: Crag Drannon

The angry sea brought chaos as its huge swells crashed upon the steep rocky cliffs of Crag Drannon. The fortress's mighty walls rose to heights of nearly 60 feet. The keep showed the ravages of war and its dark history. A devastating fire had razed one of its towers to only half the height of its sister. Built to withstand the fury of war, it withstood the attack of every army for the last 1300 years. The ancient fortress, in all its grim power, now stood cold as the whisper of death.

There in the stable yard across from the hayloft, Gascon and Ceiran stepped into the deep, muddy soil. Greeting them were two apprentices of the keep. Hoods pulled low over their faces, they were clad in coarse, dark gray robes.

They gave Gascon and Ceiran one warning, "When seated, do not, for any reason, rise from your chairs. Not until the Master comes." It was the taller, heavier of the two who spoke. During every visit to the keep, Gascon was given that same instruction.

The tall apprentice and his partner seemed rather ill at ease and anxious to be on their way. Neither one looked up much from under their hoods, so Gascon never really got a good look at their faces. That was always the case. He could not really blame them though. If he had to live here, he would not want to look around much either. They barely spoke, but what they did say only added to Gascon and Ceiran's unrest.

"It is never wise to be alone, not here," said the taller of the two, keeping his gaze down.

His tone left no question in Gascon's mind that it was truly unsafe to be alone.

They entered the intact tower and made their way up the winding staircase. Ceiran looked out one of the narrow windows and caught sight of several women being led into a decrepit building on the far side of the courtyard. The last woman, hustled by another grey clad apprentice, glanced up. Her face appeared wane and tired, and her eyes showed nothing but hopelessness. Prodded forward by the apprentice, she disappeared into the building. She felt a clawed hand on her ankle. Her breath caught in her throat. She looked down but saw nothing there.

"Keep moving," the heavy apprentice called down to Ceiran. "Lest you wish to remain here. It is your choice."

With that, he and the other apprentice turned and kept moving. Gascon glared at her in annoyance before continuing on. Ceiran swiftly followed.

"The forces at work here today seem particularly fitful," Gascon mumbled, as he pulled his thick, lavender, fur-lined cloak closer around him. "Forces I will be glad to be far from, and the sooner the better." Gascon swept away his long, brown hair from his handsome face and scanned the solitary, bleak room they entered near the top of the tower.

"Did you say something, my lord?" Ceiran asked. "I did not quite hear you."

Ceiran, Gascon's scribe turned to him. She was stunning. Her Auburn hair, thick with loose curls, danced about her oval face with a soft grace that framed it perfectly. She had sharp, light brown eyes and pencil thin lips that curved in a most flattering smile. She wore a long tunic beneath a shorter white one with flowers of gold and silver stitched into the plunging neckline that accentuated her small but pert cleavage.

"When I say something you need to hear," Gascon disdainfully uttered, his brown eyes lingering on her chest. "Believe me, you will hear it."

Though he greatly enjoyed looking at her, he treated anyone whom he thought was lower than his station with contempt. Gascon tolerated her presence here because he hated coming to this unearthly place on his own. He would never admit that aloud, of course.

"I understand being here makes you nervous," Gascon was trying overly hard to sound calm, himself. "But please, try to remember you are here on official business of the Weaver's Council, and your behavior is a direct reflection on me. Do not embarrass me."

"Apologies, my Lord," she said, looking down at the parchment, quill, and ink bottle she carried with her constantly. "I will ... work on my composure."

"Well, see that you do. We have important business at hand."

He tried to ease his fears by constantly reminding himself that in this grim fortress, he was a representative of The Great Muse herself. He was a Herrod of the First Order. His was in a position of authority.

He took note of how rapidly the pair descended the staircase after leaving them in the room. The boom of the heavy door at the base of the tower signaled that the apprentices had left.

The room in which they were relegated to wait had two openings. One was an arched window, unobstructed by protective glass, thus allowing the cold and damp of the ocean mist to enter freely. The other was a doorway, which faced the center of the tower.

Gascon and Ceiran sat down, seemingly alone in the dark tower, though it was said that no one was ever really alone in Crag Drannon. They were in the center of the room on plush, deep chairs with wine red, satin cushions. Talustrian by design, they matched the deep bandoo fur rug spread out beneath. How oddly out of sorts the comfortable chairs seemed in their surroundings.

"All of this luxurious, opulent furniture wasted in a bleak tower that no one, other than the dead, seem to frequent," Gascon spoke aloud. All the pieces would have cost the price of a small farm. Gascon liked that. Indeed, Gascon liked anything connected to money, but more to the point, to power.

To be sure, power was the thing. Gascon mused to himself.

Aside from the finely crafted chairs and beautiful rug, the room had only one other furnishing, an oil lamp that hung directly over their heads in the center of the ceiling.

Gascon looked about. "My, how the Necromancers do seem to enjoy their petty torments."

The comfort of the furnishings, indeed, served to keep them feeling very out of place. That seemed to be the point. The dim light of the lamp, fed by a sickly smelling oil, thick and yellowish that resembled the scent of embalmer's fluid, was barely able to stave off the darkness, which threatened to consume the room. This made the room seem stiflingly small. Even with the open window, any air that gusted in only seemed to send the putrid scent fully into their nostrils as opposed to clearing it from the room. That too seemed to be the point.

The arched window also let in the effects of the gloomy weather. A stormy sky obscured any light that would have been let in by the window. A day without storm clouds looming overhead in this portion of the Known Kingdoms was rare, indeed.

The chairs Gascon and Ceiran sat in faced the open window and put them in the unpleasant position of having their backs to the open doorway. With no door on the hinges, it opened directly into the pitch black of the stairwell. The minutes seemed like hours while they sat listening to the loud thunder of the crashing waves. Those, however, were not the sounds that caused either of them unease. The other sounds, much quieter and closer, heard only when the mighty ocean receded to gather strength for its next barrage, sent a chill to the marrow of their bones.

"Did you hear that, my Lord?" Ceiran asked.

"It was ... the wind. Nothing more," Gascon replied.

Whispers. They swore they could hear whispers coming from just beyond that gaping doorway, whispers that sometimes sounded as if they came from within the very room itself. Some sounded like the cries of an anguished soul, soft and distant. Others sounded darker, deep rumblings of someone angry, of something vile.

Then there were the footsteps. They both heard someone walking on the lower landings of the tower. Those steps creaked up the stairwell and occasionally stopped outside that dreadful, open doorway. Each time Gascon and Ceiran craned their necks around, hoping to see the man with whom they had business, they were met only with the cold darkness of the tower. Doors below would creak and occasionally slam shut, sending a thundering echo up the desolate stairwell.

Gascon almost jumped halfway out of his stockings at the sound of whispered conversation coming from the corner behind him. He turned quickly and was left with only a quick shiver down his spine and the sense that something unseen hovered nearby.

Ceiran also examined the corner of the room. Gascon turned to her, trying to mask his own nervousness with irritation.

"Please stop jumping about like that," he scolded, not for one moment acknowledging that it was he who jumped. "One would think you had never been in a castle before. Honestly, I am beginning to seriously doubt whether I should have raised you to my chief scribe."

Ceiran looked away.

Gascon tried to keep his wits about him, not letting the feeling of dread that pervaded the tower dull his senses or his nerve. His hunger for power kept him in that chair; it would see him through. Gascon was a Weaver. He was a spinner of yarns whose current job was to ensure that only the correct information about the Necromancers and their dealings was publicized. He and his fellow Weavers were the screen through which the people of the Known Kingdoms viewed the Necromancers. He was the filter through which the truth was told. A truth that was far darker than any sung about in fireside tales.

"Well, this is unacceptable," Gascon finally said. "I am of the mind to leave this instant. I am a Herrod of the First Order, after all, sent on business of The Great Muse herself! How dare they keep me waiting all this time?" All he needed to do was walk through that doorway. That black, looming doorway, on whose other side beckoned the cold dark of The Flaming Tower.

"And what of the warning?" Ceiran asked. "That we remain seated." She wanted to leave as surely as he did, but she would not be fool enough to get up first.

"Yes … that. Well … I suppose it would be rude to not give them another few minutes more. It would be a shame to waste the trek up here after all. What is that awful stench?"

Gascon caught a faint smell. He could not put his finger on it. Distinctively different from that of the lamp's heavy oil, it quickly overpowered it. The smell seemed to emanate from somewhere beyond the doorway. It was a strong, sickly scent. It was a scent he recognized, but what, exactly?

His skin crawled with apprehension and fright as he

pinpointed the odor. It was the putrid stench of burnt human flesh.

Ceiran covered her nose with a dainty hand. "I feel very unsafe here."

"Calm yourself," he quietly reassured her. "If the Necromancers meant for harm to befall us, they certainly would not have gone to the trouble of furnishing us such comfortable amenities."

"Not so," a deep voice whispered from the right side of Gascon's chair. "Lochrin Zaid was quite comfortable before he transitioned."

This time Gascon and Ceiran did turn. That was the most recent whispered voice they had heard, the voice for which they had waited. It was the voice of Lord Ronulen, one of the highest of the order of Necromancers.

"My dear Brother Ronulen …," Gascon began but stopped abruptly when he turned to find the imposing wizard not to his side, where he had heard his whispered voice, but standing in the doorway of the room. "… Greetings. But where is your Lord, Necromverde Cartigas? Will he be joining us?" Gascon hoped he had finished his sentence quickly enough to mask his surprise regarding the dark Necromancer's position.

"Brother Gascon," Ronulen pronounced. "I do apologize for my tardy arrival. And my master and supreme Lord of Crag Drannon, Lord Cartigas, sends his apologies as well. Affairs in the Keep have him duly detained." As he finished and the sound of crashing surf filled the void left vacant by his booming, baritone voice, Ronulen swept his dark cloak forward and around in a small bow. The tall man turned his dark, almost black eyes on Ceiran. "I was told you brought a companion. I was not told of her beauty though." Ronulen bowed again, though this time, he bowed more deeply.

"I ... am flattered, Lord Ronulen," Ceiran responded, giving her own seated bow.

"Well, you were significantly tardy, to say the least ...," Gascon began, as he turned around in his chair to face the window. His own retracted breath nearly choked him as Gascon turned to face the Necromancer now towering ominously in front of him, not more than an arm's length away. "But ... forgiveness is the backbone of strength, after all."

Any pretense of not being taken aback by the sudden and shocking movement of the tall Necromancer was lost in the surprise in Gascon's eyes, as well as his spluttering speech. Ceiran pretended not to notice as she prepared to write.

"It would appear congratulations are in order, Brother Gascon," Ronulen began in his bellowing voice. As he spoke, he turned to face Gascon and sat down in a chair of the finest cedar, gathering his black robes around him. That chair had not been there prior to their arrival. "To become Herrod at such a young age is impressive, indeed. And to be a Herrod of the First, well, it is an honor that speaks for itself, to be sure."

"My thanks in return for your most kind acknowledgement of my *new* station," Gascon replied, his pride more than apparent. "You may rest assured in knowing that the responsibilities inherent to my new position will in no way interfere with my duties to you and the Necromancers."

"To be sure," was all that Ronulen said. His tone was not at all menacing but left no doubt that that fact was never in question.

"Brother Ronulen," Gascon began, clearing his throat. "If we might delve into the matter that brings me to your keep ..."

"Of course," Ronulen interrupted. "We do have several issues to address."

"Now, Brother Ronulen, as the new Herrod for the region, I must discuss with you what I feel would be the wisest strategies for reaching the commoners with news of the work in which you are involved."

"The work in which we are involved ...," Ronulen began, "will benefit humankind for the rest of its existence."

"Most assuredly," replied Gascon. He needed to tread cautiously here, as the common perception about the goings on at Crag Drannon had nothing to do with benefiting humankind. "But the good work being done is sadly ... overshadowed by an outward demeanor that is anything but friendly.

"We need to demonstrate to the masses that the Necromancers of the Western Watch are ... guardians. Yes, that's it, guardians and safekeepers of the good of the common people. You see, Ronulen, recently events in the surrounding countryside have left the people ... unnerved."

"To what events do you refer?" Ronulen asked, easing back into his chair.

"Disappearances," Gascon began. "People, commoners, disappearing in the night. I am not saying that you had anything to do with it. But well ... the masses seem to think you do. The fact of the matter is ... if I may speak candidly ... that although your efforts to cure disease and prolong the span of human life are of the greatest import, the methods with which you carry out your work are ... well ... frightening"

"Fear!" Ronulen bellowed. "What greater emotion is there than fear? Fear teaches us; it drives us, motivates us to do more ... to be more ... than what we are.

"You show me a frightened man, and I will show you a man who is truly alive. I do not need to ease feelings of dread in local communities. Mine is a mission most sacred."

The room still shook with the power of the Ronulen's baritone words. Gascon had to bring the mood of the room to a more temperate tone.

"My apologies, Ronulen," Gascon began, sounding far more meek than he had intended. "I meant no disrespect. On behalf of all on the Council of Herrods and of all Weavers in general, let me say that we wholeheartedly agree with, and support, the work you do. We Weavers have had a long-standing tradition of spreading the word and deeds of the Necromancers for several hundred years. That is a tradition that I most assuredly wish to continue. And continue it in fine fashion.

"I only bring up fear because ... because ... well, yours is the task of prolonging life, yes, of healing. Mine is a job of promoting image, of altering perception."

"Some may say of warping it," was Ronulen's reply. "I know well the history our two brotherhoods share. You may save your lesson for your trainee. I also know well, due mainly in part to that very history which binds us, that your methods for spreading news throughout the kingdoms are often lacking in certain key ... elements. Truth being chief among them. So before you lecture me on fear, perhaps we should discuss honesty."

Ceiran looked on in concern. No one spoke to a Herrod of the First Order in such a manner. She kept her focus on her notes.

"Brother Ronulen," Gascon continued. "Our methods ..."

"Your methods are wise," Ronulen interrupted. "You must understand; my life's work is my passion. You must forgive me for raising my voice to a Herrod, especially one of the First Order. I apologize to you as well, Lady," the dark Magus continued with a more tempered air. "I merely wanted to reassure you that what we do here is for the good of mankind. I know how the commoners perceive us, as I know it is your task to make sure that perception is favorable."

"Indeed," Gascon replied.

"Indeed," the huge man repeated quietly. "Indeed. Now, what other concerns have you?"

"Well," Gascon continued. He shuddered at bringing up this next point. "There have been whispers that … that the Grimward have been seen hunting in the deepest parts of the forest. I pray, for all our sakes, that that is not the case."

"The Grimward were creations of the darkest parts of our magics. They were a necessity in ridding the world of the Oracles and their magics in the Apocalypse of the Mourning Night. A necessary evil, as it were. That, though, was close to a thousand years ago. We have held to our agreement with the Magi of the other Strands of Magics to never again create those dread warriors. We hold that promise still."

"Well," Gascon exhaled deeply. "That is a relief. All will be most glad to hear that news."

"Now, what is it you want?" Ronulen asked.

"Well, Brother Ronulen," Gascon cleared his throat before continuing. "In regards to what I need in order to assist in … promoting … a better image is information, really. I would like a full accounting on the benefits of your work. Also, I would like to go over several strategies I would like to implement to better get the news of those benefits to the people. Commoners are, after all, a very talkative sort. I need to discuss with you how I plan to get them to say what we want them to hear."

With a dismissive wave of his large hand, Ronulen silenced Gascon. Again, Ceiran was shocked to see Gascon handled in such a manner.

"Your strategies are, I am sure, going to prove quite effective," Ronulen said. "You shall have information and more. Lord Cartigas has instructed me to leave the Keep and stay at our school in Farmalkin. It is only a half-day's ride from your residence in Laingarn. In that way, you can communicate with him through me without having to make the long and arduous trek here. But that is not what I meant by the question." Leaning in, he glanced briefly at Ceiran. Gascon understood the meaning of that look.

"Anything you have to say to me, you may say in front of this one," Gascon said. "She is my loyal servant."

Ceiran, knowing what was to come was strictly, 'off the record,' set down her quill.

"Very well," Ronulen seemed satisfied by Gascon's answer. "What is it *you* want? You will have the complete support of the Necromancers about any news you wish to spread. My master has long admired your work and trusts that you would not have been raised to such a lofty position without being fully worthy of such admiration. But what I want to know is, what do *you* want? We have been following your exploits for some time and recognize great leadership when we see it.

"That is why, when the Council of Herrods asked if the Necromancers would rather have a Herrod represent them who was more tenured in the position, I told them that my Lord responded a resounding, 'No.' After all, you have handled all our business in your lesser capacities quite effectively. No, we felt there was no reason to bring someone else into our dealings.

"I want you to consider this, Lord Gascon, Herrod of the First Order, Keeper of the news of the Necromancers of the Western Watch, ours could be a relationship that could prove quite ... fruitful to both of us."

At last Gascon saw it. Finally, Gascon knew for fact what he had sensed all along. The mighty dark Lord Cartigas did recognize his power. This was all ... just a test.

"Anything that could benefit the Necromancers would certainly be … acceptable to me. I desire only what is best for us both," Gascon knew he had won Ronulen over.

"I think our relationship will prove quite beneficial for us both. Beneficial," Ronulen lingered for a moment, "and lucrative."

The greed in Gascon's brown eyes was apparent.

"I had to be sure I could trust you, Lord Gascon," Ronulen said, a strange upturn in his lip passing for what must be, to him, a smile.

A test! Gascon knew it was all a test. After all, a Herrod of the First Order was no one with whom to trifle. He was a man of power. He was a man to be reckoned with.

"Brother Ronulen," Gascon began with all the bluster and pomp a Weaver could muster. "It will be my honor to uphold the lofty regard with which you and your mighty master hold me. And let me say, you will be greatly pleased by our new working relationship."

"Of that I have no doubt. Now, if you would be so kind, I have duties to attend here in the solitude of the tower. You will find your carriage waiting for you down below. We shall speak again soon."

"As you wish, Brother Ronulen," Gascon turned his attention to Ceiran. "Come, Ceiran. Slow girl. Let us not keep Brother Ronulen from his duties."

Rising slowly, his legs tingled with the numbing prickles of having fallen asleep. He bowed lavishly and with a flourish before leaving. The torches held in the wall sconces along the spiraling staircase were all now lit, which made the doorway seem much less imposing, at least, for a Herrod of the First Order.

Ceiran rose as well. Her bow was delicate and well-practiced. "It has been … a pleasure, Lord Ronulen."

"Indeed," Ronulen stood and bowed to her. "I am

sure our paths will cross again in the near future."

As Gascon and Ceiran quickly left the room, Ronulen gave that strange smile once again. Gascon would serve them well. After a few moments, Ronulen heard the resounding boom of the door at the base of the tower slamming shut.

"The greedy are so easily manipulated," where Ronulen's voice was a strong baritone, the man who just spoke did so with a booming bass. Entering the room was the dark Master of Crag Drannon, the most powerful Necromancer in the world, Necromverde Cartigas.

As Cartigas approached, Ronulen bowed deeply. The Lord of Crag Drannon never seemed to walk exactly; it seemed he moved with more of a glide. It was impossible to see his feet, as the towering man, even taller than Ronulen, wore heavy woolen robes of the darkest black that fell to the ground. His cloak, though not as coarse as his robes, was every bit as black and dragged behind him in a small train, outlines of faint silver runes barely noticeable along its edges. One would think that anyone wearing that much material would be falling over himself every third or fourth step, but Lord Cartigas moved with the grace of a dancer at a royal court. It was most peculiar of a man of his height and broadness of shoulder.

"My Lord," Ronulen said. "It seems we will be well-served by that one."

"Yes, we will," Lord Cartigas moved to the window. Necromverde Cartigas, High Lord of the Necromancer's of the Western Watch, always wore the hood of his voluminous cloak pulled low over his face, setting his countenance deep within the darkness thereof.

As the large man stood at the window, he let the hood

fall back, revealing a head that was bandaged from just below his ears to the top of his forehead, leaving only a balding crown to be seen. The crown of his head was perhaps his best feature as some sort of dark sorcery had ravaged the rest of it, leaving him forever bandaged and deeply scarred. Those bandages, marred with sickly yellow and brown splotches, spoke of wounds beneath that would perpetually blister, never seeming to heal. Whatever dark magic had damaged his face spared his vocal faculties, leaving him a voice more rich and beautiful than his scarred face could ever be.

"I do so enjoy the feel of the ocean's mist. It is so soothing on my skin," he said as he turned and made his way to the high backed chair. A small end table and porcelain washbasin magically appeared by its side. He sat down and gestured for Ronulen to sit across from him where Gascon had earlier. Ronulen sat immediately.

Lord Cartigas stared at Ronulen for a time without saying a word. Staring, that is, if anyone could stare at anything through a thick layer of bandages covering their eyes.

"The time of the Great Reawakening will soon be at hand," Lord Cartigas finally said. As he spoke, he unraveled the puss-soiled bandages slowly and deliberately unwrapping layer upon layer of foul-smelling material and gingerly placing them into the porcelain basin. Each layer released more and more of the stench of decaying flesh into the air. The smell did not seem to bother Ronulen in the least.

"All is being made ready," Ronulen said. "We are gaining vessels for use daily. Our numbers grow in strength."

Removing the final bandage, Ronulen sat before a visage of pain. Twisted by horrible magic, the face of the mighty Necromancer was a decaying husk. The skin, where it was not rotting outright, was gray and stretched tightly over the bone. Where once his nose rested, now only holes remained. The rest of his face was nothing but withered skin rife with the crust of dried mucus. His upper lip was nearly non-existent, having been burned back to the point that a portion of his teeth was always visible.

His eyes, though, were the most disconcerting of his features. He had none. Two deep, vacuous pits stared pointedly at Ronulen. They seemed slick with some sort of beige film, which would well at the base and run down the Necromancer's gaunt cheekbones like some sort of perverted tears. The smell was stifling.

"All of our growing numbers are worthless if we do not have the Pride," Cartigas's booming voice echoed in the small room. "We shall not make the same mistake as did the Oracles, underestimating the Caredon Cycle."

"The cyclical ebb and flow of the world's energy," Ronulen stated.

"Yes," Cartigas continued. "Every thousand years, the amount of magical energy in the world is at its peak. The Oracles sought to control it and bring about a new era in the world by using that energy to completely destroy the dark energies of the magics, the energies we Necromancers draw upon for our strength."

"Their mistake ripped the world apart," Ronulen mused.

"Indeed," Cartigas agreed. "In our fight to defeat the Oracles, the world was torn asunder, leaving zones of magical chaos torn across the kingdoms like great, festering scars."

"The Great Rift."

"Along with other, smaller areas of magical unrest, though equally as unpredictable as the Rift," Cartigas continued, turning back to face Ronulen. "They did not see that the world was irreparably split apart in that great battle—

the apocalypse now known as the Mourning Night—because the forces of positive magics cannot do away with negative magics. Indeed, they cannot survive, one without the other."

"The prophecy," Ronulen said.

"The Prophecy of the Magics says that the world will be brought into its new era by those who can embrace all sides of the magics. That is why now, as we reach the next peak in the thousand-year Caredon Cycle, we must have the final piece of the puzzle to ensure our victory."

"The Pride," Ronulen whispered, almost in awe.

"The Pride," Cartigas confirmed. "The Pride will allow us to create a new dawn, a beginning where we can merge the forces of the Life Magics with the forces of the Death Magics. In merging them, we will create new life. A world where the living and dead are one." Cartigas was growing in intensity as he continued. "Think of it, Ronulen. We will create a new race of beings, a stronger race. One that needn't fear the pull of death. We will be a people who will live as dead, immortals with limitless potential."

"It will be a glorious new beginning for man," Ronulen spoke with the fevered pitch of a true believer.

"We will be the masters of this new race. The Pride is the key," Cartigas continued. "Without the Pride, we will not have the power to bend the magical forces necessary to merge the world of the dead with that of the living." Cartigas took a deep breath. "It is prophesized that he who is meant to lead us must be living." He gestured to himself. "As you can see, my time on this plane grows short. Without the Pride to make me whole, I will not be able to lead us to the New Dawn. I cannot transition to the other planes."

"You will not, my Lord," Ronulen said, with a bow.

"Our magics exact a heavy price on these mortal husks," Cartigas said, referring to his damaged body. "Our potential is so limited by the confines of life. It is only in our

49

union with death that we can truly tap into the powers that are our right." Cartigas gestured to Ronulen's hands. "I see that even you are beginning to bear the weight of Necromantic power."

Ronulen rubbed his gloved hands together. "I yearn to be as blessed by the glorious decay as you are, my Lord."

"Perhaps one day, you shall be. Without the Pride to strengthen and renew us, our weak, mortal shells will expire too soon. The Pride is the key. With the Pride, I will be made whole. With the Pride, I will be the ruler of a new world. With the Pride, I will lead us to ultimate glory. It must be so. It *will* be so," Cartigas's voice rolled like thunder. "The kingdoms will fall in line with us."

"The kingdoms will always bow to power." Ronulen said.

"True. And the battle for the New Dawn will soon be upon us. We do not have much time. Even now, the Pride's power grows, bubbling just below the surface, seeking to be unleashed."

Ronulen's eyes burned with desire. "I have felt those bubbles erupt from time to time, causing great ripples in the flow of the magics."

"We all have, those of us skilled enough to sense such things. The twentieth winter of life will soon visit the Pride, that is the critical year. The Pride's magics will then manifest fully. We will not have this chance again. We must claim the Pride by that time!" Cartigas spoke with almost a growl in his voice.

"The Pride will be found soon, my Lord," Ronulen replied, with a bow. "Our search will be successful."

"It had better be," Cartigas said. The finality of his words hung ominously in the air. "All of our plans rest on that."

3: Master

As Kellis was about to strike, a sudden, high-pitched blast filled the gully at the very moment the blade should have torn into Corwyn's flesh. Crisp and powerful, the sound caused Corwyn to wince in pain as its shrill tone echoed. It had the same effect on the two attackers; they turned about completely and shook their heads to clear the loud noise from their ears. Growing in pitch and intensity, it gained strength with every passing moment and rang throughout the enclosed space. Though in a daze, Corwyn was able to bring his hands to his ears, his injured back and ribs burning with the painful movement.

Had he been able to focus on anything other than the echo of the piercing notes, Corwyn would have heard the howls of the other men since they, too, cried out in pain. The sound filled his ears, his mind, and his very soul with a deafening intensity. Fighting as much he could, Corwyn could feel himself slipping into unconsciousness. He noticed the waning focus on his Heart's Eye, his senses growing numb. When consciousness finally left him, Corwyn's last thought was that the notes, though deafening and powerful, were strangely beautiful and perfect in pitch.

Darkness closed in around him.

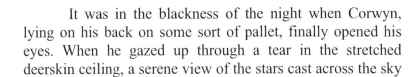

It was in the blackness of the night when Corwyn, lying on his back on some sort of pallet, finally opened his eyes. When he gazed up through a tear in the stretched deerskin ceiling, a serene view of the stars cast across the sky greeted him. He took a full-measured account of his surroundings as his eyes adjusted.

Corwyn lifted his head and was all too quickly reminded of the recent battle he was in. Given the injuries he had sustained, he was pleasantly surprised by how little pain he felt. Noticing for the first time that he was shirtless, Corwyn saw that his midsection was tightly bandaged. The faint scent of mint and rose petals from beneath the bandages indicated that some sort of ointment had been placed on the injuries. When moving, he could feel the soothing effects of the healing balm.

Corwyn realized he was inside the Weaver's Hut. Large bones of wild caribou served as vertical foundation posts, strapped with various lashings of cord and vines to smaller deer bones attached at odd, disjointed angles to each other. The rocky, uneven granite of the gully was the home's rear wall.

The hut was rather spacious, some 10 feet from gully wall to the stretched, piecemeal animal skins that enclosed it. Wreaths of garlic and other wild herbs hung on the large foundation bones that lent the structure its shape and gave the hut a very earthy, comforting scent. Candlelight bled subtly throughout. Books and maps of every make and size cluttered any space that some strange trinket or ornament had not taken up. It was just as Corwyn remembered.

Rising to search for his belongings, he blushed to find himself only in his smallclothes; even his boots had been taken off. He found everything in a cluttered pile on a small, dark, wooden table.

Corwyn quickly put on his soft, rust colored pants. When he grabbed his beige shirt, he noticed that the short sleeves had been removed and his shirt had been stitched where the blade had torn through. Bringing his shirt to his nose, he breathed in the scent of lavender. It had also been laundered. How long had he been unconscious?

In the corner of the hut, Corwyn spied his leather boots and bracers, as well as his greatest possession, Taryn, in its leather tooled scabbard. He grasped the mighty sword's hilt and immediately felt comforted by the familiarity of its weight and touch.

As was his preference, Corwyn strapped Taryn over his shoulder, closed his eyes, and took a deep breath. Now fully dressed, he focused his consciousness through his Heart's Eye and was relieved to sense the presence of the mysterious woman.

May the Heavens be praised. Corwyn thought with relief. *She lives.* He opened his eyes, released his focus, and pulled the hut's flap open. He nearly tripped over himself in shock when a huge, snarling wolf greeted him. The wolf was enormous, black as pitch, and obviously not happy to see him in the least.

"Whoa! Easy now!" he exclaimed, one hand instinctively going to Taryn's hilt.

Looking out into the night, Corwyn saw an old woman approach. A second large wolf accompanied her; its coat was white as winter snow.

"Mama ... Mama Weaver?" Corwyn called out. "Is that you?"

"Of course, it is I," she said, reaching the hut's entrance alongside the first wolf. "Who else would I be?" She turned her attention to the snarling, black beast. "Hush, Peaches."

The wolf whimpered like a small pup, instantly settling at her command. Corwyn released his grip on the hilt, lowering his arms in as unthreatening a manner as possible. She turned her attention back to Corwyn.

Dressed in a tattered, sleeveless dress of faded, multi-colored silk, the woman seemed a collection of bones and odd angles, all shoved into weather worn skin that appeared tan and tough as the hides that made up her hut.

"Well, you certainly slept long enough," she began. "One would think I was running an inn by the way you rested. Now, the real question is ... who are you?"

"I am Corwyn Du'Serradyn, Mama. Surely, you remember me?"

Mama Weaver stared quizzically at Corwyn for several long moments. "No," she flatly responded. "I remember nothing. Peaches ... Cream." When she snapped her fingers, the two wolves were up instantly, hackles raised, snarling once again.

Wanting to convince her of who he was, Corwyn gave his brightest smile. "See, Mama Weaver," he said cautiously. "It is indeed I. I have returned from the Glass Tower."

Mama Weaver arched an eyebrow. A look of disbelief crossed her face.

"Please, you must believe me. Trust me, I mean you no harm," Corwyn lifted his arms up, palms open toward her in an attempt to look meek and unassuming. He was afraid he was about to be made wolf meal when sudden recognition filled her dark eyes.

"Corwyn!" she declared, a large smile crossing her face. "Corwyn Du'Serradyn! By all the stars in the sky! Come here, child!"

She stepped forward and wrapped Corwyn in a loving embrace. Both the wolves tilted their heads in uncertainty.

Corwyn hugged her back immediately. He looked fondly at the old woman. She already appeared ancient when he left for the Glass Tower five winters ago. Now her hair, completely silver with age, was pulled into a tight tail and hung down to the midpoint of her back. Fine wrinkles covered every inch of tan, baggy skin. Her eyes, though, black pools of reflective depth, were as expressive as a child's. They had a glint in them that was either gleefully mischievous or slightly unhinged. Corwyn could not be sure which, though he leaned toward the latter. He was glad to see her here, still alive, and gave her another big hug.

"Oh, come now, Corwyn," she said happily. "Let an old woman go before you crush her to dust."

Corwyn pulled away, knowing full well that it would take more than a hug to damage this tough lady.

She turned to the two wolves. "What are you two doing, standing around here? Go on!"

After she threw two bones she had pulled out from a small bag at her waist, the wolves lost all interest in Corwyn and chased after the chew snacks.

"Please, I must know," Corwyn said, suddenly. "The woman that was here with me ..."

"Is resting comfortably by the fire," Mama Weaver interjected, waving him off.

"Thank you," he said, "for all that you have done, dressing my wounds. I was sure I had met my fate. What happened? How long was I unconscious?"

"For as long as was necessary, boy, and not a moment longer."

"Wren!" Corwyn exclaimed. "I must go and find my friend! He helped me save the woman." Corwyn remembered leaving Wren to deal with the attacker. The fact that the same man had shown up in the gully to attack Corwyn did not bode well for Wren.

Mama Weaver put a comforting hand on Corwyn's shoulder. "You nearly died, child," she said. As surprisingly good as he felt, he was still weak from the ordeal. "Now you wish to go running out into the Nortgard in the middle of the night? And to think ... people call me crazy."

Corwyn had to admit her words had merit. It would be difficult enough backtracking across the Nortgard to find the trail during the day. At night, with the creatures of the forest out and active, it would prove far more challenging.

"At first light then," he said.

"Yes, yes. At first light," she mimicked as she moved by him quickly into the hut's interior. She rifled through stacks of strewn paper and map parchment on the far table. After sifting through several weatherworn books and pieces of parchment, she smiled in satisfaction.

Mama Weaver moved with purpose and passed Corwyn without so much as a second glance and headed outside. "Come, warm yourself by the fire."

Corwyn followed quickly into the cool, crisp night. The hearty scent of the forest mixed with that of roasted quail. He had not realized how hungry he was, but upon smelling the delicious bird roasting on a spit over a large fire some 20 yards away, he grew suddenly famished.

On a thick pillow by the fire's edge sat the mysterious woman. She had on a dark olive cloak, which she wore with the hood over her head. She raised her head and smiled when she saw Mama Weaver approach. Corwyn noticed how much improved her bruising had gotten. Surely he could not have been asleep that long?

Corwyn always moved stealthily, even without meaning to, and took her by surprise as he stepped into the circle of firelight. Her eyes grew large as teacups. She fearfully spun to her knees, dropping buttocks to heels, and bowed with her arms before her, head to the ground.

Corwyn's eyes grew nearly as large as hers and stopped his approach, raising his hands in a pacifying gesture. "No, please," he began. "There is no need for that."

"Get up, girl," Mama Weaver said as she sat down on another large cushion. Immediately, Peaches and Cream joined to lie comfortably beside her. She then gestured at Corwyn. "I've known this one since before he knew to clean his rump. You have no need to fear him."

The woman raised her head. She seemed no less wary, watching Corwyn with eyes filled with suspicion and doubt, but she did finally sit up. However, she did not get off of her knees.

Corwyn approached the fire slowly, making his moves very deliberate. He did not want to do anything to frighten the woman further.

Mama Weaver watched his ginger approach. "Is there something wrong? Are you still hurt?"

"Well, no," Corwyn began. "I just ..."

"Well, be on with it and sit, then," Mama Weaver interrupted. "You are moving like an arthritic old crone."

With that, Corwyn hastily gathered himself and sat. The quiet stranger just stared, not taking her eyes from him.

Mama Weaver took the spit from the fire set it on a nearby plate, shoving it at Corwyn.

"Here," she said. "Eat. We have already dined."

Corwyn ripped into the quail without so much as a second's wait, the hot flesh barely slowing him as he tore into piece after piece of the succulent bird. Singed fingers were a small price to pay for the brilliantly seasoned meal.

As he continued to eat, juice dripping down his chin, Mama Weaver produced a wine skin from behind her and tossed it his direction, along with a small hand towel.

"Take your time, boy. It's not like the bird is going to fly away," she chided. "And wipe your mouth. Apparently, they don't teach manners at the Glass Tower."

Corwyn looked down in slight embarrassment. In his starved condition, he had completely let his manners slide.

"My apologies, Mama Weaver," he said.

He wiped his face, mouth still full of food. Mama Weaver shook her head, and with a condescending glance in Corwyn's direction, she continued. "I believe introductions are in order. Corwyn Du'Serradyn, I would like to introduce you to Velladriana Ral. Velladriana, this is Corwyn Du'Serradyn. Oslyn of the Glass Tower."

"I am not fully Oslyn yet, Mama Weaver," Corwyn corrected. "I am on my Testing."

Corwyn set down his plate and stood, which made Velladriana jump slightly. He gave a most gracious and formal bow before sitting back down. For her part, Velladriana gave a tiny nod, never taking her cautious stare from him.

Corwyn saw that she was now clothed in a plain brown dress. Even with the high cut of the neckline embellished with a small touch of frilly lace, the dress did little to hide her ample bosom.

"You know, as an Oslyn, I must say, you have let your duty as her protector slide quite a bit."

"Protector," Corwyn began. "No, you don't understand. I found her in that condition and brought her here in the hopes of escaping her captors ..."

"I know, I know. She told me what little she remembered," Mama Weaver stated.

"What happened to them?" Corwyn asked.

"Well, you took care of one, and my babies here took care of the other two."

Corwyn paused from eating and stared into the fire for several moments. Never having taken a life before, he was not sure how to come to terms with the fact that he had killed someone. Whether the killer deserved it was another matter completely. A man had lost his life, and Corwyn was the one who took it. While he sat contemplating what he had done, Mama Weaver reached over and took his plate of half-eaten quail and threw it to the wolves. They tore into the bird, devouring it in seconds.

"My babies love quail. Thank you, dear boy. However did you know?" she asked the question with total sincerity, as if he had indeed prepared the meal for them.

"Mama, I ..." Corwyn stammered for a moment. Mama Weaver looked at him innocently, the odd glint returning to her eyes. There was no point in making too much of it. "I am so happy they found it to their liking."

Having barely taken the edge off of his hunger, Corwyn was deflated to see the wolves licking away the remnants of quail from their jaws. At least they seemed satisfied. He thought he registered the slightest of smiles cross Velladriana's face.

"Music!" Mama Weaver suddenly declared. "We need music!"

Without another word, she got up and headed quickly for her hut, followed closely by the wolves. She was very spry for one so old. Mama Weaver's sudden departure made Velladriana more apprehensive. Her pale knuckles tensing on her lap grew even whiter.

Corwyn attempted to relieve the tension. "Velladriana," he cautiously began. "That is a beautiful name. It is indeed Lyndrian, is it not?" She stared at him, as if bracing herself for some impending beating. "My family had ancestors that lived near Lyndria. Though that was ages ago."

Still, Velladriana only stared.

Corwyn looked around, unsure of where to next take the very one-sided conversation. Scanning the gully, dark as it was, he was unable to make out either corpses or graves. How had the old woman disposed of three burly ruffians? Turning his attention back to Velladriana, Corwyn saw her eyes clearly for the first time. They were ice blue like the bergs floating off of the Anterin Glacier. She was striking, even with the mix of perpetual angst and wariness evident in her gaze.

Corwyn tried changing the subject. However, social dealings with women had always baffled him. This instance proved to be no different. "Mama Weaver is most unique, is she not?" Again, he was met with silence. "She has known my family for many, many years. My father started bringing my brother and me here to the Nortgard after our mother died. She thought the forest too dangerous for children, but my father loved it here. We would always make it a point to visit with Mama." Statues registered more emotion than Velladriana did. "Long ago, she was a very prominent Weaver. Do you ... do you know what a Weaver is?"

"Yes, I know what a Weaver is," Velladriana spoke softly. Her stilted accent was indeed Lyndrian and gave her words a unique tone.

"Oh ... good, good," Corwyn, feeling that the ice might be breaking between them at last, continued. "At one time, she was a Herrod of the First Order and served the court of the legendary King Haldrian, himself."

Velladriana resumed her statue-like silence. Corwyn searched for some way to get her talking again. "Uh, your face ... it looks much better than when I first saw it."

That was not it. Velladriana's cold blue eyes narrowed at the comment.

"I mean to say ... you are not so bruised and swollen," Corwyn shut his mouth. Perhaps silence was best.

"Music!" Mama Weaver came dancing back to the fire with a small lute in her hands. Made of maple, the fretted instrument had a teardrop shaped soundboard. Mama Weaver sat down gracefully. As always, the wolves accompanied her, lying protectively at her sides. With the lute resting comfortably in her arms, she suddenly bore the poised demeanor of a bard of the highest caliber. Any and all traces of her kookiness melted away when she started strumming the lute strings with the delicate savvy of a virtuoso.

She teased the notes, manipulating them so that the created sound tantalized with a subtle grace. As she continued, the notes were a perfect accompaniment to the ones previous. She breathed the music, keeping the soft tempo of her fingers in constant harmony with her steady breath. Each wave of notes seemed to dance through the air, washing down upon Corwyn and Velladriana like a fairy's kiss, barely detectable, yet utterly unforgettable.

Turning to look at Velladriana, Corwyn saw that she was relaxing for the first time, allowing the gentle refrain to carry her to a place of peace. He wondered how often, in what must have been the most difficult of lives, was she able to reach this place of peacefulness. Her blue eyes leveled their gaze upon Mama Weaver, but what she saw was clearly lifetimes away. She was quite beautiful.

The music played for what seemed like an eternity, yet it strangely felt as though no time had passed at all. Mama Weaver, whose eyes had been closed since she began, suddenly opened them.

"Tell me," she began, turning her gaze to Corwyn. "What brings you back to the northland?"

"Home. I am headed to Silverton to look for my brother."

"Alek," Mama Weaver sighed, audible just above the haunting melody of the lute.

"Have you any knowledge of him?" Corwyn's tone grew more cheerful at the mention of his brother's name. "Is he all right? Does he reside in Silverton still?"

"Alas, child, I lost touch with him soon after you departed for the Tower. The last I had heard, he was indeed alive but had left with some relatives. He is no longer to be found at your childhood home."

Home, he thought with no small measure of melancholy. *What does it mean to be home?*

"Do you know where he was taken?" Corwyn asked. His saddened gaze pulled at Mama Weaver's heart.

"When last I heard, it was to the city of Tanner's Landing."

The mention of Tanner's Landing brought thoughts of Wren back into Corwyn's mind. That was the destination that he and Wren were to have deposited old, foul smelling Terridous the Bold. Corwyn looked to the entrance of the gully. Somewhere beyond those granite walls was his friend and their charge. Indeed, it was all he could do to stay put and not rush off into the night and search them out. Only his curiosity regarding the Lyndrian woman matched his growing guilt about staying.

"Now that Velladriana is safe here with you, Mama, I will leave in the morning to search for Wren." He looked over at Velladriana, her blue eyes studying him intently. "He assisted me in rescuing you."

"I owe him my thanks," she said. She looked down, suddenly very self-conscious. "As I do you."

That last came out as barely a whisper. She was not used to showing kindness to men. As her bruises could attest, she was not used to receiving kindness from them either.

"You owe me nothing," Corwyn stated, softly. "It was my duty and honor."

He too, looked down, lost in thought.

Ever as they spoke, Mama Weaver continued her soft playing. She never let the music stop. Corwyn's mood had obviously brought a heavy melancholy down around the campfire. Even the wolves seemed saddened.

"Gifts!" Mama Weaver shouted suddenly, her demeanor completely changing. "One cannot have music without presents. It was a tradition in the courts of old to offer gifts to one's guests, and it is so rare that I have any. Guests ... not gifts!"

At that, she stopped playing, giving a hearty laugh and picked up the books and parchments she had brought out earlier.

"We need no gifts, Mama," Corwyn stated. "Your hospitality has been gift enough."

"Nonsense," Mama Weaver rebuked. "You will not tell me how to entertain guests in my own home. It is gifts you are due, and gifts you will have." She then looked at Velladriana, giving her a sly wink. "Men ... you always have to keep them in line, dear. Remember that."

"Now, Velladriana Ral, I have for you an old manuscript. I acquired it on my travels. It is Lyndrian, a retelling of the ancient fables of your homeland. Now ... where is it?" Mama Weaver handed Velladriana the various books. "Here, hold these for me, would you? That's a girl"

"Thank you," Velladriana said, meekly. "But I ..."

"Hush, child," Mama Weaver dismissed her offhandedly. "You sound as foolish as the boy here. You can accept it, and you will."

Velladriana did not know how to react as Mama Weaver continued to hand her old books and pieces of parchment. Corwyn noticed Velladriana suddenly did not look well at all. She had taken on a very removed demeanor, her eyes growing vacant. It was not something Mama Weaver noticed, busy as she was rummaging through her books and parchment. Corwyn was about to voice his concern when Velladriana suddenly lurched forward as if a bolt of electricity shot completely through her. Her eyes widened, and she exhaled. It was as if all the air had been sucked from her lungs. She convulsed for a moment, eyes staring toward the heavens, and spoke in a voice not her own. No longer stilted with her Lyndrian accent, it was a voice deep and ancient that bellowed forth in a language Corwyn did not understand.

"Velladriana!" Corwyn shouted. The moment she had convulsed, his Heart's Eye flared as if suddenly infused with energy.

"By the gods," Mama Weaver whispered in shock. The wolves sprang to their feet, hackles raised, howling into the night.

Velladriana dropped her gaze, locking Corwyn and Mama Weaver in that strange, empty stare. Her eyes were glossed over, their stark blue replaced by a milky gray film, looking almost lifeless. When her gaze met Corwyn's, he could not help feeling as though a piece of his soul was being pulled from him. He felt like death itself was surrounding him, smothering him in its icy grasp. Fear threatened to overtake him. Instinctively, he reached for Taryn's hilt. He saw Mama Weaver clutch her chest, as well, as if forcing her soul to remain where it was.

"*Il gardis manthea!*" was the last thing Velladriana called out before her body had a final spasm and she collapsed back onto her cushion. Slick with sweat, she lay shivering by the fire.

In an instant, Mama Weaver was at Velladriana's side. The moment Velladriana collapsed, the strange sensation Corwyn felt was gone. Though not a warm night, it felt positively hot relative to the stark chill he had just experienced.

"Shhh, child," Mama Weaver consoled, putting Velladriana's head in her lap. "You are all right. You are all right."

Velladriana regained her composure soon enough, breathing in deeply the cool night air as she sat up on her own. She looked at Mama Weaver, taken aback by what she had felt. "What ... what was that?" Velladriana's voice was a whisper.

"Do not fear, child. You will be fine."

"What just happened?" Corwyn asked, finally removing his hand from Taryn's hilt. He could not escape the sensation that rushed through his Heart's Eye when Velladriana convulsed, nor the cold and dread that followed.

"That is what we are going to find out, boy. The truth of it lies in her words." Mama Weaver turned to Velladriana. "What do you remember, dear?"

Velladriana took a deep breath.

"Well," she began slowly, her voice very unsteady. "I was gazing at your fire when I felt myself becoming numb like my soul was leaving my body. Then," she paused for a moment, taking a steadying breath. "I ... I felt an energy rush through me, cold and powerful. The ... the next thing I remember is being in your lap, looking at you."

"You do not remember what you said?" Mama Weaver asked.

"No."

Velladriana looked down, wringing her hands nervously.

"You spoke something in Lyndrian," Corwyn stated. "Though you did not sound like you do now."

"That was not Lyndrian," Mama Weaver countered.

Velladriana looked up at them both.

"Well, it certainly was not the common tongue, nor any other I have ever heard spoken," Corwyn continued.

"No one has heard what she has spoken, not for a thousand years." Mama Weaver looked with compassion upon Velladriana. "This was not the first time this has happened, was it, my dear?"

Velladriana stared at Mama Weaver for a moment before weakly shaking her head. "No," she said in a whisper. She seemed on the verge of tears, but she did not allow them to come.

"What did she say?" Corwyn asked.

"It was prophecy," Mama Weaver began. "A prophecy ancient as the world. Few know it in its original tongue. Fewer still can recite the words so clearly."

"How is it you understand it?" Corwyn was truly curious.

"I am not as young as I look," Mama Weaver said with a flat stare and cleared her throat before continuing. Her voice was melodic and powerful, not at all what one would expect to come from a body so old and frail in appearance. "Man begets man as time holds fast. Life begets death as destinies passed. Weapons of power are wielded to sunder; both man and time, in death they plunder. Whose hand doth touch the Wheel of Fate to hurt in love, to heal in hate. When prophecy foretold does come to be, man is lost to himself and eternity. The master of a new age has arrived. Balanced to bring what is meant to be, balanced on the edge of destiny."

"What ... what does all that mean?" Corwyn asked.

Mama Weaver gestured for her lute, which Corwyn handed to her from across the fire.

"Listen to me children, as I speak the tale," Mama Weaver started singing and playing her lute. Again, the music had a hypnotic effect. "Of lives forsaken, and worlds left frail. It was the time of Oracles, their magic of life ripped the world with light, harmony made strife. It was a time when great cities stretched into the heavens, when beings of thought danced with creatures of flesh. The foolish were wizened, the wicked made chaste, once bountiful fields were ever laid waist. The light turned to darkness, once pleasure now pain, the dead bore the living, a horrid refrain. We were saved by the darkness, saved from the light, saved from ourselves ..."

"To the Mourning Night." Corwyn finished the line without thinking. It was as if Mama Weaver had pulled the words out of him. He blinked as if emerging from a trance. "The shattering of the world. It is a story well told. The strand of magic known as the School of Life from which the Oracles sprung forth grew too powerful, its Magi too corrupt. They tore the world, causing the Great Rift. It was the main reason for the creation of the Oslyn order."

"It is the Great Rift that separates the east from the west," Velladriana's voice was barely audible. "The impassable barrier that separates freedom from slavery." Her voice trailed off listlessly, her eyes staring once again at sights far removed.

"Were it not for the power of the Necromancers, the Oracles would have destroyed the world with their purging light," Corwyn knew the histories quite well. "We are forever indebted to the School of the Soul and the strand of Necromantic magics."

"Yes, child, so it is written," began Mama Weaver. "The Oracles grew in power, using their premonition to foresee what they believed was a utopia. But they pushed too hungrily. Their magics of light, instead of becoming a beacon for life, instead burned with ambition and threatened to burn the world to cinders."

"You sound as if you do not believe," Corwyn said with doubt. "Surely you, who have seen so much of the kingdoms, so much of the world, know this to be true."

"It is true that I have seen much of this world and others besides," Mama Weaver spoke cryptically. "But as is often the case, what is written is only part of the story.

"The Necromancers saved the world, true enough, they saved the world," she said, leaning forward for added effect, "to destroy it themselves."

With that, the music stopped.

Corwyn and Velladriana shared uncertain glances. Most people would take what Mama Weaver spoke of as near blasphemy. Corwyn had been taught throughout his training that though Necromantic magics were born of unnatural dealings with many forces considered perverse, they were now harnessed for the betterment of all beings. For close to a thousand years, the Necromancers had been looked upon as the saviors of the entire planet of Tarune, not merely the Known Kingdoms.

"I believe you," Velladriana stated plainly. "I have seen too much hate to believe that this is how the world was meant to be."

"And you are correct in that assessment, child," Mama Weaver said, as she set her lute down with the gentleness of a mother laying down her child.

"Tell me, Velladriana," Mama Weaver began. "Have you heard of the Magi's Pride?"

Velladriana shook her head no.

"What you just did, child, was summon magics far greater than most could issue forth. Necromantic magic to be exact."

"How is that possible?" Velladriana was aghast.

"You, yourself, said that this has happened before. Though, I would wager, not as powerfully as it just did. No need to answer, I see the truth of it in your eyes. Everything happens for a reason, you see. Fate did not deal us this reunion by chance," Mama Weaver turned to look at Corwyn, "nor did it deal her accidentally to you."

"I do not understand," Velladriana stated.

"When you gazed at us, Corwyn and I both felt as though our souls were being emptied, being replaced by the dread shiver of death." She looked at Corwyn, he nodded his head yes. "None but the most powerful of Necromancers could have summoned magics that can attack the very soul. Even had you studied for decades in the dark art, had you not the inherent strength, that sort of spell would have been as useless as if Corwyn or I had tried to cast it. And yet here you are, wielding might you could not possibly fathom," she spoke with growing earnestness. "Having saved the world in the battle of the Morning Night, the Necromancers feel that the Magi's Pride is theirs to claim. I have listened to the wind. I have heard the conversations that the Necromancers wish to keep hushed."

Listening to the wind was how Weavers described their ability to communicate over vast distances through sound and song. Weavers were more than bards, singing bawdy songs in taverns and courts. They were historians, record keepers, gatherers and senders of information, and at times, gossip mongers and spin doctors of propaganda. Weavers communicated through the wind, and apparently, Mama Weaver had learned to listen in on the windborn conversations of others.

"The Pride is not a feeling," Mama Weaver stated. "It is a being. This being would make all the Necromantic Magi proud. This being would be their Pride. Only, she is more than just a Necromancer. She is equally capable of harnessing the magics of the Oracles, as well. Making her the Magi's Pride."

"History tells us that it's the one person who will bring balance and restore order to the Strands of the Magics. All who have lived in the shadow of the Mourning Night shall share the Magi's' Pride." Corwyn's voice was soft and reflective.

"History is written by the victors, after all," Mama Weaver stood and looked at them both. "This being would come from not one single Strand, but belong to all the Strands. It's the greatest power any of the four Strands of the Magics have ever courted."

Everyone pondered those words.

"The Pride has finally been born. The dark Magi have used many a fell craft to discover this. If the Pride falls into their hands, they can shape the world into their image. The dead will be born and the living exterminated. This plane of existence will become a hellish underworld with the Necromancers in complete control."

"What are you saying?" Corwyn asked.

"The final words that you spoke, '*Il gardis manthea,*' do you have any idea what they mean?" Mama Weaver asked Velladriana.

Velladriana shook her head no. "I have never heard them before."

"They are from the ancient tongue. They mean … I am the master." She stared intently at Velladriana. "A power within you is being awakened, a power greater than that of even the strongest Magi, even the mightest of Necromantic Magi. You, child, I fear, are the Magi's Pride. And if that is the case, then you are no longer safe here. You must leave at first light. The Necromancers will be coming for you. And you," she turned toward Corwyn, "have been appointed to keep her safe."

"What?" he asked, stunned by what Mama Weaver was saying. Corwyn locked eyes with Velladriana, who stared back in a quiet stillness.

"Finding her was no accident, boy," Mama Weaver declared. "In the lateness of this hour, your destinies are intertwined. Corwyn Du'Serradyn, Oslyn of the Glass Tower, in your charge lays the salvation of the world!"

70

In the depths of Crag Drannon, darkness stirred. Lord Cartigas stepped onto the balcony of a room in the Flaming Tower, looking eastward across the Tearfall Mountains and toward the mighty Nortgard Forest. As a sinister smile stretched across his decaying mouth, his eyeless sockets locked onto something in the distance.

"Now," he whispered, his voice rolling like distant thunder. "The Pride has been awakened."

4: The Trek East

The dawn began with a peal of thunder, crisp and powerful, in the distance. The sun, barely visible in the eastern sky behind the thick cloud cover, set a gray cast on the day. Here in the northland, the clouds moved quickly, gathering strength and momentum, pushed by the winds. Corwyn rolled up the weathered map that Mama Weaver had given him, setting it aside with no small measure of concern. He had barely slept at all. Choosing to remain by the fire as opposed to sleeping within the confines of Mama Weaver's hut had been a decision born of concern and confusion. He told Mama Weaver that he wanted to keep watch as well as study the map she had given him. Her amused cackle told him exactly what she thought about that idea, but she had not attempted to stop him.

A fool, indeed, Corwyn thought, as he stretched the stiffness from his bones. His injured back and shoulder felt good, very good. They were virtually pain free. In truth, he wanted to sleep by the fire, now nothing more than faintly glowing embers embedded in thick ash, because he did his best thinking when he was alone. After the revelation from the night before, he needed the very best of his thoughts, now more than ever.

Mama Weaver had told him it was his destiny to escort the strange, hauntingly beautiful Lyndrian to where she would be safe. It was difficult for him to grasp the erratic turns his life had so quickly seemed to take. He was being asked to forsake his duty to his people, his dreams for himself, to escort a foreigner from the far side of the Great Rift, no less, to a place he did not recognize. He needed time to ponder this fully, far more time than he knew he had.

Corwyn's thoughts went to his brother Alek. He hoped Alek was happy and strong. He hoped to see Alek again, to find him once he had re-established himself in Silverton. The sad irony was that, had he been able to get Terridous to Tanner's Landing, fate would have dealt him far closer to his brother than he could have wished. Now, it seemed that Corwyn was to be denied even that.

Then there was Wren, poor, brave Wren. Corwyn's sadness was multiplied in the cold light of the clouded morning. Thinking of his friend, he wiped away a tear running down his cheek. In truth, though, Corwyn could not shake himself free of the feeling of betrayal that haunted him. He should not have listened to Mama Weaver and pushed into the Nortgard, despite the hour, despite the dangers, and gone to find what happened to his friend. Was it Mama Weaver's wisdom that had stayed his departure or his own cowardice?

"It was both," Corwyn said aloud, with finality. Hearing it made it more real. In the stark light of the slate morning, he needed to hear the truth. He should have returned to his friend.

Wiping tears that now came freely, Corwyn tightened his bracers and checked that Taryn was strapped firmly onto his back. He would move quickly, retracing his steps from his harrowing escape. He would find what happened to Wren … and Terridous. Another wave of guilt flashed over him. Tightness seemed to crush his chest. By following his Heart's Eye, Corwyn had abandoned the old Magus. He had also abandoned his duty. How was it that he could have done so much wrong in his attempt to do right? The pain he felt was completely his making, and he would have to own it as such.

"Ready for the road? That is good."

Corwyn spun at the sound of Mama Weaver's voice. She had emerged from the hut and approached Corwyn,

Peaches and Cream, as always, by her side. Forcing himself to calm down, he gave her a nod and quickly turned away, not wishing for her to see his bloodshot, brown eyes.

"Good morning, Mama Weaver," he said with his back turned.

"The goodness of it is yet to be seen," she said. Putting a hand on his shoulder, she turned him to face her. Stress and concern, along with dried tears mixed with dirt, was etched on his face. "It looks as if you have been fighting yourself all night out here by the fire."

Fool, he thought. *In my blubbering I let an old woman and two huge wolves sneak right up behind me. Wren would never have let that happen. What am I doing here?*

About to speak, Corwyn took a deep breath. Mama Weaver, though, was quicker to the point.

"Yes, you are ready for the road, Corwyn Du'Serradyn, but which road is it? That is the question."

"I must find him," Corwyn choked, his words heavy. "I must find my friend. I ... I left him to die."

"You did no such thing, child," she said, looking at him peacefully. Her manner was very soothing. "You were moved to do what was right. Had you not acted, that poor girl would be dead ... or worse. Oh, yes. There are some fates in this world far worse than death. You see, fate led you to her, and you both to me. You rescued her from villains. You saved her life."

"And him, Mama, I left him to die."

"Faugh!" Mama Weaver's patience was growing thin. "I have heard enough. The life of an Oslyn is full of risk. You know that, as did he. He died protecting one weaker than himself. Ask yourself, what better death is there for an Oslyn?"

Corwyn looked on at Mama Weaver, unable to quite grasp his thoughts. She was right, he knew, and yet, he could not allow himself to fully believe it.

"But ... but if I could find him, he may still be alive."

"You slept for close to a week, child, near death as you were," Mama Weaver held understanding in her voice once more. "I am sure your fellow Oslyn was skilled in woodlore. Do you not think he would have found you in that time?"

The reality of it hit Corwyn full bore. He did not realize he had been unconscious for so long. As heavy as his heart was for Wren, his burden was doubled when he thought of Terridous. Filthy, yes. A criminal, absolutely, but he did not deserve to be left to the will of the Nortgard. After a week, there was no way that the old man could have survived, certainly not shackled as he was. In his mind, Corwyn had now killed three people. The murderer he would grow to accept as duty, Wren and Terridous he would forever carry as a duty failed. Was this what it was to be an Oslyn?

Mama Weaver saw the internal struggle on Corwyn's face. "You must move forward now, Corwyn. It is the only way."

Corwyn looked at her as if seeing her for the first time. He shook his head to clear his mind. He needed to think and turned away for a few moments. He gathered himself before facing her.

"We must talk, Mama. About last night ..."

"Talk," she interrupted. Corwyn saw the strike coming quite clearly and could have easily evaded it. Nonetheless, he stoically accepted Mama Weaver's slap across his cheek. He thought it rude to do otherwise. "There is no more time for talk, dear boy. All has been made ready. It is time to move. Yes, the time to move is now."

"You are promised to assist those in need, my young Corwyn." A slight bit of mischief glinted in her eyes. "I may be crazy, but I am sane enough to know that."

Corwyn could not argue with that logic, though he wished he had the strength to do so. Velladriana did need his help; that much was true. Hired assassins had accosted her, after all. Moreover, his Heart's Eye, it had ... pulled him towards her. It was as if his soul had somehow sought her out. It was a feeling that was still beyond him. None of his training in the Glass Tower had prepared him for the tug he felt when Velladriana was near. That feeling was very strange. The strength of his Heart's Eye pull to Velladriana was undeniable.

Seeing apprehension in his eyes, Mama Weaver took his hands in hers. "This is the most important undertaking of your young life, Corwyn," she began. "You must believe when I tell you, you will be doing far more good for the world by getting Velladriana to safety than you ever could in any other way."

"Yes, but safety?" Corwyn countered. "Mama Weaver, I studied the map you handed me. I studied it late into the hours of the night."

"Ah, good," she said, releasing his hands. "It is good to be prepared."

"Yes, but that is just it," Corwyn said with concern. "The map is to a place further east, a place called Mount Elderstone. Apparently, this Elderstone is in the northeast in the northern mountains, toward the Eastfall Moors."

"Yes, that's right," she said, as she walked back to the hut and pulled back the flap of a front door. "You can read a map, thank the heavens for that. You see, I knew you were destined for this." She cackled.

"I have studied extensively the maps of the northland while I was at the Glass Tower," he called. "There is no

Mount Elderstone! It does not exist on any map save this one." He could not make it any clearer than that, picking up the map and shaking it for added effect.

Mama Weaver stopped and turned to look at him. "You think too much and see too little," she smiled. "I thought we had been through all this last night?" With that she turned and entered the hut. "Velladriana," she called. "It is time to be about it."

Peaches and Cream lay down at the hut's entrance. They seemed to look at Corwyn as if he were the crazy one.

Mama Weaver suddenly stuck her head back out of the hut's flap. "There is a basin on the other side of the hut, filled with water and mint leaves. Make your wash and be ready to leave with all haste."

Corwyn looked on for a moment.

"Forget your mind, boy," Mama Weaver said. "What does your soul tell you?"

With that, she disappeared into the hut and began riffling about loudly. He knew she was right. His soul told him he must help Velladriana. He only wished he had more time to think it through. He walked to the basin, scrubbed his teeth with the mint, and washed his face.

Within only a minute or two, both Mama Weaver and Velladriana emerged from the hut. Velladriana was now wearing hunting clothes, a stout coat of brown with sturdy breeches of the same color and high leather boots of the northern style. She also wore a thin, gray cape with a hood that she pulled low. It concealed her half-shaven head quite effectively.

Mama Weaver handed Corwyn a large pack full of supplies with two sleeping rolls tied to the sides. Corwyn took his sword from his back and belted it to his left side. He strapped the pack of supplies onto his back. She then walked off quickly, gesturing for him to follow. He fell in behind

78

Velladriana. His presence seemed to put her instantly at guard. She coldly stared at him out of the corner of her eyes. It was odd. Most people felt more comfortable with an Oslyn near, not less so. These were peculiar circumstances, indeed.

Walking through the gully's narrow opening, they emerged into the dense forest.

"Now," Mama Weaver said. "The North Road lies ahead, just a few miles from here. I have listened to the wind this morning, and there is no mention of Velladriana at all. But the longer she is tardy in reaching whatever foul place her attackers had planned to take her, the more questions will surely be raised.

"There is enough gold in the pack for horses, along with two sturdy cloaks of bandoo fur. Really, how an Oslyn is supposed to make it through the Nortgard without a good bandoo cloak is beyond me. I also put more of the healing balm in the pack. Apply it to any new injuries I am sure you will get. I included a vial of the magical elixir I used to speed your recovery. It is quite potent, so use it sparingly. I am sad to part with it, as it is works wonders on my bunions. However, you will be in far more need of it than I. These are the gifts I have for you.

"Now, mark me well. There is a saddler on the outskirts of Silverton, some five miles from the city proper, who has good horse stock. Sadly, I wish I could give you more, but this will have to do." She dismissed Corwyn's protests with a wave. "Get on the road, follow the map, and stay out of trouble. I know you want to see your home again, Corwyn. But if you enter the city, you, of all people, will be recognized."

"Mama, without horses, we will have a long road to reach Silverton."

Mama Weaver looked at Corwyn intently. "That is why you must take the direct route. The shortest distance between two points is, after all, a straight line."

"Jundin's Pass," Corwyn said in realization, looking concerned. "You mean for us to go through the Pass?"

"What is Jundin's Pass?" Velladriana asked.

"Jundin's Pass is a wasteland in the north," Corwyn expressed. "It is a result of the Apocalypse of the Mourning Night, similar to the Great Rift. It is a scar on the world, a deadly scar."

"Similar," Mama Weaver conceded. "However, not the same. It is a short expanse of land. Unlike the Rift, it is navigable, and the magics actually work there."

"It is a dangerous expanse of land. Many dangers lay in wait for traders and trappers fool enough to opt for that quick route as opposed to taking the winding North Road," Corwyn corrected. "Perhaps if we—"

"There is no more time, boy!" Mama Weaver exclaimed. "You do not yet fully understand. Every moment you stay here is a moment closer the Necromancers are to finding you. Time is against you as are forces more powerful than you could comprehend." She saw the look of worry darkening Corwyn's features and smiled, softening her tone. "Trust a crazy, old hag."

Looking in her eyes, Corwyn knew it was time to be off. He wrapped her in a loving embrace. "You are not a crazy, old hag, Mama."

"Why, whoever said I was?"

"Goodbye, Mama," he said softly. He cleared his throat and turned to Velladriana. "Let's be off then."

Velladriana gave Mama Weaver a strong hug of her own. "Thank you," she said. "Few have shown me the kindness you have."

80

Mama Weaver returned the hug. "I know men have hurt you all of your life, my child," she said, looking deeply into Velladriana's ice blue eyes. "But this one, you can trust. He was led to you for a reason. Hold faith in that."

"I will ... try."

"It is a long, hard road you walk. Your strength will see you to its end. Hold faith," with that, Mama Weaver waved her away. "A road made harder if you lose your guide. Go on." Mama Weaver smiled.

Velladriana returned the smile and went off to catch up with Corwyn. Mama Weaver watched them depart, deeply concerned. The wolves circled her restlessly. She turned to re-enter the gully. She had listened to the wind for many hours. No one spoke of Velladriana ... yet. However, those who had ordered her kidnapping would try again.

She looked back longingly as the two walked beyond her sight. She knew Corwyn would be hard pressed to do what he must. Mama Weaver understood how much he longed to find his brother, how he wished to re-establish some semblance of normalcy to his life. She was saddened that he was not destined to be normal, no matter how much he wished it. The Glass Tower had made Corwyn a powerful warrior; of that there was no doubt. However, when looking into his deep brown eyes, she still saw the sensitive boy who had left so long ago.

"High Ones, I hope I have done enough for the savior of our world," she prayed as she turned back to her gully. She had taken what measures she could. She would listen to the wind at sunset and pray to the gods in the meantime.

Corwyn and Velladriana found the North Road easily. It was not more than a four-hour hike from Mama Weaver's home to the road, which wound its way along the border of the Nortgard. Connecting the smaller frontier communities like Silverton to larger civilized hubs, such as Tanner's Landing, the North Road was a lifeline for the peoples living at the edge of the expansive wilderness.

Corwyn and Velladriana spent that time in relative silence. He tried to engage Velladriana on multiple occasions. He even explained the plants and animals that they saw on their trek—it took his mind off of the heaviness he carried in his heart. He spoke of the enormous redwood trees, the mighty oaks and aromatic glens of cedar and birch. He showed her what deer trails looked like and how to spot the scat of predatory animals.

"Look!" he shouted suddenly, pointing to the sky visible through the thick trees. "A griffox." He pointed out the enormous, hawk-like creature as it flew overhead. "They are virtually extinct in all but the most remote places of the kingdoms.

"At one time, they had been domesticated and used as aerial mounts. Did you know that? They do better in the cold, so you never really see them in the south. Now, alas, you do not really see them anywhere, anymore."

Velladriana looked up at the impressive creature as it flew past. She looked in awe at the sight of the foreign animal.

"Their numbers are now so diminished that only the wealthiest of the rich can afford to keep them at all. Impressive creatures, I have always thought it sad to think of such regal creatures as pets. It is a rare sight to see one. The largest can carry up to four riders."

He watched the griffox sail gracefully overhead toward the high peaks of the northern Nortgard Forest. He truly hoped he could ride one someday.

Turning back to Velladriana, he saw that again his efforts at conversation were met with silence and that cold, ever-cautious stare. They walked on quietly, greeted only by their own footfalls and the sounds of the wild forest around them. After a bit more travel, the forested terrain began to change.

The plush greenery of the thick forest canopy thinned out. Trees, once vibrant with life, grew sparse. Withered husks of dying trees became more prevalent. The forest shrubbery was withering here, replaced instead by boggy, marsh-like terrain. The North Road meandered off. They moved off of it, letting that last trace of civilization wind away, reclaimed by the thickness of the woods.

Looking about, he took full account of their surroundings. "Let us stop and take a moment to eat before the terrain turns truly sour," Corwyn said.

They were approaching Jundin's Pass. The dying landscape was the first sign it was near. With any luck, they would get through the pass quickly with no creatures taking account of their passage. That was his hope at least.

They sat down on the soft grass beneath the shade of a large oak tree that was still strong and full of life. Corwyn handed Velladriana some of the dried cheese and fruit that Mama Weaver had provided, along with the wineskin filled with water. Breaking off a small amount of cheese for himself, Corwyn settled into what he was sure would be a quiet meal.

"Oslyn are killers?" Velladriana asked.

Caught by surprise by the suddenness of the question, Corwyn spluttered and nearly spit out his water, most of it running down his chin.

"What?" he coughed, as he choked down the last swallow of water. He was always surprised when she initiated conversation, rare as that circumstance was. This time was no different, as the soaked front of his shirt could attest. "An Oslyn?" He cleared his throat, wiping his chin. "No, not killers. Not precisely. That is to say ... we do kill. Only when there is the greatest need to do so. And never out of anger, only out of duty. I mean, of course we do. That is an inherent part of it, you see. Yes, we kill. But only when we have to." Corwyn wondered why he could never halt the flow of unnecessary words that his mouth vomited when speaking to a member of the opposite sex, especially one so pretty as Velladriana. "An Oslyn is a warrior ... and a peacekeeper. Yes, I suppose peacekeeper explains it well. We ... keep the peace." His sigh suggested he should have shut up a few sentences earlier.

"And you live in this forest?" she asked.

Corwyn looked around for a moment, taking the forest in. "I did. A long time ago. I have been training at a place called the Glass Tower. It is far from here, in lands to the south. Are you familiar with the kingdoms to the west of the Great Rift?"

"I know nothing of this place," she said. Stating that truth seemed to make her feel as out of place as she truly was.

"Well," Corwyn continued, sensing her sorrow. "As I said, it is far from here. After leaving the Glass Tower, Oslyn are given their choice of assignments. Most often, we return to our homelands.

"I came home because the only Oslyn here in the northland are normally found in the larger cities of Tanner's Landing or even Felder's Gate. Those cities are far from here, and by the very nature of their size and population, crime is more prevalent. They are in great need of—"

"Peacekeeping," Velladriana finished his statement. She heard in his voice that he was beginning to ramble. She thought it best to stop him before he began. He smiled slightly, obviously sensing the same thing. She did not quite smile, though a brightness did lighten the severity of her gaze.

"I know how challenging life can be for these northern peoples. I feel like I can do far more good here on the northern frontier than ever I could in the great cities. That is why I will return to protect my people and my home." Corwyn was proud of himself. He did not ramble whatsoever that time. "What is life like in Lyndria?" Corwyn asked, feeling that a bridge of connection had finally been made.

She instinctively pulled the hood of her cloak low, defensively ensuring her head was covered. She looked up at Corwyn from beneath the lowered hood, her blue eyes cautious and uncertain.

"It is ..." she began, after long moments. "Harsh. It is ... very harsh." She looked down, her hand instinctively going to her slave loop of hair before she quickly lowered it back to her lap. So much of this distant, new country was strange to her. The lush green forest she was traveling through, along with the numerous areas her captors had dragged her to, were so different from her homeland. Lyndria was a harsh, barren landscape, at best. As a slave, it was harsher, still. She did not know what to make of this land or its inhabitants. Most especially, she did not know what to make of her new predicament. She was terrified by the energies that had so fully consumed her the night before. She was confused by what they foreshadowed. Looking over at

Corwyn, she did not know what to make of her talkative travelling companion, either.

"I hope you will find life easier here," Corwyn said sincerely.

This time, Velladriana answered only with silence. Mama Weaver said she could trust this man. Strangely, she truly believed that odd lady. He was well-built and soft-spoken. However, pretty faces and broad shoulders all too often hid the souls of monsters. Mama Weaver also told her that Corwyn had slain one of her dangerous captors in her defense. That was no small feat. Velladriana had seen the assassins' brutality and sword skills on several occasions.

As Velladriana sat in silence, she knew only time would tell if that faith Mama Weaver asked her to have could be well founded.

"Well, it is time to be off," Corwyn said. He put the supplies away and slung the pack over his shoulders. He offered Velladriana a hand, but she got up on her own. "The terrain will be a bit more difficult, but it is best we keep a hurried pace."

The pace Corwyn set was quick. Velladriana, her legs honed though years of hard labor, had no trouble keeping up. The terrain of the Nortgard was very hilly and near Jundin's Pass was no different. The marsh and bogs, along with the scarcity of trees, made for unobstructed views. As the hills rose up around them, Corywn pressed hard to make the quickest route through what was becoming a very depressing landscape.

Instead of green foliage, the land was gray and barren. The peat bogs gave off a sickly scent. A low hanging mist perpetually floated, casting an eerie film over the ground. In the distance, strange cries could be heard.

"There are many creatures in your forest," Velladriana spoke, almost in a whisper. "Not at all like the lands near the Rift."

"You have been to the Great Rift?" Corwyn asked, extremely curious.

Velladriana's mood darkened. "No one of right mind ever goes to the Rift. Though I have been near it."

"What is it like?"

"It is dark with an angry sky," her eyes narrowed. "The sun never shines there; light never penetrates, only storms. Storms … and darkness." She was speaking of the stuff of children's nightmares as if it were nothing more than a walk along the beach.

After a couple hours of steady marching, accompanied only by the scent of rotting peat and the howls of strange, distant animals, Velladriana truly felt the oppressiveness around her. She now knew why Corwyn sought to be through it so quickly. He pointed to an opening between the large hills in the distance.

"There … the opening to Jundin's Pass."

5: Neophytes

The fullness of the moon and its bright light did little to lighten the mood of the lone figure that stood uneasily beneath its glow. There was nothing that could warm the disposition of young Crispin Claxis. Given the journey Crispin was about to undertake, he doubted whether he would ever feel any warmth again.

It was never an easy calling, that of a young neophyte summoned to one of the great disciplines of the Magi, which was made even more difficult in this instance because of the school extending the summons. Young Crispin was destined for the Dark Spire of Crag Devlin to become a Necromancer.

It was with a shudder that Crispin pulled himself from these despairing thoughts. It was never his desire, or even intention, to follow in the footsteps of the great Magi from whom he was descended. All his ability had ever visited upon him was nothing but trouble. His family called it a gift.

Finally, after having vanished for so many long years, there was a Claxis who demonstrated the ability for harnessing the Life's Spark of the Magics. Now, the Clan Claxis could hold its name once again in the gloried circles of conversation amongst the elite, for the Life Spark had returned.

"Gift, my arse," muttered Crispin.

Though the night was in no way cold, Crispin pulled the fabric of his coarse woolen cloak tighter about him. Pulling the hood down low, Crispin sunk further into its depths and deeper into his self-pity. Allowed only the thin, white robes of a neophyte magus, unmarked leather sandals, and a woolen cloak of black, Crispin mourned his current situation.

"Why couldn't I have been a Lifer or a Rager? Goblin's tears, I would have even been happy with an elemental strand. But this ..." Crispin looked at his meager belongings with no small degree of disgust, "this is ... just reprehensible. I mean, honestly," Crispin spoke aloud, more to comfort himself with the sound of his own voice than anything else. "Any other strand of the Magics would have at least sent me off with a celebration. I should have at least gotten a party out of this wretched deal. If nothing else, a comfortable cloak. Goblin's tears."

Crispin pulled his cloak closer, its coarse fabric only adding to his discomfort as it scratched his soft skin. Crispin's sorry state was not completely his fault though. It was as much the fault of his more-than-comfortable lifestyle on his family's expansive estate on the Locksdale Foothills that was to blame for his present condition, as was the Necromantic calling that placed him there. Crispin had never wanted for anything in his life. His was a position of relative ease: the fourth son of the fourth son of the Grand Magus Prespertin Claxis, final Grand Magus of the Clan Claxis.

Were it not for the yearly ceremonial testing held at the Grand Court during the summer solstice, a testing offered to all the royal families of the Magi, of which the Clan Claxis were still considered a part, Crispin's gift may have gone by entirely unnoticed. Alas, for Crispin, whose only hard work had ever been to find new ways to go by unnoticed, there were many discerning eyes watching him closely on the day of his test.

It was those eyes that marked Crispin a Necromancer. The tests are geared not only to find neophytes from the numbers of the masses, but also, to determine to which strand of the Magics those neophytes would gravitate.

Since the dreaded Sightless Oracle was put down at the end of the Second Age at the hands of the Necromancers, their power had grown virtually unchecked. Where once Necromancy was viewed with disgust, it was now embraced as the magical art that saved the world. It was peculiar, indeed, the forms that modern heroes take.

That thought almost returned a smile to Crispin's lips, were it not accompanied by a sudden revulsion. Though having lived through only 16 winters of life, Crispin knew all too disturbingly that the sound that greeted his ears was far from normal. He heard silence. He heard only cold, empty silence. The wood owls had grown still.

Standing on the edge of his family's property on the main road that connected Locksdale to the larger, walled community of Dun Sparrow to the north would normally be an idea that only a fool would have entertained. Although Locksdale was a community well within the lawful lands of Canodria where the Civil Guard had patrols constantly moving up and down the road proper, there were bands of wolves and lone, solitary thieves that occasionally hunted in the woods after dark. On a night like tonight when the moon was at its fullest, a pudgy youngster of barely 16 winters would stick out like exactly what he was, an easy target.

Crispin sensed the impending approach of death, and it sought only him. When the Necromancers chose a neophyte, they took immediate steps to ensure that youngster understood how far removed from daily life they were to be taken. No farewell celebrations marked their departure, no gifts from their families. No, only a marking on the right hand, a sigil formed from the ashes of the dead, to clearly demark a new member into an ancient fold.

So, here he now stood. Looking down, Crispin cringed in grief and regret when the sigil that the Necromancer Maudgrim placed on his hand at the conclusion of his test glowed a faint red. It served as a homing beacon for the minions of the Necromancers, the beings whose sole purpose was to collect the newest class of neophytes and take them to their respective training towers. Though Crispin knew well why the sigil he bore was glowing a faint amber hue, it did nothing to make him feel any comfort in his current situation. It was never an easy thing to know that death was approaching.

The mist was growing thicker as the night wore on. Crispin knew this mist had its origins in Necromantic sorcery since he could sense the sources of the magics clearly. He also noticed that there was a faint whispering in the light breeze blowing softly about him. It was a weeping, strange and sad, as if the night sensed the impending cold and mourned for him.

A sudden moan of dismay traveled across the grasslands, followed by wagon wheels grinding on the hard earthen road. His carriage approached.

Again, that dread moan bellowed across the land, rising in volume. The mist thickened around Crispin's now shivering form. How cold it had become. He was shocked at how quickly the beautiful serenity of the eve had been transformed into a ghastly setting of despair. He could literally feel the mist about him, pulling on his cloak, trying to rob the warmth from the marrow of his bones.

Suddenly feeling a cold hand on his ankle, Crispin leapt in shock. Turning quickly, Crispin saw no one there. Then a tug on the back of his cloak alarmed him. He spun round, only to feel another tug, this time pulling on the back of his hood. It was as if the mist had solidified in form, reaching for him with skeletal hands, beckoning him to the world beyond.

Crispin began to panic, swinging frantically with his arms in a fruitless attempt to knock these mist-shrouded hands away. He turned, again and again, striking at what seemed to be a hand at his throat, a claw on his thigh, a pinch at his ribs, only to come up empty.

That soft weeping was more constant now. Crispin heard it as the strained cries of the dead, begging him to lend them his warmth.

"*So cold, my love. Come and warm us with your embrace. Let us taste of your goodness and be made whole. Come to us and bleed us your love,*" These were only a few of the calls that made their way to Crispin's ears. "*We taste your warmth, my love. Bleed us your warmth.*"

"Stop it!" Crispin shouted, closing his eyes and covering his ears in an attempt to keep out the morbid whispers. "Leave me alone!"

Crispin's yell drowned out all other sound. He fell to his knees, shaking uncontrollably as he kept his eyes shut and his ears covered. After a few moments, Crispin noticed that the whispering had silenced. Daring to open his eyes, he looked into the thick mist. He knew it was too much to ask to have the night grow clear, but at least the voices and the grasping hands had ceased their torments.

Removing his hands from his ears, Crispin cautiously scanned the area and rose. Still shaking, he tried to control his fear and raging emotions.

Control and bravery had never been his forte, unfortunately. He quickly found himself sobbing, tears streaming down his face.

"You have done well," came a booming voice from behind.

"Aaah!" Crispin yelled as he turned quickly, swinging with a wild, poorly delivered strike. Unlike the other times, this time Crispin made contact with something all too solid. Stepping from the mist stood a giant of a man, easily seven feet at the shoulder, with a gaunt face of an ashen, gray hue and huge, bulbous, lifeless eyes.

Terrified by the huge being but strangely comforted at seeing something tangible, Crispin was about to breathe a sigh of relief when the huge creature easily lifted him up off of his feet, as if he weighed as much as a cloak. Opening the rear door, the giant threw him into the back of a covered wagon. Crispin fell with a thud onto the hard floor, shaken and more than a little upset. There was nothing to hold back his emotions this time. Tears and sobs spewed out uncontrollably.

"Would you please stop blubbering?" ordered a feminine voice from behind him.

Crispin was fully prepared to scold her for interrupting what was going to be a good, and well-deserved, cry. His reprimand caught in his throat, however, at seeing a fully furnished living area, complete with cots along the wall and a dining table nailed to the center of the interior. A large candle that burned weakly at the table's center, casting large, dancing shadows throughout the interior, illuminated the space.

Crispin could not help but notice that the decorations were cold and bare and seemed to reject comfort completely for functionality. But it was the sheer size of the space, fully twice the size inside of the wagon as it was on the outside, which took him aback. He had, of course, seen this type of magic before, but it was still off-putting, given his circumstances.

"You are quite safe. For now, anyway," said the female voice. "We are their neophytes. They are not going to harm us … yet."

Scanning for the voice, Crispin saw a small, unassuming form seated toward the forward-most portion of the wagon's interior. A small hole torn into the fabric of the wagon's covering allowed Crispin to see just past the small figure the huge form of the being he encountered earlier seemingly hitching itself to a yolk and harness.

Noticing Crispin's stare, the pint-sized female spoke. "That is a Greel. More dead than alive. It serves the Necromancers."

As if on cue, the Greel suddenly lifted and the front end of the wagon rose slightly, pulling the wagon along. The lurching motion of the wagon dumped Crispin once again on his rather bruised buttocks. The Greel let out a low, ominous moan, the very same moan that greeted him earlier.

As the wagon jostled along the road, the small girl made no effort to move. She merely watched Crispin make several vain attempts to establish his footing, only to lose his balance over and over. Finally maneuvering himself to a wooden chair by the center table, he was able to assume some measure of composure as he sat down.

"You are very graceful, Magus," she mocked. "Let us hope you cast better than you keep your balance."

"Shut up!" was the only retort that found its way to Crispin's lips, "And ..."

"Leave you alone?" the female again mocked him in a perfect imitation of his voice. "Yes, I heard you pleading outside. Very heroic. Maybe the dead won't want a sissy. Is that what it is you hope?"

Anger quickly replaced any fright that remained in Crispin.

"You shut your mouth, or I'll ... I'll ..." Crispin searched for some witty, biting statement of reprimand. "I'll shut it for you!" That was all he could muster.

"Well, we wouldn't want that, now would we?"

Sarcasm dripped from her every word.

Perhaps silence was the best weapon to employ at a time such as this. This woman was obviously a lower class cast about. He would not be goaded into an argument with this ... peasant. It was utterly beneath him and—

"Aaah!" Crispin shouted as the Greel suddenly lurched forward, picking up speed at an astonishing rate. The sudden increase in tempo sent him launching, once again, to the floor. It was with pure dismay that he noticed the peasant had not moved an inch.

Righting himself quickly, Crispin crawled back to the chair. His bottom was far too tender to absorb much more punishment. He sullenly turned to face the rear of the wagon. Oh, how he wished for another life.

"Greel can run as fast as horses for short stretches of time. Did you know that?" the female asked. "Strong as oxen, too. Brighter than most people would think. Although—"

"Would you please shut your mouth?" Crispin shouted over his shoulder. He was quite impressed with himself that there was no measure of crying apparent in his voice.

"No," was the simple response. "No, I won't shut it."

Crispin felt his anger growing with each passing second.

"I thought you said you'd shut it for me," she goaded.

This time, Crispin was able to catch himself on the table, though his shock nearly sent him to the floor again. Spinning around, Crispin was staring eye to eye with the little, female trollop. She was sitting next to him, having made her way across the jouncing wagon without so much as a sound.

Crispin could not make out any distinctive features since she had the hood of her black, woolen cloak pulled close. He did notice how thin she appeared though. Obviously, meals were a rare accommodation for this runt. As, apparently, were baths.

"What are you doing? Get back to the far end of the wagon where you belong," screeched Crispin. "I have nothing to say to you."

The female neophyte lifted an empty, pale hand. Also quite dirty beneath the fingernails, Crispin quickly noticed. With a flourish worthy of the finest court entertainer, there suddenly appeared a handkerchief resting in her palm. "Take it. Grimy cheeks do not a Necromancer make."

With that, she tried to dry Crispin's tears, only to have her hand smacked away. Or rather, would have been smacked. This little female dodged his hand as if the move had come from his grandmother. In the blink of his astonished eyes, she had the handkerchief right back in front of his face as if he had not moved at all.

After a moment's consideration, Crispin reached out, carefully, and took the handkerchief, though he did take it with a magnanimous sniff for good measure. The wagon continued to bounce roughly while he wiped his face.

"I suppose you expect me to thank you, now?" Crispin said, eyes closed as the handkerchief made its way across his brow.

"No," she said, having returned to her original spot at the far end of the wagon. "I don't expect too much of anything from you."

Crispin opened his eyes quickly, again astonished at her aptitude for quick, silent movement.

"Well, here you are, then," Crispin raised the now soiled handkerchief in her direction. "Thank you … I suppose."

"I blush at such heartfelt sentiment."

Goblin's tears, but the little street urchin had a way with sarcasm. She virtually oozed with it.

"You keep it," she continued. "I have others."

Crispin folded the handkerchief neatly, more to have something to do during the uncomfortable journey than for anything else. Unconsciously, he raised it to his face and dabbed his nose. It had the faint scent of lavender. Perhaps she did not smell so badly.

"I can't ever recall the road to Dun Sparrow being so pocked and rough-hewn," he said. "It is obvious the civil planners are not keeping up with the duties of the interior." There, that should once again set order to things. Surely, this street person could not fathom the depths of civil engineering.

Let's hear her sarcastic retort to that, he thought, amusedly.

"We haven't been on the road for the past half hour," was her reply.

Crispin made his way carefully to the front of the wagon. He stabilized himself on the rough wooden planks that made up the lower, uncanvassed wagon base. Looking through the tear in the canvas flap, just past the hulking shoulders of the Greel, he could barely make out the terrain. The unearthly fog traveled with them, no doubt meant to obscure them from anyone's view. He did see that the ground was clearly not the hard-packed surface or cobbled stone that marked a road of Canodria.

"Like I said, Greel are strong as oxen," she went on. "They don't tire like normal beings. So long as the wagon wheels stay sturdy, the Greel will move all night. No fear of broken bones either."

Crispin turned and gently slid to the floor. It was every bit as comfortable as those gods-accursed chairs and easier to maintain balance on. Here, Crispin caught his first glimpse of the mysterious female, as beautiful green eyes shown ever so briefly in the candlelight. Almost as if she sensed he had seen too much, she instinctively drew her hood further down, sinking into its darkness.

"How do you know so much about these Greel things?"

"How do you know so little?" she retorted. "You're a Claxis, correct? Grandson of the Grand Magus Prespertin Claxis? Oh, I know all about you."

"How did you know that? My appointment was not made public." Crispin was truly concerned.

"You'd be surprised by what I know, Claxis. You'd be surprised. I know that a rich, snotty noble like yourself has access to all the books in the Known Kingdoms on either side of the Rift. But do you read them? Not hardly. Your hands haven't seen a hard day's work in your life, and if my arse was as lily soft as yours, I'd have been crying too."

Crispin arose in disdain. Only to get knocked into the wagon's frame by a particularly uneven patch of ground and sat back with a thud. Quickly, though, he rose to his knees, coming eye to eye with the small whelp. He steadied himself before he spoke.

"Now see here," he began, "I have read more books in my life than you possibly could get your filthy, grubby little fingers on in 10 lifetimes. I just chose to concentrate on other fields of study. And as for hard work, I've done more than my share. Work that you and yours obviously don't have or can't keep, judging by your hygiene. And ... and ..."

"And what?" Her quiet tone suddenly took on quite a dangerous edge for one so slender. Crispin wasn't quite sure what she might do ... or what he could do to stop her.

"And ... my arse is just fine!"

With that, he turned and sat. That should teach her, speaking to one of her betters in such a manner.

What happened next completely shocked Crispin. She laughed. Full throated and hearty.

"I like you, Claxis," she spat. "Damn me for a fool, but I do."

How vulgar. Crispin hoped that the neophyte classes would be segregated to male and female sections.

"Please stop calling me Claxis," he said, after inching away from her spittle. "If we must be forced to cohabitate, for the time being ... you may call me Crispin."

At that, the little street urchin with the sarcastic tongue slid back her hood, revealing a face that was very pretty. And very young. Crispin saw raven black hair, cut short, almost in the style of most Canodrian boys. It did nothing to age her face, and if anything, only added to her youthful appearance. Overall, her face had a waifish, fairy-like quality. But it was her eyes, emerald pools of strength, which caught the candlelight with such brilliance that he could barely look away, that held his attention so intently.

"Why, you're just a girl."

At that, she suddenly rose and sent a sandaled foot right into Crispin's chest, sending him fully to the wagon's hard, wooden floor. In an instant, before he could catch his breath, she was standing over him, her glare leaving no doubt about her mood.

"Now you listen, Crispin Claxis, and listen well," she began. "I am every bit as much woman as you are man, if you can call yourself that. I have seen 16 winters come the Feasttide, and I'll not hear otherwise. Understand!"

"Yes. Yes. Understood," Crispin stammered as she moved clear of him. He had never met anyone who was so insulted by age. He thought women always wanted to be remarked upon about how young they looked. Well, it must be a lower class trait. "I only meant that you looked young."

"Well I'm not," she stated flatly.

Crispin rubbed his chest as he sat up. He was fully prepared to give her a piece of his mind. How dare she *strike* one of her betters? Although upon further reflection, he thought better of sharing any more of his mind with her. Not that he was scared, of course. He just did not feel like handing her the thrashing she deserved. She had, after all, offered him a handkerchief.

They continued on in silence for quite some time. She had repositioned herself at the rear of the wagon. She did not look at him at all. Strangely, he drew little comfort from that.

"Well, do you have a name?" Crispin finally spoke. "Or are we meant to suffer this road in silence?"

She turned her gaze to him slowly. "I thought you wanted my mouth shut?"

Crispin rolled his eyes in irritation. *Girls*, he thought. He looked at her again. *Women*, he mentally amended.

"My name is Dolthaia."

Dolthaia, quite a lovely name for a street rat. Crispin thought.

Crispin rose and carefully approached Dolthaia. He sat down in one of the uncomfortable, straight-backed wooden chairs and handed her the handkerchief.

"Here," he began. "I will not forget the kindness."

Dolthaia looked at the dirty handkerchief and dismissed it with a small smile. "You keep it. I have others."

That rang peculiarly with Crispin. "Yes, you said that. But how exactly? We are not supposed to carry any personal items with us. Not even a handkerchief, let alone more than one. Surely *you* know that?" Hah, Crispin could ladle out the sarcasm quite well, himself.

Dolthaia looked at him plainly.

"Magic," she stated, as if that answered it.

Crispin was rather perplexed by the response. Necromancers were not known for their ability to conjure objects into being. To be sure, the very powerful could in some instances, but that ability belonged more to an elementalist. Odd, also, that he did not feel a Life Spark at her conjuring. All magics are different, of course, as are the people who wield them, but he did have a gift for sensing the usage of magic. Strange that he did not register the sensation with her.

"Have you read nothing about the Necromancers?" Dolthaia asked, genuinely curious.

"Honestly, I tried not to think about it. I thought it best just to let the training begin." Crispin gave a half-hearted chuckle.

"We should rest," Dolthaia stated. "It will be sunrise soon."

Not quite content to leave the conversation lie, Crispin continued. "What is the worst that can happen? I mean, we are their neophytes. Certainly, they will scare us, try to bend us to their will. Bend me, I say. I am easily persuadable. The less I know, the better. After all, it is not like they are going to kill us, right?"

Dolthaia just stared at him with those piercing green eyes for a time. She seemed to be taking a full accounting of him.

"They are Necromancers," she said, finally. "To embrace the art, we have to touch the Spark from beyond this life. To embrace the Spark, killing us is exactly what they have to do."

She was serious. She was dead serious. Crispin's buttocks must have already gotten stronger because he hardly felt it this time as he collapsed to the floor.

"Kill us?" Crispin whispered.

"That is the first test of a neophyte," Dolthaia stated. "We have to die."

At that moment, Crispin was very thankful for Dolthaia's handkerchief.

6: Maars Wills It

B ands of light from the rising sun poured through the clouds and highlighted portions of the terrain as if the gods had chosen only small sections to bask fully in radiance. Torgatu looked out toward the western horizon onto wide swaths of open land dotted with rocky outcroppings, some that rose as high as 20 feet, and widely spaced copses of dogwood, maple, and spruce trees, only now beginning to don their autumn coats. Like arms to the Sharp River, streams snaked across the landscape.

There was one section though, not basked in any radiance whatsoever. One section that the gods' love nor the sun's rays would never fully touch, no matter how directly they shown down upon that point. It was that section, which held Torgatu's focus. A small thicket of spruce trees near a large outcropping of rock and very close to a meandering stream of moderate size held Torgatu at the ready. That copse contained the prize. Torgatu would claim it today; he and his band would retrieve it for the glory of the true gods, for the glory of the Lector Maars himself. Spotters had caught the trail the night before. It was indeed fortunate that Torgatu was able to assemble a group and get them into position so quickly. It was rare to catch the trail of a Necromantic wagon, bearing its neophytes to their dread service. It was even more so to come away from a confrontation with Necromantic Magics unscathed.

"How goes the watch, Torgatu?" came a call from behind. "Any movement?"

Torgatu did not need to turn to know who addressed him; her voice was distinct and clear as the morning sun. Maltia approached with a confident gait. Tall and though Canodrian by birth, she wore her long, blonde hair braided in the Talustrian style. She was all business. Torgatu respected that about her.

Her leather, sleeveless jerkin was neatly kept, with a light green blouse underneath. She wore trousers of thick amber material, well-suited for riding. Fashion for her was a form of function, nothing more. With a short sword and a dirk strapped to either side of her sturdy black belt, she cut a most formidable figure. Never one to be called pretty, she never grieved over the lack of attention from men. She was a good soldier; that was all that concerned Torgatu.

Finally turning to face her as she approached, Torgatu adjusted his padded-leather jerkin. His dark eyes glowered with a hungry anticipation as he unconsciously fingered the heavy, curved dagger at his waist. "None. They are still as the dead."

"As they soon will be. When do we strike?" she asked.

"Soon," he spoke with eagerness. "As the sun rises, their powers grow weak. We will strike in the heat of the day, with the sun's full radiance shining down to mark witness to our glory. Today, we strike a blow for all that is good and just." Torgatu looked up towards the thickening cloud cover. "Though we may lose some of our advantage if the sun cannot burn its way through this increasing cover." He turned to look at her. "Let's move forward."

"Yes, sir," she replied, as she raised her right hand in a salute that was picture perfect. Maltia then turned and headed to her mount.

The best time to strike was when the sun was highest in the sky. He did not know how many neophytes the wagon carried, but that mattered little. Even one less new Necromancer was a mighty blow for the cause of truth. Though innocent now, these neophytes would soon become corrupt and darkened by the Necromancers and their magics. He was really doing them a favor. Their deaths would be quick and painless, that he would assure. Today they would die, but they would die with their innocence intact. *After all,* he thought. *Maars wills it.*

Having relieved himself and feeling several pounds lighter, Crispin walked leisurely back toward the wagon. The last few days had passed without incident—minus having to put up with his ill-bred companion, of course—and he hoped that trend would continue. The wagon was camped in a rather thick copse of trees, nestled within their deep, green branches. The rocks the trees grew around stretched high into the morning sky and cast their shadows in a westerly direction against the rays of the rising sun.

For a creation of Necromantic magics, the Greel had picked a very tranquil place to stop. In the clear reason that accompanies the light of day, the Necromancers did not seem all that bad.

But eventually, the sun must set. He thought sadly. For now, however, the surroundings were quite hospitable, despite the early hour.

Looking about, Crispin wondered as to where the Greel could have gone. Where was the large thing? A creature that size certainly could not just up and disappear. Perhaps, those creatures vanished at dawn? That would be a small blessing unto itself.

Crispin heard light footfalls coming from the wagon and knew that meant the approach of Dolthaia. She was certainly a stealthy, little thing. Crispin was certain that sort of skill was required, given her common background. Commoners were always best seen and not heard. She was

105

unlike any girl he had ever met. Uncouth, to be sure. Classless and crass at the utmost and purposefully sarcastic, she definitely did not have the refinement to which he was accustomed. She did have the most alluring green eyes though.

At her approach, Crispin walked over to a small boulder near the stream and sat down. He felt the slight tingle of the magics nearby. It must have been emanating from the wagon. Crispin noted that the boulder was very smooth to the touch.

He had acted very awkwardly when he first encountered Dolthaia. Today, though, he was going to be the cutting image of composure. He would not be outdone in a showing of poise-under-pressure by a common street rat, however pretty and wise she might be.

Being a noble made him inherently self-assured. *Yes, he thought as he leaned slightly back. I am the picture of ease.*

That picture of ease turned quickly into a caricature of fright when the boulder suddenly moved. Crispin yelped and fell to the mossy ground. It slowly stood and removed a large cloak. The Greel stood before him.

"Ha! Damn me for a fool, Claxis, but you are good for a laugh!" Dolthaia chuckled. She neared him and offered him a hand. "You act as if you'd never seen a Cloak of Blending before."

Crispin arose in agitation without accepting her help. So it was the power of the cloak that he had felt. He should have been more alert.

A Cloak of Blending was a rather weakly enchanted item as far as that all went. It was only effective when its wearer remained perfectly still. It bestowed upon its wearer the ability to take the shape and appearance of anything in the surrounding area of the same basic size. So long as one stayed completely still, one could blend in perfectly anywhere.

He was more than a bit surprised that this mindless creature could use such an item. Although how much intelligence did it truly take to kneel into a ball and cover oneself?

Dolthaia approached the Greel slowly, its pasty expression barely registering her presence as it looked down at her. The massive size of the Necromantic creation magnified her tiny frame. Whereas she was perhaps five feet tall at most, the Greel towered over her by at least three-and-a-half more feet.

At slightly under six feet, Crispin towered over her too, but the disparity in size he now witnessed was almost comical. In the deathly mist and dark of night in which Crispin first encountered the thing, he could not fully take in its mass and size. The Greel was enormous.

"Thank you for bearing us so safely, thus far," she began. Dolthaia's voice was soft and comforting. "What is your name?"

The Greel only stared down at her. Its ashen, gaunt face and huge, bulbous eyes looked a mockery of life. Covered in only a sleeveless, gray tunic and matching pants, its swollen mass from below its thick neck was all muscle. There was no muscular definition to be seen, just rounded mounds of thickness that splayed across its torso, arms, and legs. The creature's bare feet were as unsightly as those of an oarkman, dirty and fungus ridden. Crispin noticed that this particular Greel had several toes on each foot missing. Obviously, a lack of toes did not slow the thing's pace in the slightest.

"It's all right," she said again, softly. "What is your name?"

The Greel only stared at her.

Smiling, she raised her hands in front of her face. "Watch this …"

Moving them about, she waved them one in front of the other in a flourish, making a fist with her left hand. She blew into her fist as she kept her right hand dancing about. In a quick gesture, she opened her hand and produced a small, yellow wildflower. Smiling, she offered it up to the creature. "Here, for you."

Crispin noted that she produced the flower in the same way she had the handkerchief with no trace of magical spark at all. It was such a tiny flower that he must not have registered what little spark was necessary for the conjuring. After all, he could not sense all magics.

Dolthaia reached out for the Greel's large, swollen hand. It moved back ever so slightly.

"Why are you bothering?" Crispin asked. "It obviously does not understand you. It is animated tissue, nothing more."

"The Greel live … and think," she said without turning to look at Crispin. "I just want him to know I appreciate him, is all."

"Why do you even care what that hideous thing thinks? It surely could care less about you."

"Because I do," she abruptly turned to face him. "You nobles really make me sick. Do you know that? You think that because someone is hideous, he has no heart? Is that it? Or is it merely that the Greel appears as nothing more to you than a servant? Just like the rest of us commoners."

"Don't talk to me in such a manner," Crispin countered. "You forget yourself. I brought it up because the thing is clearly unresponsive. So why waste your time?"

"Everyone appreciates a kind gesture, whether they respond or not," she turned back to the Greel and placed the wildflower on the ground at its feet. "That is for you." Turning, Dolthaia headed back to the wagon.

"Kindness, Claxis," she said as she crossed past Crispin. "I don't just reserve it for sniveling little nobles."

Perplexed, Crispin watched her walk away and climb the small stepladder positioned at the rear of the wagon. The rear door slammed shut with a solid thud. He did not understand why she was so upset. Clearly, the Greel did not understand her, or at the very least, did not care. It was a thing, nothing more. Looking back at it, he saw the huge creature looking down at the flower at its feet. It raised its head slowly, bulbous eyes, completely black, as if they were all iris, looked back at him.

It slowly donned its Cloak of Blending and turned to kneel. As it did, Crispin noticed a large piece of thornbrush protruding from the back of its left leg, just at the ankle. Thornbrush grew in abundance in southern Canodria. It was exactly as its name implied: thick, hard brush covered with long, spike-like thorns. Many a noble would plant it along the perimeter of their castle's walls, for it grew and spread like ivy, adding another layer of defense. Little red bulbs covered some varieties and made them appear quite attractive. The particular strain that stabbed into the Greel was just an ugly brown. Rather fitting for the creature it had impaled.

"Wait!" Crispin called suddenly, much to his own surprise. Also surprising Crispin, the Greel did wait. It then turned to face him. "You have a … a, spike. There, on your ankle. It's thornbrush."

The Greel looked down at its ankle, then back to Crispin.

To his great surprise, Crispin found himself approaching the huge monstrosity. Crispin bent down and reached for the piece of thornbrush. "I cannot believe I am doing this," he said to himself.

The Greel began to move away.

"Hold still," Crispin said. The Greel did exactly that. At such a close proximity to the Greel, Crispin noted that the creature had a rather foul odor. It was not as pungent as the smell of death, but it was definitely not pleasant and almost made Crispin turn away. However, he had come this far. He might as well finish what he had started.

"This might hurt a bit," Crispin said.

He grabbed a piece of the thornbrush without any wicked spikes. With a firm tug, he ripped it free from the swollen flesh of the Greel's ankle. The creature did not register any reaction at all. "Then again, maybe not."

Crispin rose quickly and backed away. The smell was pungent and sickly sweet, almost like meat that had been left in the sun for a day or two. He noticed a tiny flow of blood oozing out of the puncture the thornbrush had left. The blood did not flow freely, however, as it would have had the injury been Crispin's. Instead, it seeped like molasses, slow and steady. It seemed to thicken rapidly.

Crispin had seen, and smelled, quite enough. The Greel watched him as he tossed the thornbrush aside.

"Well," Crispin began, rather unsure of how to proceed. "Thank you … I guess. Do whatever it is you do."

With that, he headed quickly to the wagon as the Greel knelt back into its original position by the bank of the stream.

Dolthaia returned to the table and sat down. Having seen the exchange between Crispin and the Greel through a small tear in the wagon's canvas covering, she smiled despite herself. "Well done, little, spoiled Claxis," she said. "Maybe there's hope for you yet."

Entering the wagon, Crispin suddenly felt a tingle come over his body. Something felt wrong. "Dolthaia ..."

Suddenly, a powerful blast struck the side of the wagon with a loud explosion. The force of the blow launched everything in the wagon's interior. The magical candle winked out with a flash of yellow light as the heavy wooden table crashed end over end into the far side. Chairs flew everywhere, one clopped Dolthaia in the shoulder as she was rocked to the floor. The magics that enchanted the wagon shielded it from most of the effects of the magical strike.

Crispin was trying to regain his balance when a second, more powerful blast slammed into the wagon, completely overturning it. A hole had been blown open in the canvas covering on the side that bore the impact. The force of the second blast knocked Crispin and Dolthaia out of the wagon and onto the nearby ground.

The world spun to Crispin's dazed view. He heard shouts of, "Maars wills it!" It sounded like numerous people had taken up that call.

He had the vague feeling he should get away but was unable to get his legs to lift him from the soggy ground on which he sat. Looking up, he felt something warm trickling down his forehead. Why did his face feel so sticky and wet? He did not have time to register what it was when he felt a pair of small, strong hands grab him by the scruff of the collar.

Dolthaia appeared before him. She had blood streaming down from a cut on the side of her neck. She grabbed him and gave a violent shake. Her lips were moving, but Crispin could not hear any sound from the ringing in his ears.

"Come on!" Dolthaia yell.

111

He concentrated with as much focus as he could muster. Looking through the dust and debris, Crispin saw that the wagon was now completely upside-down. The small hole was now a gaping opening with smoke billowing through. Along with shouts Crispin heard the sound of arrows whizzing in the air.

"To arms! To arms! The beast moves!" He heard someone call.

"Light the arrows!" Came a response. "Fire! Maars wills it!"

Crispin could barely take an accounting of himself as Dolthaia helped him to his feet. Finally shaking his vision clear, Crispin saw chaos surround him.

To his left, Crispin saw men firing arrows at the Greel through the copse of trees. The Greel, already with two arrows protruding from its huge, swollen frame, tore off into the trees.

"It escapes!" one man yelled.

"Give chase!" called another.

"No! Hold your ranks!" called a third.

Two arrows, these with flaming tips, buzzed just above him as bowmen from his rear flank fired at the quickly retreating beast. *So much for it being of any help,* he thought with dismay.

Turning to his right, Crispin caught sight of three mounted figures, two women and a man, perhaps 20 yards away. The man and one of the women looked like soldiers, with studded leather armor and swords drawn, while the other woman wore only a loose vest of chainmail over her blouse and greaves showing from beneath a divided blue riding dress. Crispin did not need his ability to sense magic to know that she was a Battle Magus. She was preparing to cast again.

"Damn it! Return to your ranks!" the male mounted rider swore at the men giving chase to the Greel. He was clearly in charge, an air of command about him. "Lanna, quickly, destroy the wagon!" This he shouted to the female Battle Magus.

There was a strange, white mist forming on the ground around them. As the black smoke billowed from the wagon up into the air, this mist seemed to spill out from it and onto the ground. It felt cold. Crispin remembered this mist well; it had greeted him on the road the night before. Instantly, he was gripped with the same fear he had felt as he waited for the dread wagon. This time, however, the mist did not seem interested in him at all.

The female rider, her sword drawn, pointed in the direction of Crispin and Dolthaia. Her words were lost when a crack of thunder pealed with deafening intensity through the trees. A blue blast of lightning erupted from the hands of the Battle Magus and smashed into the burning wagon. The wagon exploded in a blast of blue energy and crackling wood. The force of the explosion sent Crispin and Dolthaia flying into the soft moss and bushes that grew near the water's edge, some 20 feet away.

The wagon had been destroyed too late. This was what Torgatu had feared the most. With the day fully overcast now, the direct rays of the sun were not present to help combat the death magics that the Necromancers employed. The mist rose from the ground and charged towards them, taking form at alarming speed. It began to shape itself into hideous, zombie-like torsos made of vapor with faces contorted into wicked, barely human forms. He

113

heard strange calls on the wind. *Bleed for us.* He heard voices call.

"Ignore the sounds!" Torgatu yelled.

He quickly drew a piece of flint rock and struck it to the blade of his long sword. Having been doused in highly flammable wax resin, the blade burst into flames. Without a second's delay, he touched it to Maltia's sword, which, also having been coated, immediately caught flame as well.

"Stay away from the mist and get those children!" he ordered Maltia.

"Yes, sir!" she responded, as she galloped off.

Torgatu moved his horse away from the Battle Magus as the mist creatures quickly approached. He did not want to be close to her as she loosed her next spell. The mist reached out for him in the form of two fast-moving, wicked ghouls. Keeping his wits about him, he struck at the mist with his flaming sword. The thick wax resin would keep the flame localized on the blade, and the wet cloth he used to wrap the sword's crosspiece and hilt would protect his hand from the heat. He had dealt with death magics before.

Slicing out and across his body from left to right along a descending arc, the fiery blade struck and ripped into the mist creatures as if they had solid mass. The mist creatures dissipated wherever the flames made contact. He shuddered at their screams when the creatures lost their earthly form and returned to mist. The cries of the dead were never easy on the ears of the living.

Torgatu saw the three remaining bowmen who did not give chase to the beast suddenly drop their bows, cover their ears in horror, and take off in separate directions.

"Fools!" he spat in disgust as another mist creature rose in front of him. This one spooked his horse, and it was all he could do to stay in his saddle.

A blast of fire erupted around the Battle Magus when Lanna cast a *Ring of Flame*. The basic spell tore through several ghouls as the energy dissipated around her. She was preparing another spell.

"No, Lanna! Pull back!" Torgatu yelled, as he brought his horse to heel. Like most Battle Magi, Lanna was very powerful and could summon large amounts of magical energy. Also, she was quick to act, thinking her spellcasting would see her through any situation.

Charging toward her, he realized that she did not have the time to finish her next casting. The mist rose up before her, forming into a huge wraithlike creature of horrid design. The sight literally stole his breath as he saw the mist creature dive upon her, crashing in and through her body, as well as that of her spotted horse, and sent them slamming to the ground.

She looked up at him in horror as ghostly, vaporous claws grabbed at her and seemingly yanked the youth from her body. She uttered the last portion of her final chant as a Ring of Flame formed around her and blasted into the mist.

The wailings of the dead issued forth as fire dissipated the mist around her. The damage had been done, however, as she slumped down next to the carcass of her dead horse. Both she and the animal looked as if they had been sucked dry, only withered husks that once housed vibrant, living beings. Torgatu winced.

The mist was losing its energy now. He was beginning to be able to see through it to the other side of the brush. He could make out the image of Maltia slashing her way through with the practiced strokes of a trained warrior.

Flaming arrows struck the mist where it still clung to the ground as it attempted to take shape again. The arrows tore through the mist and caused it to evaporate into nothingness. The howlings of the dead were growing steadily weaker. Trying desperately to transform into a murky claw, one final tendril of mist wrapped itself around Torgatu's arm. Even in its ever-weakening state, the mist pulled with the cold force of the dead.

Disgusted, Torgatu slashed his flaming sword in a downward arc to sever the mist and its ties to this world. Had the sun been out, it would not have been able to take form at all. Had Lanna listened to his commands, she would have stayed back and still be alive. The Necromancers had exacted a heavy toll. He would repay that loss with the neophytes' heads.

7: The Great Muse

The sounds that greeted Gascon upon entering the theater were as familiar to him as the sound of his own breathing. Weavers strummed melodic rhythms on lutes, harps, and a multitude of stringed instrument from every alcove and corner of the beautifully furnished space. The whistling elegance of flutes and other exotic woodwinds accompanied their steady strum.

Each Weaver's Theater in every town or city was built upon the same general design. A large, spacious interior tiered with balconies that led to offshoot rooms in which to conduct private business were the standard. The open main hall was built in a vaulted, beehive design. Every decoration, banister, and hallway as well as each overhang and eave were designed to enhance the acoustic majesty of the theater.

Greeting Gascon upon his entrance was Ceiran, waiting with a huge parchment scroll.

"Greetings, Lord Herrod Gascon," Ceiran said formally. "I hope this late afternoon finds you well."

"Yes, yes. Well enough, I suppose."

She took up quickly at his side, walking just behind him. "The Herrod's Council awaits your presence. I have here the list of the day's topics and minutes of the last meeting."

She extended and handed a smaller piece of rolled parchment to him. How he tired of Ceiran's endless barrage of parchments. Gascon took it with a perturbed and dismissive wave.

"Sing well," she called, as Gascon began to ascend a secluded staircase. "Bid the Great Muse my warmest."

"What!" Gascon roared, his face quickly blanching as he turned back to face Ceiran. "The Diva herself holds this council?"

"Why, yes," Ceiran said, legitimately confused. "It was in the notes I gave you this morning. The Great Muse intended to preside personally."

She barely finish that statement as the full force of Gascon's backhanded slap rang flush on her cheek, sending her to the floor. She gathered herself quickly, unwilling to exhibit any outward sign of weakness or pain.

"Next time, foolish tart, make sure you deliver any news of the Great Muse to me verbally! Do you understand?" Gascon was livid. He planned to demonstrate to the other Herrods his importance by arriving late. Never would he have dared insult the Great Muse in such a manner. Many a Herrod had lost their station by making that miscalculation.

"Yes, my Lord. It was my fault completely."

"Indeed," Gascon barked. "See that it does not happen again!" With that, Gascon moved with all haste up the winding staircase.

Regaining her feet, Ceiran quickly followed Gascon up the staircase and through the ceiling, emerging into a smaller room. The staircase led up one more level, but she remained there.

A small stool with a pedaling device attached to a long rope sat just off to one side of the central, spiraling staircase. Ceiran walked over, sat in the chair, and started pedaling. The pedals were attached to a series of pulleys, notched interconnected wheels and cranks, visible beneath open metal grates in the floor.

The mechanisms began to move and spin off of each other with a well-oiled ease. As they did so, the rope, which wound through the mechanism, stretched taut and triggered the release of a weighted, curved bone with intricate carvings and holes placed in various spots. The rope shot from a small opening in the outer wall near one of the columns and began to spin. The faster Ceiran peddled, the faster the bone-weighted rope spun.

Called a *dradar*, or wind whistle, the bone would catch the wind through its many holes as it spun and emitted a high-pitched whistling sound. The sound of the whistle escalated with each rotation, the faster Ceiran pedaled.

Gascon quickly reached the uppermost level of the spiral staircase. Stepping from the staircase, he was struck by wind as he assumed his position behind the podium. On occasions when the Great Muse joined the Herrod's Council, as was the case today, her dais would be located at the center point of the compass, a position of power, and elevated so that all had to look up to her.

With the dradar's spin reaching an appropriate resonance, Gascon cleared his throat and raised his voice in song, as the thought of the Great Muse's displeasure filled his mind. He had witnessed her anger leveled with vicious ferocity against the very Herrod who held the position prior to him. He didn't want to see that ire turned against him. She must remain pleased with him at any cost.

To become a Herrod of the First Order in the Weaver's upper echelon, only those voices capable of attaining the most perfect pitch were considered. Gascon's voice rose and matched the note of the whistling dradar, merging with it in a unified tone.

The moment the notes combined, the wind began to be pulled into the vortex of circular motion created by the dradar. Charged with the energy of Gascon's powerful baritone voice, the dradar became empowered with the ability to bend the wind itself. The spinning wind draped itself around the elevated platform like the silk canvassing of a tent being raised into position.

The very moment the blast of spinning, enchanted wind covered the dais completely, all cold and outside noise was blocked. The walls of wind, sturdier than the thickest stone, shielded Gascon completely from the elements. Rain, snow, even lightning itself would have met with as much resistance as if they had struck a castle's fortified walls.

Gascon's next sung note changed the variance of the pitch dramatically. It rang out, sending the newly formed wind ceiling swirling up into the heavens. The ceiling rose and shimmered, spinning up into the clouds like the funnel of a tornado that only Gascon could see.

Having completed the first chords of the wind song, Gascon waited. He was now at the mercy of the other Herrods. Should they choose to ignore his call—a circumstance not unheard of in the presence of the Great Muse—his wind funnel would drop back around him, closing once again to a ceiling and leaving him alone within his walls of wind.

His call was not unanswered, however, as he quickly heard four other notes merge with his own. Each note was of a slightly different pitch, but each amazingly beautiful in its elegance.

The greatest power of the Weavers was their ability to use sound as a tangible vehicle for communication over vast distances. Their songs carried more than just words though. They were also capable of transmitting visual images and scents. Anything a Weaver could sing could be communicated. The more talented the Weaver, the greater the distance the song could travel. The more brilliant the voice, the more intricate and detailed the message that could be sent. In this way, information flowed throughout the Known

Kingdoms. Weavers would sing their wind song and listen to the wind for responses. They could sing often and for sustained periods of time. Their only limitations were those set upon them by the quality of their voices or the stamina of their lungs.

As Gascon received the other notes of acceptance, he changed his singing one final time. This variance caused his voice to modulate in a strong vibrato. It joined the others and instantly caused the dense walls of wind to shimmer into the vision of an ornate palace recreation hall, complete with vistas of the most beautiful sights of each of the four regions of the Known Kingdoms.

The vibrato notes also served as a melodic shield against eavesdropping. Only those who were taught these particular series of notes could gain entrance into this particular wind song. Since no one after the apocalypse of the Mourning Night had ever learned to eavesdrop on a wind song, the participants here knew that they could speak freely, for not even the magics of the Magi could invade their song. That fact infuriated the Magi of the Kingdoms to no end.

Once he was admitted vocally into the Herrod's Council, he no longer needed to continue singing. There, facing Gascon from the other three compass points were the other Herrods of the First Order. The twins, Mara, representing the eastern lands, and her sister Zara, who represented the south, were as different as two mirror images could be. Both were gorgeous, with the sort of beauty that could enrapture both men and women with a glance. Each one was definitely her own woman. Many a failed attempt had there been to try and play each to the other, mainly because each had wants that were at complete opposition with what the other found important.

Mara, Eastern Herrod of the First Order, was almost as power hungry as Gascon was himself. Her waist-length hair, black as coal and fine as spun gossamer, she wore unadorned, flowing down her back. She was dressed simply, though elegantly, in a royal blue gown that was moderately cut at the neckline, revealing a modest amount of smooth, olive skin. Her sister, Zara, on the other hand, was passion personified. Wearing her hair in an intricate series of braids, it wrapped delicately around her beautiful oval face and cascaded down her back in elaborate tresses.

Where Mara wore a modest gown, Zara tended to leave modesty completely to her sister. She wore a more than revealing top that covered her buxom bosoms, and only her bosoms, in a swaddling of burnt orange triangular cotton, leaving her extremely toned midsection bare. Her trousers were the loose, flowing pantaloons favored by those who lived along the coastal communities.

To Gascon's right was Pelvil Galling, Western Herrod of the First Order and the only other male member of this upper echelon of Weavers. Wearing stockings that were an electric blue and fit more snuggly than did even those of Gascon, he added trademark red leather, knee-high boots. He carried a scent box dangling from a long, golden cord that he would occasionally sniff. He gestured grandly, speaking as much with his hands as with his voice. People often mistook his delicate mannerisms and high-pitched voice as signs of weakness. That was a misconception that he never played down. He had the amazing ability of always finding himself two steps away from any trouble or difficult situation. Perhaps that was because he had what was quite possibly the largest network of informants of any of the Herrods, First, Second, or Third Order.

He took in Gascon with his deep blue eyes. His smile seemed to Gascon as oily as did his pointed moustache and beard, both of which were well twisted to fine points. Though he was far older than Gascon, he showed no gray touches anywhere.

Then there was The Great Muse. She was the Grand Lady. The Diva Calindrial sat in her plush, cushioned, reclining couch of silver and gray with the presence and majesty of a queen, which, in terms of scope and power, she virtually was. Her sheer silken robe of feldspar complemented the flowing gown of fuchsia that she wore beneath. Her blonde locks flowed in great waves that fell naturally around her face in a dance of platinum grace. She wore a thin, silver headband bejeweled with small pearls. The paleness of the pearls stood in contrast to her light brown skin.

Her eyes were what caught the eye and held most people entranced from the moment they saw her. Pelvil's were blue, but hers were something more, a hue so light they almost seemed white, rung with a deep blue outer edge. Those eyes were mesmerizing and hypnotic. She locked her stare onto Gascon. Looking down from her elevated position, she and her couch seemed to be floating in air, some five feet above the others.

In these meetings, she was the only one who could move, taking her position, higher or lower, wherever she chose. If she favored someone, it was not uncommon for her to position herself right next to that person, conferring her grace and strengthening that person's position. Normally, though, the Diva Calindrial kept her position in the center, spinning gracefully to speak with whomever she chose. Now, she chose to simply take in Gascon, weighing him carefully. Her pale eyes gave away nothing but seemed to take in everything. She knew that Gascon was ambitious. She would use his ambition to further her own gains and grow the Weaver's Guild to be an even stronger force of influence in the Kingdoms.

Gascon's dealings with the Necromancers made him a commodity to be positioned with great care. She had heard that he was gaining quickly in favor with the dark Magi. She had chosen him to be the liaison between the Weavers and the Necromancers because his thirst for power allowed her to position him without having to do much more than dangle the proper carrot. Dealing with the most powerful rulers of the Known Kingdoms and making them bend to her will was what she did best.

"So glad am I that you could find the time to join us," she began. "I do hope we did not pull you from very pressing matters."

"I am so heartily sorry for having kept you waiting, my Lady," Gascon said in his most apologetic voice. It would have been inexcusable for him to speak first. "A thousand pardons I beg of you, as well as of my esteemed players." He gave a well-practiced and extravagant bow.

Mara, Zara, and Pelvil knew full well that Gascon's apology was meant only for the Diva. Had she not been here, his attitude would have been as pompous and entitled as ever it had.

"I assure you that nothing is as important to me as my commitments to you, Lady," Gascon continued. "I was not informed you were to be present until just recently."

"I see," the Diva said calmly. "It is good I am present. Lest, I fear, you may not have seen fit to attend at all." That brought a hearty laugh from the other three Herrods. The Diva merely smiled, her eyes trained on Gascon.

"I beg your forgiveness, Great Muse," Gascon said.

"Gascon, I forgive your tardiness," the Diva continued. "You are well-received. Now, we had already begun discussing the news of the day in your absence. Mara had finished her telling of Eastern events. Mara, would you grace us again with a more abridged version of events?" She turned a displeased eye to Gascon. "Just to make sure we are all current."

Mara gave Gascon a cold stare also. Once an account was given, it normally fell to that Herrod's underlings to give the retelling. "Of course, Great Muse," she said. "The song sounds freely in the East though troubles do abound that might quash its resonant tones.

"The lands whose borders touch the darkness of the Great Rift, Sorilan, Daldra, and Medioc all speak of evils rising out of the Rift itself. Being as the Rift is torn deep within the dangerous terrain of the Kyldsong Mountain range, it is very difficult to prove the claims."

"What of the claims of civil war in Daldra proper?" the Diva asked. "My sources tell me that it is not only probable but most likely imminent."

Mara knew that the Great Muse had her sources. It just infuriated her that those sources were in amongst her own. She held her circle of control closely, guarding it closely, even against the Diva herself.

"Your sources of information are correct, my Lady," Mara continued. "They are—"

"I know full well who they are, beautiful one," the Great Muse said. "Please carry on with your exquisite song."

The Great Muse knew that that small slap would sting at Mara for quite a while. It was necessary, from time to time, to let Mara know that her foundations of strength had cracks within them that carried the Diva's own signature.

"Of course, Great Muse," Mara responded quickly. She would never show that she was bothered, not in the least, and never to the Diva. "Escaped Lyndrian slaves are making their way across the Kyldsong range, avoiding the Great Rift by making the dangerous trek up and around the Frozen Circle at the top of the world. Their suppression at the hands of the powerful Therak'onian Empire must be harsh indeed.

As no news or song is able to penetrate through the Rift, this is all my informants know.

"Finally, in each Eastern country, from the largest cities to the smallest hamlets, reports of women going missing continue to spread. Not enough in any one place to cause a huge outcry as of yet. But the numbers do increase. I will notify you the moment my informants give me anything truly credible.

"With that, my account and the Song of the East are again at their end."

Mara did not hide her annoyance at having had to repeat herself. While she was speaking, the landscape behind her changed to match the various locations of which she spoke. It was a gift of the Weavers, especially the most highly skilled ones. Here, in their councils gathered in the wind song, they could create images. Hundreds, if not thousands of miles separated the Herrods and the Diva from each other, yet each looked on the others as if they were all actually in the same room. Singing images was a useful tool in communicating messages across the Kingdoms.

"Well sung, Herrod of the East. My thanks to you for your second account," the Great Muse said. She stung Mara earlier; now it was time to build her back up a bit. "You truly are one of the most gifted Herrods to hold this order. I shall continue to sing your praises across the Kingdoms."

Mara gave a small nod, her eyes registering the smallest of gleams. That tiny acknowledgement was as good as a grin from ear to ear on most anyone else. "I stand humbled, my Lady." Mara nodded again.

"Now," the Diva continued, fully satisfied. "My Herrod of the West, will you please grace us with your account?"

"The honor is mine, Great Muse. I hope my song does your presence among us justice," Pelvil began with a grandiose flurry. "The song sounds freely in the West though troubles do abound that might quash its resonant tones.

"My honored fellow Herrods," Pelvil continued. "The West is, on the whole, prosperous and peaceful. Although there are certain notes of dissension, those ring in discord across our verdant fields, tranquil cities, and glorious coastlines."

Pompous ass, Gascon thought, with no small measure of disdain.

"As was also stated by the beautiful and talented Herrod of the East, my network has informed me of a slightly increased occurrence of missing women in the West as well. These numbers are small though, and it is doubtful they are nothing more than freak occurrences, but they do bear mentioning."

"What of the Talustrians?" the Diva asked. "And please … be concise."

"Of course, gorgeous Lady," Pelvil said. He knew that the Diva was being quite diplomatic in telling him to "hurry it up, already."

"The peoples of the Talustrian Islands are preparing for the Autumnal festivities commemorating the harvest. Their ships sail wary of pirates, but their Captains, some of the best in the seas, do not fear much on the open ocean. They are quite eager to receive your presence again, Diva. The only other news is that new schools of both Elementalists and Necromancers are to begin construction on the Isles.

"Yes, we are tranquil and peaceful in the West. Some of the minor houses do jockey for position, as in all civilized lands, but those are minor games of the aristocracy, with nothing new to note that has not already been relayed to us by our various underlings.

"With that, my account and the Song of the West are at their end."

Gascon was always relieved when Pelvil was finished. This was a rather brief accounting. He had been known to wax poetic for what seemed like hours. With the presence of the Diva, whose patience was widely known to run extremely short, he was wise to keep his song brief.

"Well sung, Herrod of the West," the Great Muse said. "My thanks to you for your account. Now, my Herrod of the South, will you please grace us with your account?"

"With all honor, my Lady," Zara said, her smoky voice ever alluring. "The song sounds freely in the South though troubles do abound that might quash its resonant tones.

"Canodria is in a state of perpetual unrest. Even as the kingdom strengthens its connections with the dark Magi, the bands of the outlaw prophet Maars the Lector continue to grow. Some informants, it has been sung, believe factions of Forlmorlaine's own government have begun striking out violently against the Necromancers.

"Two accounts of arson in the small, outlying schools of Reen and Dun Medlin have resulted in several Necromantic deaths. And though the Necromancers don't necessarily look upon death with any sort of dread as do most civilized peoples, they do look very negatively upon being attacked.

"There have also been reports of Necromantic Soul Wagons, the ferries that move their neophytes to their assigned schools, being attacked and destroyed, with the neophytes either found dead or never being found at all.

"The Necromancers remain, as always, very close-mouthed about the entire situation. So it is with great interest that I look forward to the account of Gascon, our most skilled Necromantic liaison."

Zara looked very deliberately at Gascon, her sensuous demeanor belied the sincere interest she took in these happenings.

"I know your concern is sincere, Zara. Do not doubt that we will continue to sing until such time as the answers are carried on the wind. Now, please continue." The Great Muse appreciated Zara's honesty and candor. In a profession where people were tasked to spread the truth, but so few told it without embellishment, Zara was a rare jewel.

"Of course, my Lady," Zara said in her sultry tone. "The flock of this so-called prophet, Maars, holds its numbers in the foothills and gullies of Canodria. They strike and disappear along the Kerathic border and along the routes to Crag Devlin. My informants tell me that his numbers are relatively small, however, they are growing rapidly, and they are quite zealous in their devotion.

"None know where this Maars person will speak next. His position is constantly changing, but when he does speak, his flock listens most attentively.

"Devgard is indeed beset by pirates along its coast. Their shared border with Canodria is a sure place for these flocks of the prophet Maars to migrate. So my web of information gatherers is on alert for any sign that Maars is no longer content to remain confined to Canodria.

"Medioc wishes war with Canodria. Others may not wish to speak of it, but I know that King Tharster wishes to extend his reach out from his eastern home."

"Do you believe this to be true, Mara?" the Diva asked. Weavers always did well by wars. The flow of information was vital to armies on the move. The trick was to be on the winning side of that flow. As such, Weavers were indispensable in every battle. The more the Weavers knew about the onset of wars, the more prepared they could be to place themselves properly.

"There have been … whispers on the wind," Mara replied cautiously. Where Zara may have felt sure, Mara would not comment until her sources were absolutely certain. "Softly is sung the refrain of schemers prior to open war."

"I see," was the Diva's only response. "Please, Zara, carry on."

"There is much negative sentiment for the Necromancers as of late," Zara continued. "My fear is that the uprising led by this mysterious 'Maars the Lector' will gain in energy and spread throughout the south. Having a force that would enrage the dark Magi is something dangerous for us all.

"There are stories of people disappearing on treasure hunts into ancient ruins, only to emerge in other desolate haunts, often hundreds of miles away, and unaccompanied by Magi of any kind. These are silly tales, to be sure, but ones that have been floated on several winds. I expect to find nothing but am looking into these exaggerated accounts. With that, my account and the Song of the South are at their end."

"Well sung, Herrod of the South. My thanks to you for your account," the Great Muse said. "Now, my Herrod of the North, will you please grace us with your account?"

"It is my consummate pleasure and honor to serve, gracious Diva," Gascon said, bowing low.

Pelvil did so detest that little man. It was no small wonder, as the Herrod who held the title before Gascon, the disgraced Balrid, was a close friend of the Herrod of the West. It was a shame that Balrid did not see Gascon's treachery before it was too late. Pelvil did give Gascon credit for his cleverness. Gascon was a crafty one, he had to give him that.

"The song sounds freely in the North though troubles do abound that might quash its resonant tones," he began.

Singing of the political climate of the north did not concern Gascon. What troubled him was the delicate nature of his position as liaison to the Necromancers. "The northern kingdom of Aldara is strong; its frontier settlements along the mighty Nortgard Forest continue to grow and take hold."

A trained actor, Gascon could lie to a stranger that he was her son, and she would believe it. With these trained eyes on him, however, he wondered just how far he could bend the truth. No one had reported any spiritual strangeness to him. The fact that he did not ask, nor entertain those types of conversations, was beside the point. "The Lyndrian slaves escaping from around the Great Rift are stories that are ... extremely exaggerated. I am sorry to contest my talented co-player, but my informants have not confirmed the presence of even one Lyndrian."

Mara's eyes held daggers for Gascon. It was one thing to disagree privately with another Herrod's information, which happened all the time. It was entirely something else again to so blatantly deny those stories in a Council and in front of the Diva, no less!

"Where is your proof?" Mara asked. The words fell like shivers of ice from her lips.

"My proof, most captivating of singers, is that we have seen no Lyndrians," Behind him, there was only blank wind. "I meant you no disrespect, Mara of the East. I can only report what news my network of informants has gathered for me and what I can substantiate as truth. What proofs have you?"

"Lyndrians," she said with a menacing finality. Behind her, the image of a pale man with a half-shaven head and a loop of fine, black hair floated behind her.

"Enough of this!" the Diva declared. "If you children wish to quarrel, I will have a sandbox built for that very purpose. Do not bore me with your juvenile quibbling. This

131

is not a forum for debate, only exchange. You will provide your song when I command it. Never forget, it is I who spins the truth. It is I who am responsible for the content of the wind songs ... and I alone."

"Again, I fall in humble apology," Gascon's bow nearly touched his head to the floor.

"I live only to serve you, Great Lady," Mara's bow was deep and delicate.

"Let us be on with this," the Diva said. "Finish your song."

Gascon knew it was time to slip in his news of the Necromancers. "The Necromancer's of the Western Watch, they who saved us from the dread of the Mourning Night, work their magics in the solitude of Crag Drannon.

"I know not of the specifics of their magics, for a Magi I am not. I do know, however, having seen their effects first hand, that the Necromancers are making great strides in prolonging life, curing disease, and unraveling the mysteries beyond this mortal shell."

Whether they believed him or not, the other Herrods were not about to challenge his words, spoken as they were with such passion and sentiment, especially not when the Diva's mood was teetering from angry to surprised like a drunkard on a narrow walk.

"The Necromancers are quite upset by the activities in Canodria and rightly so. But they are leaving the capture and punishment of these criminals to the Canodrian Guard. As to the Rift, I assure you, I will find out with all swiftness what they think could be happening. Know full well that the Necromancers know that the responsibility of keeping the Rift contained falls squarely to them. They will do what must be done to keep it in check." Gascon took a deep breath before concluding. "With that, my account and the Song of the North are at their end."

"Well sung, Herrod of the North," The Diva looked on Gascon with great care, studying him. She relaxed back into the enveloping comfort of her silver and grey couch. "My thanks to you for your account. With that, I conclude this Council of Herrods. You have all sung well. You each have validated my beliefs in your astounding talents. Truly, I have assembled the greatest collection of talent in an age.

"Go now, all of you, and listen for my call. I will be contacting you individually as I process all we have discussed. I will tell you to what we must concentrate our focus and on what we must sing away. Go now."

Each bowed in turn. According to traditions, the Diva had the last word. Once she bid farewell, the Herrods were to leave in silence.

They began to disappear, "A moment more, Gascon. If you please?" the Diva called.

Gascon kept his notes audible, and his form quickly united into a solid whole.

"I am at your service, my Lady."

Her undivided attention was on him. She floated her image closer to him. Though just an image, she was more enticing than most women were in the flesh. She let her eyes linger, Gascon could lose himself in those eyes; most men did. He had to take care though. It was in private conversations with the Diva that people gave her far more than they had intended. It was always like that with beautiful people. She knew this, and always utilized it to full advantage.

"I have heard it whispered that these disappearing women have far more to do with the Necromancers than they let on. Is this true?" she asked.

Gascon was sincere in his response. "I know of no Necromantic involvement, Lady."

That was the truth. He had met with Brother Ronulen often in the last weeks at that dreary school in Farmalkin. Of all the vivid insights that were made known to him regarding the Necromancers and their ways, there was never once even the smallest mention of the disappearance of women. The fact that Gascon never asked was beside the point.

"The Necromancers grow in power," she purred. "Our union with them could be very fruitful for both sides."

"A fact of which they are very aware, Lady," he said. His eyes were lingering on her, as well.

"Your talent is limitless, but I am finding your knack for policy to be quite ... invigorating to behold. As you move forward with the Necromancers, please whisper to them that the Weavers will do all we must to endorse them fully. After all, they did save us so long ago." That last was almost a whisper, forcing Gascon to fully attend her with his focus. "But know this," her voice rose slightly in tone. "You are, no matter what your status is with them, a Weaver, first and foremost."

"Of course, my Lady."

"It would be such a shame to have to call upon your skills in another capacity, thus forcing me to put another Herrod in charge of our dealings with the dark Magi. Mara, perhaps?" The Diva let those words hang in the air. "But then, why would I wish to ruin all the good we are doing together?"

"You will have no need, Lady. I promise you."

"Good," the Diva purred. "Then we are secure in our ... relationship. Oh and one more thing," she said, as her form turned to dark smoke. "Do not ever keep me waiting again. Ever." With that, she and her lyrical elegance vanished to the winds.

He ended his song abruptly then. The wind funnel closed down around him. With the end of his song, the wind walls vanished immediately. The consolidation of his base of power rested in assuring those around him that the Necromancers were up to nothing so vile as the kidnapping of women. Like it or not, he had occasionally heard those whispers that floated on the wind.

In Farmalkin were Brother Ronulen and the small school of the Necromancers. He would leave on the morrow at dawn's first light. How Gascon dreaded going there. But he was a Herrod of the First Order, the Herrod of the North. He had nothing to fear. He was their equal, an equal who needed answers.

8: Jundin's Pass

As the pass drew near, Corwyn kept a brave face, but his stomach was tied in knots. What they would encounter when reaching the pass, he could only wonder. Jundin's Pass was a very dangerous place. He knew that there were creatures about. He only hoped that the larger ones, such as the rat-like horen, were not hunting as of yet. Jundin's Pass was home to many such beasts.

Thick, grayish vines extended along the ground, wrapping around the skeletal remains of the sparse trees, climbing up any open rocky spaces shielded from the sun by the high hills. Covered with thousands of tiny thorns, the vines clung to trunks and ledges, hanging off of branches like hundreds of long, intertwining snakes. The vines grew out of various, pumpkin sized gourds whose bumpy surfaces were just visible above the misty bog.

Startled by a hint of movement in the periphery of her vision, Velladriana turned to look to her right at a nearby tree, though nothing clung to its lifeless branches other than the vines.

"They are called choking creepers," Corwyn stated, referring to the vines. "They are some form of meat-eating plant. They exist nowhere else in the Nortgard other than here in Jundin's Pass. You need not worry; they will not move unless touched."

"I know. They exist in my homeland too. Though, we call them serpent weeds. They grow from the Rift." Velladriana looked at them with disgust.

The sky above momentarily blackened. The strum of tiny wings and high-pitched shrieks filled the air. Hundreds of small, black, bat-like creatures alighted on any surface not covered in vines. Their large eyes looked on hungrily out of bizarre, elongated faces. They twittered and clicked, exposing needle sharp fangs with each sound.

"Those are *bogoyles*," Corwyn said, pointing toward them. "Nasty little things, they are. Do you have those near the rift?"

"We do ... and worse."

Perhaps Wren was wrong to have wanted to seek his fame at the legendary Great Rift. Corwyn twitched suddenly, his lower back tightening. He knuckled his back beneath the heavy pack, his scar still sensitive. Apparently, his wounds had not healed as much he had thought.

"Let me take the pack for a while," Velladriana suggested, having seen Corwyn grimace in pain.

"No, no. I am fine." Corwyn gave her a small smile of reassurance. He would not have her carry his burdens.

"Your injuries were extensive. I saw how Mama Weaver tended you. You should let me help you."

"I do not need your help," he said, far more roughly than was necessary. "I can handle this burden on my own." Corwyn did not truly know if it was the burden of the pack or the burden of Velladriana to which he was referring.

Velladriana seemed to sense this. She turned her head and dropped her gaze to the ground. "If this Jundin's Pass is as dangerous as you say, I thought it would be better if you did not have to deal with the pack restricting you. That is all."

Velladriana had a point, Corwyn had to admit. The fact that her logic flew in the face of his mounting anger only made him grow more upset.

"The pack will not hinder me," Corwyn huffed. "But fine. If you want to take it, here, it is yours." He removed the pack from his back and shoved it at her like a sullen child. The release of pressure on his lower back was immediate.

Velladriana easily hoisted the heavy bag onto her back and kept moving. She was indeed very strong. Corwyn knew she was right, knew he should thank her, but he could not form the words on his lips. They walked on in silence as he fumed quietly at her for being correct.

"If it were not for me, your back would not have been injured. I am sorry."

"Sorry?" Corwyn took a steadying breath. "I am the one who is sorry. I am not even supposed to be here!" Corwyn blurted, his emotions issuing forth unrestricted. "I am not the one meant to guard the savior of the world! The Pride!"

Without realizing it, caught up as he was in the heat of the moment, Corwyn now saw that they had entered Jundin's Pass.

Fool! Corwyn thought.

The pass itself was a rather narrow canyon winding through the hills. When the sun shone, it filled the canyon with light. As such, the choking creeper vines clung only to the shaded areas, leaving the floor of the pass relatively clear. They could still hear the bogoyles flapping their wings and clicking overhead, along with other strange calls. Velladriana drew a tiny step closer to Corwyn. The air grew quite still. It was almost stale as they walked between the hills.

Reaching out with his Heart's Eye, Corwyn realized that he must be more aware. Almost instantly, his heightened senses caught the telltale sound of a vibrant 'twang.' A moment later, Velladriana gasped as the shaft of an arrow slammed into the ground in front of them.

Corwyn did not leap, having heard it let loose a moment prior. Looking in its direction, he caught sight of a bowman ducking into the rocky hills, disappearing behind cover.

Two crossbow bolts smacked into the canyon walls to either side of Corwyn and Velladriana, startling her. Again, he had heard them coming. From covered positions some 30 feet ahead of them emerged two crossbowmen, each refitting his next bolt. Along with them appeared a huge, barrel shaped man with a large, menacing cudgel in his hand. He swung the large weapon casually with the air of someone who knew how to use it.

"Stay calm," Corwyn instructed Velladriana, his sharp hearing having caught footfalls to their rear. It seemed that the situation had taken all of his nervousness and anger from him and replaced it with a practiced readiness. "They come from behind us as well."

Two voices suddenly screamed out of the entrance of the Pass, hooting and hollering as they stepped in to cut off any retreat that Corwyn or Velladriana might have planned. Sending his senses out further, he could sense small degrees of movement all around them, including that of the bowman he had seen earlier. He did not know where that person was, which made him the most dangerous foe of any he now faced.

"Well now," the huge man said, stepping forward. "What do we have here? Out for a nice stroll, are you?"

"We mean no harm," Corwyn said, putting his open hands up unthreateningly. "We only wish to get through Jundin's Pass unharmed."

"Easier said than done, that. Aye brother?" the nearest crossbowman asked the other. Twins, each had long braided hair and heavy stubble. Both wore battered, bronze breastplates over dingy jerkins and pantaloons.

"Right you are, brother. Easier said, at that," the other replied. Each brother was a mirror of the other. Each held their crossbows with the same deadly aim.

CHARLES CARPENTER & SKI-TER JONES

"We can't be like that, now can we, boys?" said the large man. His opened stained, tan shirt exposed his massive girth. Corwyn wondered if there existed a breastplate that could have covered him. "They only wish to get through unharmed. Seems an easy enough request." He gave a sinister laugh, which the two brothers, along with the woman and man to Corwyn and Velladriana's rear, shared heartily.

The large man stopped his approach. Smiling, he looked Velladriana up and down. "Well, now," he said, his smile turning from wicked to lecherous. "That one's a girl. And a nice, healthy one at that. Name's Salda, precious."

Though Velladriana had her cloak pull tightly around her, her ample curves were easily distinguishable. She lowered her head.

"Here now, love," Salda said, moving forward once again. "What have you got under that hood? Let's have a look at you."

Corwyn knew the time had come. No measure of talk would see him past this predicament. Instead of civility, he would try to influence events with aggression.

"Run for the cover of those rocks when I tell you," Corwyn whispered to Velladriana, referring to several large boulders 10 feet away on the canyon floor to their left. "It appears to me like you should be the one wearing the hood!" Corwyn called loudly to Salda. "Had I a face like yours, I would most assuredly keep it hidden."

A small chuckle erupted from the twins and the two behind Corwyn and Velladriana. The huge man turned an angry glare at Corwyn. He obviously did not like being laughed at. That was good.

"That's not the talk of someone wantin' no harm," Salda growled. He barred his teeth in a menacing snarl.

"You are more ferocious with your mouth shut," Corwyn stated. "Your lack of teeth reminds me of my grandfather. Tell me, is soup the only thing you can chew?"

Another small chuckle erupted from the crowd. This time, though, a howl of rage from the huge man accompanied the laughs.

"No one talks to Salda that way!" he yelled.

"No one talks to Salda because no one can stand the smell," Corwyn replied, moving defensively in front of Velladriana as he did so. "Get ready," he whispered to her over his shoulder.

"Aaargh!" Salda roared as he charged forward.

"Salda! Wait!" yelled the twin closest to him.

"Now!" Corwyn shouted to Velladriana, drawing Taryn in a fluid motion.

With the big man bearing down on them, neither twin had a clear shot, lest they risk hitting Salda. Velladriana made it to the relative safety of the boulders and ducked down. The woman at their rear, a thief in garb as shabby as that of the twins, ran toward Velladriana immediately, while the other man who blocked the pass's exit with her drew his long sword and charged at Corwyn.

With Velladriana temporarily shielded from the crossbow shots, Corwyn focused on finding a route of escape.

Charging forward, Corwyn drew Taryn up in a defensive block. Salda brought the huge cudgel crashing down, a blow Corwyn easily sidestepped. His high block was a feint, meant to put the large man off balance with the power of his blow. It did just that. With nothing to strike, Salda's heavy swing brought him out of control. The cudgel came crashing down as Corwyn pulled in his blade and whipped it out in an arc that tore deeply into Salda's large thigh.

"No!" Salda screamed, falling to one knee.

Corwyn, sensing the next impending attack, turned to intercept the swordsman's slash. Far smaller and quicker than Salda, this fighter wore weathered, dark leather armor and knew how to move with a sword. Corwyn blocked the strike and tried to get to Velladriana.

Corwyn saw the twins moving around, trying to find a position to fire. So long as he was amongst their companions, they had no clear shot.

"No!" Corwyn heard Velladriana yell. From the corner of his eye, he caught sight of her struggling with the woman. Velladriana had removed the pack and was using it as a shield. The other woman was trying to rip it from her hands.

Salda got up, sheer fury driving him forward, and attacked. He swung mightily, a blow that Corwyn intercepted and deflected. Salda's bulk gave Corwyn a bit more cover as he made his way toward Velladriana.

An arrow slammed into the ground at Corwyn's feet. The person with the longbow had reemerged. Apparently, he was not concerned with hitting his fellow rouges.

Re-engaging, the swordsman in the leather armor drew his blade up, stabbing forward. Corwyn smacked the blade wide and whipped Taryn back across his centerline, slashing deeply across the fighter's leather breastplate. Injured, he fell back from the force of the blow as Corwyn dodged another attack from Salda. Another arrow slammed into the rocks near Velladriana.

"Ratten!" The woman yelled out to the leather-clad swordsman.

Her distraction gave Velladriana the opening she needed. Falling backwards, she kicked with all her might, catching the woman in the chest and launching her off of her feet. She fell with a thud a few feet away. Velladriana, pack still in her possession, ducked behind the boulder as both another arrow and crossbow bolt came inches from hitting her.

"You're dead!" Salda howled at Corwyn. Behind him, Ratten was regaining his balance.

"Help me!" yelled one of the twins from behind them. Ferocious growls echoed in the canyon.

Salda continued his attack on Corwyn. The large man was off balance with rage. His attacks were wild.

"Horen!" yelled the other crossbowman. He turned his crossbow away from Corwyn and fired it at the large creature that had attacked his brother.

Not only one but several of the large, rat-like creatures approached from deeper within the canyon. Their huge haunches and shoulders, heavily muscled and covered in thick layers of tightly woven hair, gave them the look of being covered in battle armor. Long claws, equally adept for digging out burrows as for ripping apart prey, scratched the ground in anticipation. Their long, hairless tails whipped excitedly behind them. One of the beasts dove atop the first twin who shouted, biting down and ending his life with a sickening crunch of snapped bone.

The creatures were bigger and broader than even Mama Weaver's large wolves. Elongated, rodent-like faces, with jaws lined with rows of sharp teeth and set with large black eyes, stared hungrily at the scene. They had hundreds of small, writhing appendages protruding from their large snouts, giving the appearance of maggot-covered flesh. They were actually organs that heightened their sense of smell, allowing the horen to sniff out the smallest sources of food from miles away. Drawn into the pass by the sounds of battle and the scent of blood, the beasts were worked into a feeding frenzy with the prospect of easy prey so haphazardly stumbled upon. Once the beasts were moved to feed, they would attack anything.

Corwyn broke off his attack and ran for Velladriana as Salda and Ratten, aware of the far more dangerous foes, turned towards the horen.

Sensing an arrow heading straight for Velladriana, Corwyn dove and placed himself in the line of fire. Her eyes widened with panic. The arrow ripped with tremendous force across his upper shoulder, slicing open a gash as it slammed into the canyon wall. Corwyn fell atop her in a heap.

The woman, regaining her senses, turned to run, immediately triggering the horens' predatory response. In a bound, one of the creatures jumped atop the fleeing female thief and closed its vicious jaws down on her head and neck. It ripped through and freed copious amounts of blood and gore onto the canyon floor. The horen gorged hungrily.

While the horen ate, Velladriana moved out from under Corwyn. The gash was bloody but far from life threatening. The sounds of men shouting and creatures howling filled the canyon as Corwyn got to his knees, shaking off the impact and the searing pain in his shoulder. He saw the look of relief in Velladriana's eyes. Any lower and the arrow would have torn out of his chest, ending his journey. He grabbed Taryn and helped Velladriana to her feet.

The bowman was now firing at the various horen that Salda, Ratten, and the remaining twin were fighting. More of the creatures were approaching; clearly, this was an entire den of the sickening animals. Wasting no time, Corwyn led Velladriana around the boulders. Salda was pounding on one of the beasts with his cudgel, several arrows and crossbow bolts sticking out of its tough hide. The twin now slashing at another two with a sword of his own, trying desperately to fend them off. Having suffered a vicious bite in the fight, he was bleeding from his side. Ratten was fighting another, though the wound he suffered at Corwyn's hands had slowed him immensely.

Corwyn picked his moment and pulled Velladriana along. They ran past the beast that was engaging Salda and headed further into the canyon. Salda slammed his cudgel into the horen's head, slaying it as two more arrows found their mark in the creature's side.

As Corwyn ran past, he slashed Taryn low at a horen that moved into his path. Taryn's razor sharp edge caught the creature in the head, cleaving a vicious gash that killed the creature where it stood. Immediately, another pursued Corwyn and Velladriana who were making their way down the canyon floor.

From his distant vantage point, the bowman saw that the day had been lost and disappeared from sight.

"I'm not done with you yet!" Salda yelled, as another horen leapt atop him. The big man bashed the creature as another joined. The force of their weight took Salda to the ground. The sounds of torn muscles and crushed bones soon replaced his screams.

"Keep running!" Corwyn instructed Velladriana.

"But—"

"Go!" Corwyn yelled. "Please!"

Corwyn turned and unleashed Taryn with all the fury he could muster, slashing through the horen that was giving chase. The sword bit deeply into its tough hide, ripping through its haunches.

Afterward, Corwyn ran towards Velladriana. Behind them, he heard the sounds of the horen chasing the bandits down and eating them alive.

Corwyn reached into a small compartment on his belt and produced a dozen gray pellets, each no larger than the size of his thumbnail. "Keep running!" he yelled.

The canyon narrowed markedly up ahead. As they entered the narrowest portion of the pass, Corwyn dropped the pellets to the ground. Upon impact, long spikes erupted from each pellet.

They could hear the agonized howls of the horen who had just stomped on the spiked pellets. Two horens came up lame. However, three more leapt over them and kept up the chase.

Corwyn knew that they would not outrun the horen on the valley floor. Having caught up to Velladriana, Corwyn grabbed her and pulled her up to a narrow trail on the left side of the canyon walls. With the narrowing of the pass, the walls created more areas of shade. The choking creeper vines growing along the walls were taking back the pass here.

The horen followed up the path and were gaining on them. Ahead, Corwyn saw what was easily a five-foot section missing. Velladriana paused for just a second, and Corwyn grabbed her hand and yanked her forward.

"Jump!" he yelled, as they both took a running leap.

He made the distance easily. She though, with the pack on her back, caught her foot on the far ledge. Corwyn pulled her across, and they kept up their run.

"Keep going!"

With that, Corwyn turned and engaged the first horen to leap across the broken path. He had a dangerous idea, but it was the only gamble left.

The horen leapt atop him as he fell onto his back, accepting the creature's full rush. Pulling his feet in, Corwyn caught the heavy beast in the belly and kicked with all his might. He sent the horen over the ledge and down into the choking creepers below.

Upon contact with the falling creature, the vines whipped out at lightning speed, wrapping the struggling animal in their deadly embrace. The creature shrieked as its life was squeezed out.

Corwyn was up in an instant and continued running along the path, kicking any and all rocks and loose gravel that he could find down onto the deadly vines to wake them all.

Choking creepers did not need much food to live, conserving their strength by staying perfectly still, as any other harmless—though ugly—vine might. However, once in motion, they, like the horen, would lash out at anything that moved. That was Corwyn's hope. The vines extended and launched from where they clung along the pass walls, firing up onto the path. Corwyn ran with all speed, the vines firing out behind him, just missing by inches. The vines struck the trail and wall with such force that they chipped the very stone.

He was gaining on Velladriana who was very fast. The vines below her had not begun to move yet. Corwyn hoped that they could outrun the wave of hungry vegetation.

Corwyn heard more howls of pain. Daring a brief look back, he saw a large horen quickly being constricted. The third still followed closely, just barely escaping. It now ran as much to kill its prey as it did to survive.

The pass wound to the right some 50 yards ahead. From his angle, Corwyn saw another large section had fallen away. This one, though, was at least twice as long as the first. He picked up speed to gain on Velladriana, the horen nipping at their heels.

Corwyn knew that he could make the jump. He also knew that Velladriana could not. As they approached the edge, Corwyn hooked Velladriana by the waist in his left arm.

"Hold on!" Corwyn leapt with all the power his legs could muster. The horen leapt behind them.

The moment he launched them into the air, he knew his leap would not get them both across. Summoning all his strength, he threw Velladriana forward. She crashed onto the path, rolling to a stop in a jumbled heap. Corwyn, Taryn still in his right hand, slammed into the ledge on the far side. Half of his body was on the path, his lower body hanging over the edge. The impact of his collision with the far ledge knocked Taryn free of his grasp, his momentum sliding him backwards. Corwyn dug his fingers into the hard-packed path with all his might and stopped his backward slide.

The horen howled as it leapt. It could not get its heavy body all the way across and snapped viciously as it fell behind Corwyn and down into the vines. The moment it crashed into the creepers, it was enveloped, awakening all the vines that clung to that portion of the pass.

Velladriana helped Corwyn up, only to have him shove her back harshly.

"Keep running!"

As if on cue, vines started firing up the path, once again. One caught Velladriana's leg, wrapping itself in a death squeeze, and pulled her over.

"Corwyn!"

Corwyn was up onto the ledge, grabbing Taryn and slashing through the vine with a quick stroke. With no time to lose, he again pushed her forward.

She stopped as she heard Corwyn hit the ground; several vines that had caught his ankle were dragging him down. He slashed himself free just before he was yanked over the ledge of the path.

Getting up quickly, Corwyn sprinted with all that he was worth, grabbing Velladriana and pulling her along as the vines struck out again and again. They reached a bend just as several large vines whipped out, nearly skewering them as they ran past. Around the bend, the path cleared. Corwyn and

Velladriana pulled up, sucking in all the air they could. Behind them, they saw the writhing mass of choking creepers settling back down into the shade of the lower pass walls. They had escaped.

Velladriana shrieked as dozens of bogoyles suddenly assaulted them, the small creatures landing and nipping at any place they could. Corwyn waved his arms to clear them, grabbing her and setting off, once more.

"They are drawn to our perspiration," he said, moving her along. "So long as we stay moving, they will not bother us."

It was true, the moment they picked up their pace, the annoying little creatures scattered into the sky, landing on nearby ledges, waiting for the travelers to stop again.

Soon enough, the path wound its way back to the floor of Jundin's Pass. With the choking creepers relegated to the far walls, Corwyn knew they were safe of that threat at least.

"If our luck holds, we will make the rest of the way through Jundin's Pass unharmed," Corwyn huffed, as they ran.

Velladriana looked at Corwyn's bleeding shoulder. "This is luck?"

"Yes, very lucky, indeed."

A short time later, they came out from Jundin's Pass and were back in the marshlands that surrounded it on all sides. Within an hour of exiting, they were back in the lush embrace of the deep Nortgard woods. The sun was beginning to set, its final rays casting hues of warm orange and purple light through the dappled canopy of thick trees.

They stopped at a small stream so that Corwyn could address his wound. He did not drink any of the healing elixir that Mama Weaver had provided, saving that for an injury that was truly life threatening. Instead, he applied some healing balm to his shoulder and with Velladriana's help, strapped on a field bandage. She was actually quite adept at dressing wounds. He assumed she had to be, given the difficulties of the life she had been through.

"I think it best we make camp here for the night. We will reach the North Road in the morning."

Shortly after, Corwyn had a strong blaze filling their campsite with its light, casting dancing shadows along the nearby birch, maples, and oaks that surrounded them. Once the fire had taken well, Corwyn sat and doled out more of their humble rations. Velladriana noticed that he gave her the largest portions of the dried cheese and fruit. In the sky, they could see brilliant expanses of stars visible through the patchwork clouds that floated overhead.

Velladriana took note of how quiet Corwyn had become. She knew that if he had not placed his body between hers and that arrow, her journey in these strange lands would have come to an abrupt end. She also knew that his quick thinking and reactions had saved her from both the horen and the serpent weeds, or choking creepers, as they were known here. She had never had someone so valiantly risk his life for hers. She saw the fatigue of battle set firmly on him.

"I owe you my thanks again," she said.

"You owe me nothing. I said I would keep you safe, and so I shall."

With that, Velladriana settled down, wrapping herself in her bandoo cloak.

"You were wrong about what you said earlier."

Corwyn looked at her quizzically, unsure as to what she meant.

"If I am indeed the Pride Mama Weaver speaks of, then you are the one I want guarding me." With that, she rolled over and attempted to sleep.

Corwyn said nothing further. He merely gazed into the fire. Twice now, he had almost lost his life in defense of this mysterious woman. That did not bother him as such. What did bother him was whether he could actually see Velladriana to safety. He silently hoped that Mama Weaver had placed her faith in the right man. Given the losses he had suffered and the confusion that wracked his thoughts, he could not be sure. Whether he was ready or not, he knew that this, now, was his duty. It was not a duty that he would have chosen for himself, but then, duty did not ask the readiness of its charges … it demanded it of them. He heavily thought on it while looking over at her. His duty was now protecting Velladriana, the slave from the east.

9: The Saddlery

Corwyn and Velladriana were on the move early the next morning. Within a few hours, they ran back into the North Road. Corwyn thought it best to travel just off of it, moving with the cover of the bushes and trees. The ground was relatively level here, so they made time just as easily off the path as they would have on it. Corwyn knew that stealth would be their greatest asset. The North Road was relatively untraveled, but more people used it now than Corwyn ever remembered using it in his youth.

As they descended from the depths of the Nortgard, Corwyn and Velladriana rounded a bend in the terrain and were greeted by an impressive sight. The deep thickness of the forest cover thinned, and the road began winding down at an increasing grade. There over a vast valley, green with trees and life was Silverton. It stood some five miles away but was more imposing than Corwyn remembered.

Built on the hillside, the city was tiered to optimize space and the defensible position it had at the valley's end. The city walls, huge structures of timber and reinforced masonry, stood some 20 plus feet in the air. Ramparts and towers positioned along the tops of the walls gave ample defensive strength. Even the homes themselves had been improved upon. The largest one he recalled from his youth paled in comparison to the structures he was able to see from this vantage point. There were many tracts of land that had been cleared, and small farms and homesteads were visible outside of the town. Silverton seemed to have grown up as much as he had.

He was impressed, though his feeling of saddness redoubled. He knew that things would have changed since he was gone, but he had not anticipated them changing to such a degree. When he was a child, Silverton had been nothing more than a trader's outpost. It served as a home for trappers, hunters, and those who wished to carve out a living in the forest. It was a town of perhaps a thousand people.

Now, several winters later, he was staring at what he was sure was a town that held close to ten times that number. It was no longer a town. It could almost be called a small city. Corwyn did not know if it was the change he was witnessing that saddened him or if it was the fact that he would not be able to visit his childhood home that made his heart so heavy.

"I thought you said it was small?" Velladriana asked, sensing Corwyn's mood.

"It was," he said, softly. "Long ago."

With that, they continued on. It made sense that there should be a saddlery on the outskirts of the town. The horses would need their space after all.

"Let's pick up the pace," he said. "We should be at the saddlery soon."

Leisurely leaning against the hitching post, Dolver smoked his long, bone carved pipe. His sturdy, athletic frame was dressed in the simple garb of a trapper. His stern presence seemed to indicate that he was something far more than that. He scratched his bearded chin with a leather-gloved hand. His other hand tossed his pouch of smoke weed. His sword was strapped casually to his side. He was in the middle of a conversation with Worrick, a stout and stocky man also clad in trapper's gear.

Dolver looked sternly at Worrick. "Listen closely, I don't care if it is just you and me and the bloody horses. If you ever mention our 'cargo' as girls again or as anything other than our 'cargo,' I'll gut you myself and leave you to bleed out in the bloody forest." Dovler's stare left no room for interpretation.

Worrick quickly cleared his throat, looking truly apologetic. "I'm sorry, Dolver. I am. I just was wonderin', is all."

Dolver sneered at the comment. "Wonder in silence. That is how we do our business, in silence and in the dark. All I know is that the gold is heavy in my purse. We're getting paid to deliver the cargo, alive or dead, but alive pays better. That is all the fuss that needs concern you."

"The gold is heavy in our purses," Worrick repeated Dolver's remark.

"Bloody right. Now, if you want to survive in this business, shut your mouth, open your ears, and sharpen your knives. It's time to be off. We can't wait any longer."

Worrick turned and walked off to find their third partner, Brenner, behind the saddlery.

It was true. They were being paid handsomely. Kidnapping women did not bother Dolver. He had done far worse to women for less, for much less. He did not care why the women needed to be taken as long as the gold was right. The only reason he was concerned about the condition of the five he had shackled in their cage-wagon, hidden far from the saddlery and deep within the woods, was that they were worth more alive. He was rather surprised at Worrick's curiosity. Worrick was new to the trade, but if he kept wagging his tongue, he would soon find it cut out, along with his heart.

While Dolver was finishing his pipe, he caught sight of two travelers coming out from the forest along the side of the road. Interesting that they would not be traveling on it.

The man was in beige, wearing a sleeveless shirt that exposed well-muscled arms and bracers that were too fine for any common woodsman. Many would have missed that but not Dolver. This stranger also had a sword of fine construction strapped to his side and walked with a very confident gait, which spoke of ability with the impressive weapon. His companion, though, was the one who really caught Dolver's attention.

She was tall and shapely yet lean. She had strength to her stride and strong shoulders beneath her gray cape. Her legs were long and solid, also indicating strength.

A good ride. He thought wickedly. Why would she be wearing her hood pulled down so low on a cloudy day such as this? Then he saw it. His sharp vision noticed what many would have missed. Dolver saw the lower portion of a slave loop bobble out from beneath the hood. The fact that the pale woman was so aware of it, hiding it back beneath her hood so self-consciously, marked her for who she was.

"Lyndrian," Dolver whispered, greedily. Not all Lyndrians were slaves, of course. Nor did they all have the loop. However, Lyndrians sat highest atop the list of women who were being sought.

What is a Lyndrian doing here, leagues from her home? And on this side of the Rift, no less? Dolver thought. The why of it did not matter to him all that much though. This fool Lyndrian should have cut her loop off when she had the chance. If she had, he would have thought her nothing more than some pale northern girl. She would have been nothing worth his time or effort. A Lyndrian, however, that was well worth his effort. Even dead, a Lyndrian would be worth five times as much all the women he had caged in the wagon.

Alive ... Dolver thought, his eyes narrowing greedily. Alive, she was well worth his effort, indeed. He got up and headed toward the back of the saddlery as the two interesting travelers entered the front.

Dolver always followed his instincts. After all, it had been those same instincts that had kept him alive for over a decade in a trade that was not known for its longevity.

Anyway, He thought. *Even if I am wrong, accidents happen in the northland all the time. People die; it just happens.* Dolver looked around as he approached Worrick and Brenner. It was a particularly slow day on the North Road. With the town's patrol having passed by nearly an hour ago, he knew there would not be another coming this way for some time. He readjusted the collar of his stout, white shirt to cover the suicide sigil, the mark of a master assassin, which it hid beneath.

Corwyn and Velladriana entered the saddlery and went up to the large man behind the counter. The man was fiddling with a horseshoe lock and did not look up from his work.

"Excuse me, sir," Corwyn began. "We are in need of horses."

"Well, you've come to the right place then. Name's Tornvil. This here's my shop." As he spoke, Tornvil set his craft down and wiped his filthy hands on the front of his dirty apron. Tall and bulky, with a round midsection, Tornvil was a rugged man. His reddish beard hung to his mid-chest, and his frame spoke of years of hard-earned, frontier strength. Shirtless beneath his apron, he seemed a man who was all business. Finally looking up, he recognized Velladriana, giving her a small bow. "It is good to see you again, lass. I see your time with Mama was well spent."

The exchange concerned Corwyn, his hand inching ever so slowly to Taryn's hilt. "How do you know this woman?"

"I know her because I have met her before," Tornvil stated, flatly. "I would have met you, but Mama Weaver said you were sleeping like a newborn babe."

Corwyn was more than a bit surprised. So this was the help Mama Weaver had promised. He let his hand relax away from Taryn.

"We require two mounts," Corwyn began. "And with all haste."

"Three," came a female voice. "And they're already ready."

From a side room emerged a spritely young lady. She approached Corwyn and Velladriana with a warm, inviting smile. "Name's Harper," she said, settling next to them with an easy grace. "Tornvil's my uncle."

Where Tornvil's hair and beard were reddish, Harper's hair was positively aflame. It was the brightest, most vibrant red that Corwyn had ever seen in his life. The similarity between the two ended there.

Harper had a round face, whereas Velladriana's lines were sharp and striking. Harper had high cheekbones and a nose that was slightly hawkish yet seemed to work on her face. Her light, speckled hazel eyes were full of mirth and warmth, which was in complete contrast to the ice blue of Velladriana's. Her lips curved into a smile that seemed to swallow her entire face, and she had a glint in her eyes that was slightly reminiscent of the mischief found in Mama Weaver's. Lean of form, she donned riding breeches and a doublet of dark brown.

Where Velladriana was taller and shapelier, Harper was thinner and had a more airy quality to her. Corwyn looked at Harper curiously. She returned his gaze with a knowing look. Her smile was slightly quizzical.

"Three?" he questioned. "I'm sorry. But have you met us before as well?"

"Nope," she responded happily. "But I know you. Both of you."

"Best be on your way if you're to be back soon, Harper," Tornvil said. "I can't stop you from going. The gods know that is true, but I need you back before sundown. Lots of beasts have been coming out of the deep wood. Your folks would roll over in their graves if I got you eaten."

Harper leaned over and gave Tornvil a kiss on his cheek. The large man tried to suppress a smile.

"I'm not getting eaten today. I promise you that, uncle," she said with the smile that never seemed to leave her face. She then slung a thick, leather pouch with a single strap over her shoulder. The pouch had several long tassels with beads at the end of each, which clinked lightly as she moved.

Corwyn could not help but observe that this Harper was more in command of their relationship than her uncle ever would be. He pulled out the small sack of gold coins that Mama Weaver had given him.

"Your money's no good here," Tornvil said, waving away Corwyn's attempts at payment. "Some still believe in a Mama's love. By the way, I saw your handiwork on one of those dead men. Well done." That last was said with a knowing look.

Corwyn did not know how to reply to being complemented for taking a man's life.

"How did you …?" he stammered.

"I check on Mama Weaver pretty regularly," Tornvil said with a smile. "Help her keep things tidy. Come now, boy, didn't you wonder what happened to the bodies you and

Peaches and Cream handled? The dead don't police themselves, you know." Tornvil let out a booming laugh.

It was true. Corwyn had not given much thought as to what had happened to the corpses of the men he had fought in the gully.

"I did not think any still knew of her," Corwyn said.

"Most don't," Harper responded. "To most, she is just a story now. The crazy old Weaver who lives in the forest."

"No one has seen her out of the forest in years," Tornvil added. "All believe her dead."

"Then, how is it that you still know of her?" Corwyn asked.

"Just because no one has seen her doesn't mean that she hasn't been seen," Harper said with a wink. She definitely sounded like Mama Weaver, that was certain. Corwyn wanted to trust her, but he would remain cautious.

"Harper'll get you to a good easterly trail," Tornvil continued. "Then back before sundown." He said that last with a good deal of emphasis. Apparently, this Harper did not take well to instructions.

"Back before sundown," she repeated playfully.

"I just need to bring out a couple things from the back," Tornvil said. "Give me a minute, and you're on your way."

"Many thanks," Corwyn responded to him.

Tornvil had to duck to fit through the door into a back room. Corwyn saw a small bellows and furnace glowing in the far corner. That room was where Tornvil would repair the horseshoes with which he shod his mounts. It seemed to be well-ventilated, with a portion of a large open window visible from his angle.

"Hi, name's Harper," she said to Velladriana.

"Velladriana," she responded, almost in a whisper.

"Do you like horses?" Harper asked her.

160

"Some."

Harper had to strain to hear her. "Well," she went on, "you'll like this one."

Harper chatted with Velladriana about the friendly nature of her horse, a beautiful gray mare, one of the three out front. Corwyn walked to one of the front windows and looked out at the horse line. Unease suddenly swept over him. It seemed quiet. It seemed too quiet. He quickly turned and walked back to the two women.

"It is time to go," Corwyn announced. "Harper, I—"

Seeing a flash of movement from behind Harper, Corwyn reacted with lightning speed.

"Ahh!" Harper gasped as Corwyn grabbed her and pulled her to the ground. He yanked Velladriana down as he dropped as well, gaining them cover behind the high counter of the main room.

The dagger had implanted in the far wall of the room, its hilt vibrating from the force. Had he been a moment slower, it would have struck Harper right between her shoulder blades. Someone had thrown it from the back room that Tornvil had entered only moments before.

"Here now," Dolver called to them. "Those are some quick reflexes you have. Come out, and no one else has to die!"

"Else?" Harper worriedly said. Her eyes grew large with fright. "Uncle!" Harper leapt toward the back room with the open furnace. Corwyn had no time to grab her and jumped after her.

"Stay down!" he yelled to Velladriana. By instinct, Corwyn reached into his Heart's Eye.

Springing through the doorway, Corwyn tackled a distraught Harper and landed on her just as the downward stroke of a hand axe buried itself into the thick supply pack he wore on his back.

Corwyn spun off the now hysterical Harper and fired a low kick into the leg of a large, wooden workman's table that crowded the center of the room, sending it toward Worrick. Corwyn's movement freed the axe from Worrick's hand, leaving it stuck in the heavy pack. Corwyn sprang to his feet and ducked low as Brenner jumped atop the table and slashed with his short sword, coming within inches of Corwyn's head.

Harper crawled to her uncle, who was face down in an ever-increasing pool of his own blood, a dagger protruding from his back. Attacked from behind. That was the signature of a coward … or an assassin.

Corwyn was in the thick of it. The space was too confined for him to draw Taryn. Instead, rotating on his feet in a semi-circle, he removed the heavy pack, grabbed the straps, and whipped it around. Doing so just as Brenner reversed the direction of his sword slash, Corwyn blocked the returning strike with his pack. He moved to evade a strike from Worrick who, armed with a second hand axe, swung at Corwyn's exposed side. These men were well-trained in fighting in cramped quarters.

Corwyn launched a fast side kick into Worrick's knee, buckling Worrick and sending him back a pace as Corwyn simultaneously dropped to a crouch and dove under the table. Again, Corwyn's reflexes saved him from having his head slashed off by another strike from the speedy and balanced Brenner.

Corwyn had to do something about the assassin atop the table while negating the advantage of striking from an elevated platform. Corwyn pushed at the table from underneath, his muscles tightening with the strain as he exploded into a standing position, pressing the table upward further by extending his arms.

"Watch it!" Brenner yelled, obviously taken completely off guard by the display of strength. Brenner was thrown off the table and crashed backward, slamming into the furnace and dropping to his knees. The impact sent sparks flying throughout the room and knocked several of the red-hot irons out of the glowing embers. One fell on a large pile of chaff used to stoke the furnace and lit it immediately on fire. Fed by the breeze coming through the window, the flames raced quickly. In moments, the entire half of the wall was aflame.

"No!" Velladriana yelled from the other room.

Worrick had regained his balance, and though slightly wobbled, was still strong enough to re-engage Corwyn. With the large table now thrown to the side, there was more room for Corwyn to navigate, though still not enough to draw his sword and utilize it with any effect.

Corwyn had to get to Velladriana. He ducked to avoid a quick downward slash of Worrick's axe and launched three rapid-fire punches into Worrick's midsection. The assassin was strong. Corwyn felt solid muscle upon contact. However, he was strong as well and felt a rib crack with his third strike.

"Arrgh!" Worrick instinctively dropped his left arm down to cover his ribs. That was the opening Corwyn needed. He did not delay. He rose and launched an arching elbow smash with his right arm into the side of Worrick's face while simultaneously using his left hand to grab Worrick's lowered left wrist and pull him off balance and onto the upturned table. Worrick crashed with a thud, stunned but not unconscious.

Brenner got to his feet and raised his short sword and dirk to face Corwyn.

"Uncle!" Harper cried inconsolably.

Velladriana screamed from the other room. Corwyn reached into his leather belt pouch and produced several throwing blades. Brenner thought better of engaging this skilled warrior, and instead, turned his attention to the hapless Harper.

The smoke was filling the room, beginning to choke off both oxygen and visibility. Corwyn launched two of the throwing blades at Brenner. One struck Brenner in the shoulder, the other in the thigh. Brenner yelled in pain as he fell to one knee. Corwyn hoped it gave him the time he needed. He dashed back into the front room.

Through the smoke, he could barely make out the large form trying to pull a kicking, and punching Velladriana out the front door. Corwyn sprang over the counter and launched himself through the thickening black smoke toward the attacker.

Launching a kick, Corwyn smashed it into Dolver's chest, sending him out the front door and down the small wooden steps leading to the entrance. Dolver crashed with force and lost his breath.

The alarm bells were loudly sounding within Silverton's walls. The smoke had obviously risen to a point to where it was clearly seen in the town. Fire was not something taken lightly when living in the forest. Soon, there would be Magi here, using their spells of cold and water to extinguish the flames. That was, of course, if there were any Magi in the town at all.

Within the burning saddlery, Corwyn landed on his feet and tried to help Velladriana to hers.

"Velladriana!" Corwyn yelled over the crackling of the burning building. "It is I! Corwyn!"

Velladriana looked up and barely made out Corwyn's face through the increasing smoke.

"Corwyn!" she said in surprise, as he pulled her up. Grabbing her, he immediately ran back into the other room. He ducked and pulled Velladriana low with him.

Harper did not want to leave the body of her uncle. She was waving an iron poker in a vain attempt to stave off the assassin.

Corwyn launched another throwing blade. This one slashed Brenner in the neck. He immediately dropped his dirk and clutched his bleeding wound. Suddenly, with a loud crack, a burning crossbeam snapped from the ceiling and came crashing down on Brenner's head. He fell in an unconscious heap. The inferno raged around them.

Now moved only by his need for survival, Worrick charged forward in a desperate attempt to escape the burning building. He struck quickly at Corwyn. Armed with a large dagger, Worrick wanted to get out the back as the flames spread into the front room. Corwyn was now in his way.

"Get Harper!" Corwyn yelled to Velladriana, as he engaged Worrick. Velladriana ran over to the kneeling Harper.

Worrick was fast, striking quickly at Corwyn whose bracers proved their use in deflecting two well-delivered, high strikes. The thick, well-made bracers were scratched but otherwise undamaged.

Corwyn fired a snapping front kick into Worrick's abdomen, followed by two more. The speed at which Corwyn struck, along with Worrick's earlier injury, quickly turned the tide of attack to favor Corwyn.

They would all soon perish in the flames if they did not get away. Harper and Velladriana's coughs hacked noisily in the smoke filled room.

Worrick charged forward again. Corwyn stood his ground, engaged Worrick's dagger hand with his own while twisting and shifting his hip into the assassin's injured gut. Using the assassin's momentum against him, Corwyn slung him over, whipping Worrick to the ground near Harper with such force that the jarring impact dislocated the man's hip.

Corwyn reached for Harper when she suddenly seemed to gain awareness of where she was. She screamed and drove the hot poker into the assassin's sternum in the meaty portion where his neck met his chest. The assassin gurgled as blood spewed from both his neck and mouth. Bubbles of red spittle dripped down his cheek and chin. He was most assuredly out of the fight now.

Corwyn grabbed Harper who stared at the dead man in sudden horror. The heat of anger and loss guided her to strike instinctively. Corwyn knew full well that nothing could prepare one for the weighted aftermath of the killing stroke.

"Harper!" Corwyn shouted at the stunned girl. "Harper! We must leave now! Harper!" Corwyn shook her from her shock with that last call. She came quickly back to reality. Her eyes were red with tears; his were just as bloodshot from all the smoke.

"Come on!" he shouted and grabbed Velladriana and Harper and pulled them into the front room. The flames danced along the doorway, consuming all of the wooden structure.

"The other man!" Velladriana shouted through her coughs as she pointed outside.

Corwyn crouched by the door. He knew Velladriana was right. The assassin was out there waiting for them.

The building was almost fully engulfed now. The smoke was suffocating, and the heat was growing more and more stifling. Corwyn had to think of something quickly. He suddenly drew upon an idea.

"Get ready!" he shouted over the flames. "When I come back, get right behind me and run to the horses as fast as you can! Do you understand?"

"Yes!" Velladriana yelled.

Harper nodded as she coughed almost to the point of vomiting.

166

Corwyn took a deep breath and charged back into the smoke and flames, heading into the burning back room.

"Corwyn!" Velladriana called, her coughing redoubled by the inhalation of smoke. She and Harper waited at the open doorway for several long moments. The smoke now billowed freely out the front. They were going to have to run out in moments or risk suffocating and burning.

They heard Corwyn yell out from the inferno at the rear of the saddlery and his heavy footfalls through the crackle of burning wood.

"Run!" he shouted, as he emerged from the smoke, carrying something large and bulky on his back. He burst out the front door. Velladriana and Harper followed immediately behind him.

They leapt the distance from the steps to the dirt easily. Weighed down as he was, Corwyn was quite able to keep up with the women. The prospect of burning to death did wonders for their pace.

As soon as Corwyn emerged from the smoking structure, he sensed through his Heart's Eye the energy of the crossbow bolts. Dropping whatever he was carrying to the right, he shielded the women from the attack.

"Get on the horses!" he yelled as they ran past.

In the light of the day away from the obscuring smoke, Corwyn dropped the large bulk of Tornvil to the ground. His heavy form serving as a shield in which were embedded two well-aimed bolts.

Corwyn dove to a roll, ending up in a crouch, and launched his final throwing blades in a lightning fast series of whipping motions. One of the blades struck Dolver in the arm, slashing his bicep and sending a spray of blood into the air. Dolver's final shot fired wide of his target as he dove behind a watering trough for cover. Corwyn turned swiftly and jumped in one fluid motion onto his horse, a sleek stallion of reddish-brown.

"Come, we must ride quickly!" Corwyn yelled.

Velladriana and Harper rapidly mounted their mares. Harper suddenly saw the body of her uncle lying in the dirt.

"Uncle!" she yelled, reaching out in a sad attempt to somehow call him to her.

Corwyn rode to her side. "We must ride, or his death will have been in vain." He knew they had to move. He heeled his horse to a gallop and was about to grab Harper's reins when she suddenly sprang into action, heeling her horse as well.

"Ha!" Velladriana shouted, heeling her mare to gallop.

Corwyn saw no sign of the assassin over his shoulder. Though he was not used to killing, Corwyn truly wished he had not left the murderer alive.

They galloped hard up the North Road for the next three miles, putting distance between themselves and the assassin. Corwyn had not seen any sign that the man was following, but he still wanted to keep a fast pace. The smoke from the burning saddlery appeared to be coming from the town itself. He felt a stab of sadness grip his heart when he looked at the heavy black smoke plumb into the sky, mixing with the slate gray of the clouds.

This is not the homecoming I foresaw at all. Corwyn thought.

Corwyn saw Velladriana riding for all she was worth; she was scared … but alive. He turned to look at Harper. Her eyes were set sternly forward. She had not looked back at all during their escape, not once. His perspective suddenly shifted. The loss of the opportunity to return home did not loom as large compared to the loss Harper had been dealt. As they made their way back into the dense Nortgard, he wondered what they would encounter next.

10: Pleas & Betrayal

Crispin rose with a loud ringing in his ears. He strained to make out what Dolthaia was saying.

"Crispin! Run!" Dolthaia shouted. The sound suddenly rushed back into his ears.

Dolthaia saw that he was coming out of his daze. "Move now! Come on! We have to move now!"

Crispin gripped her arm as she helped him up. They made their unsteady way down the stream, splashing uneasily as their wobbly steps brought them to the far bank. Staying low, they took off at a run when they reached the other side. The shrub and brush gave way to taller reeds as they moved along, and they were quickly able to run fully upright, at least for a time. Dolthaia led the way, clasping Crispin's hand tightly in hers. She was very fast for someone with legs so short. He stumbled every third or fourth step. Were it not for her solid hold on his hand, he would have long since fallen.

"Wait," he gasped, drawing up short. He clutched at a vicious stitch in his side. "I can't ... I can't breathe."

"If you don't keep running, you'll never breathe again."

She yanked him along. His pace quickened once again. He could not argue in the face of such straightforward logic.

"Don't you quit moving those prissy, little, noble feet!" she yelled over her shoulder, as if sensing he was about to collapse. "I haven't been caught by the Guard yet, and I don't plan on starting now!"

The next copse of trees was a straight shot for them across open ground. Along the stream, the brush and reeds were quite high. Perhaps, if they could make it to that copse, they could somehow disappear amongst the plants and make good their escape. They barely reached the copse before Crispin collapsed in a sweaty, gasping heap beneath a large tree.

"I just ... I just ..." he could barely take a breath.

Dolthaia slumped next to him. Though winded, she had run for her life before and was quickly preparing to take flight again.

"Come on," she gasped, sucking in as much air as she could. "We have to push on and get to the bank of the stream. We can hide in those thick reeds."

Crispin was literally gulping air. He had not run this far since ... he had never run this far.

"Go on without me," he wheezed. "Just go. I won't betray where you are. Just leave me."

"Did you hear those shouts? Those are followers of Maars the Lector. They have no love lost for Necromancers."

"But ... but we aren't Necromancers yet."

Dolthaia grabbed his right wrist and turned it to show him the back of his own hand where the Necromantic sigil had glowed faintly.

"But we will be," she said softly. "That is all that will matter to them."

Crispin closed his eyes in despair. This could not be happening. It was bad enough that he was destined for the morbid life—and quite possibly death—of a Necromancer. Now, to add insult to injury, the small but ever growing minions of the radical Maars the Lector were hunting him. This was not how his life was supposed to be. What had happened to the galas and boating trips down the River Ennin? When he opened his eyes, Dolthaia registered the desperation in them.

"You want to die here? Fine." With that, she started to rise.

"Wait. You can't leave me."

Dolthaia grabbed him and dragged him into the reeds. "Come on."

They disappeared into the tall plants near the water's edge.

Maltia stomped through the brush at the stream's shore. Her trained eyes focused on where the two children had lain hidden. Torgatu approached. He had doused his sword in the waters of the stream, though hers remained aflame. Sunlight was beginning to break through some of the cloud cover. The light of day had dispatched the last of the Necromantic mist.

"Too little, too late," Torgatu said with a shrug when he saw the sky through the thick branches of the trees. "Where are they?"

"They made haste across the stream," she pointed in the direction that Crispin and Dolthaia had run. "Out toward the other riverbank. They are on foot. They will not get far."

"Give chase quickly." Torgatu ordered. One of his men, Dantin, and another bowman, Selis, approached. "Selis, ride out with Maltia and bring me back those Necromancers. I will be along once I have ensured this area is secure."

"Yes, sir!" Selis quickly responded. He rode up next to Maltia.

"They are Necromancers despite their age," Torgatu warned. "Do not underestimate them, or you will share Lanna's fate."

"Never!" Maltia yelled as she heeled her steed to gallop. "Maars wills it!"

"Maars wills it!" Selis repeated in earnest and sped off on his horse to catch up with Maltia.

Bow slung on his back, Dantin rode forward. He was a farmer before finding truth and following Maars.

"Report," Torgatu commanded Dantin.

"Well," he began. "Regar went to find Molk and Kal, who took off after that ugly Greel."

"Fools! I told you all to hold your ranks," Torgatu spat in disgust. "Greel are cowardly creatures. They are not going to sacrifice themselves for a couple of neophytes. They are pack mules, nothing more! If they die, their souls are completely given over to the dark Magi. Don't you think they would want to avoid that for as long as possible?"

Dantin shriveled under Torgatu's harsh tone.

"I suppose I would," Dantin said, quietly.

"Of course you would! Greel may be dumb as cows, but even a cow wants to live. Fools all!" Torgatu took a deep breath to calm himself. He turned his mount around and inspected the area. Taking out a long, slender vial, Torgatu pulled the stopper and sprinkled the clear liquid on the ground where the wagon once stood. The water spattered harmlessly on the dirt.

"What is that, sir?" Dantin asked.

"Water blessed by the Mystics of Aldara," he said. "Had there been any Necromantic magics still active here, the water would have sizzled upon impact with the defiled earth."

"Oh," was all Dantin responded.

Torgatu knew that it was the wagon that served as the talisman for the dark magics. With the wagon gone, so too were their energies. Still, he would quickly spread the water over the entire area before taking up the chase for the Necromantic neophytes. He would allow no trace of the vile magics to be left behind.

Finishing with the water, Torgatu turned to Dantin. "Remain here. Regar will bring Molk and Kal back to this location. I go now to finish this."

"Yes, sir!" Dantin said, giving a salute.

Torgatu turned and heeled his mount to a gallop, splashing though the steam and after his fleeing targets.

Dolthaia kept pushing them forward, but she too was feeling the effect of fatigue. Her desire to avoid capture had set her survival instincts on full alert. She had seen too much suffering at the hands of others in her young life. She would not be taken easily, not by any stretch of the imagination.

While they moved with labored breaths, blood mixed with sweat stung their eyes. They were forced to hold up their soaked robes. The weight was beginning to bear heavily upon them.

"Dolthaia, stop. I need to rest. I really can't go on."

Dolthaia, hearing him fall, turned back to him.

"Come on," she panted. "I know it's hard. But we have no choice. We have to move."

His body, though unaccustomed as it was to any physical exertion greater than strolling along the grounds of his estate, was unresponsive. He sat for long moments, wanting to move, yet unable. The sound of hoof beats closing in rapidly brought renewed fear, and with it, adrenaline. He and Dolthaia locked eyes, wide with worry. He forced his burning muscles to push forward. Their pursuers had found their trail. The hunters were drawing near. Why was this happening to him? He was a noble after all.

"There!" He heard a female call. "I've picked up their trail there!"

Dolthaia grabbed Crispin's arm, pulling him into the reed-filled water.

It makes no difference. Crispin thought sadly. *It is not like I have any strength left to use anyway. I don't want to die.*

Dolthaia, eyes ever alert and watchful, looked at Crispin.

"Shhh. Stop crying," she whispered. "They are coming. They will hear you."

Crispin tried to stop, but every inhalation he used to try to calm his breathing only came out like a strained gargle that sounded even worse.

"If you don't get a hold of yourself, Claxis, they are going to kill us," she spoke quietly with as much force as she dared.

"I … am … trying," Crispin squeezed each word through a gasp of strained emotion. With all else failing, he dunked his head into the water. The bubbles were just as loud.

Dolthaia lifted his head. They both froze as the hoof beats pulled up short from their location. She had hoped that the riders would gallop past them. They must have a trained tracker amongst their ranks. The horses now approached at a cautious saunter.

"They are close," Maltia said.

She was good. Dolthaia thought. Living on the streets, Dolthaia was taught to always cover her tracks. Torn brambles and broken reeds left a distinctive trail for those careful enough to look. She knew there was no escaping the female rider.

"Come out," Maltia called. "There is no getting away. Come out and save yourself and us a great deal of trouble. It will be fine."

Fine, indeed, Crispin thought. *You're not the ones who are going to be killed, are you? Goblin's tears.*

Dolthaia looked with pleading eyes at Crispin. She knew that the blubbering was just moments away from starting again.

"Come now," Maltia called again. "You know we will find you. Everything will be all right. We want to help you."

Dolthaia's cheeks reddened in anger at the blatant lies in her words. Why was it that those in authority always sought to impose their will and then mask that obligation with lies and falsehoods? She had heard the like too often for her own comfort.

Barely visible now through the thicket of reeds, Dolthaia and Crispin saw the tip of Maltia's flaming blade come into partial view. The musky scent of the burning wax resin grew stronger. It was only a matter of moments now.

A third galloping rider was closing in fast. At the sound of his approach, Maltia turned her horse and moved back the way she had come.

"What news?" It was the commanding voice.

"They are close, Torgatu."

Torgatu, that name sounded strangely familiar to Crispin. Where had he heard it before? *Another noble, perhaps?* That thought filled Crispin with a small measure of hope. Perhaps he could reason with this Torgatu. Anything would be better than dealing with these other ruffian commoners. Small hope was better than no hope, after all.

Crispin looked to Dolthaia. She could not read the expression on his face, though it was not as fearful as it had once been. She grabbed his arm, her eyes begging him to be still.

"They took to the water," Maltia continued. "They must indeed be near. They could not have traveled too much further afoot."

Torgatu approached the water's edge.

"Torch the shoreline brush," he commanded. "The drier bushes will smoke them out.

"Yes, sir," Maltia replied.

Crispin heard the crackling sound of dry brush being lit. They were in no danger of getting burned. The reeds and plants at the water's edge would not catch at all. The smoke, nevertheless, would drive them out and sting their eyes and already sore lungs in the process.

Torgatu, the name suddenly came into clear focus in Crispin's mind. He was the hero of the Battle of the Kerathic Plains. He was indeed given the rank of nobility. A lesser noble, to be sure, but a noble nonetheless. It was time for Crispin to make his move.

"Wait!" Crispin called from the reeds. "I am coming out."

Dolthaia went pale. Perhaps in lighting the brush, they could have escaped in the smoke. Perhaps they could have made a run for it. Anything was better than giving up. *Blasted nobles and their foolish misconceptions of their worth in the world!* She thought. Now, it was Dolthaia who wanted to cry.

Crispin moved from the reeds on unsteady legs. His body ached from being tossed about by both the explosions and the hard run. The chill water had now added stiffness to his joints. How he hated physical exertion.

Stepping up onto the bank, Crispin looked a sad sight indeed. His white robes, soaked and see-through down to his linen underclothes, clung to his chubby midsection and gathered in dripping puddles around his skinny, chicken-like legs. The water pooling beneath him gave the appearance that he was wetting himself. Crispin took a deep breath and steadied his breathing.

"My name is Lord Crispin Claxis of the Clan Claxis, Son of Ronnell Claxis, son of the Grand Magus Prespertin Claxis, Defender of the Realm and Chief Counsel to King Forlmorlaine of Canodria. I wish to address Lord Torgatu, Defender of the Realm and hero of the Battle of the Kerathic Plains."

So far, he had shed no tears. That was a good thing.

"You address Torgatu."

"I would ask you to halt these aggressive actions," Crispin continued. "Surely, you can see that I am of no harm to you."

"None now, Necromancer," Selis spat. "You and yours took my mum and wife, you did. The Lector Maars calls you demons, and I know it to be true."

"Silence, Selis," Torgatu commanded.

"Yes, sir," Selis said quickly. He would not say another word, but his eyes held their hatred of Crispin firmly.

"I am no demon, I assure you," Crispin said. "Nor am I even a Necromancer. This is all just a terrible misunderstanding. A horrible, terrible misunderstanding."

"You are not a Necromancer yet," Maltia countered. "But you soon will be. Yours may have saved the world once, but we see the truth of you now."

"Take your ease, Maltia," Torgatu said calmly. Then he addressed Crispin. "You are a neophyte, marked by the auburn sigil of death on your hand."

"Yes, but I did not ask to be marked with the sigil of death," Crispin's voice began to take on a pleading tone. "Believe me. I wanted to be an Elementalist or a Conjurer Evoker. I would have even chosen Rager if I could. Please, you must understand—"

"Enough of this," Torgatu interrupted. "None of us chooses our destinies; we embrace them as they are presented. Think you that I would choose to hunt children on the Canodrian flats? This is ill business, and I am quick to be done with it. Now, where is the other one?"

"She ... has fled," Crispin said flatly. If there was one thing that life in a noble house taught someone, it was how to lie. "Further down the river. She kept running. I could not keep her pace." Crispin pointed behind him to show them the direction.

"Fine," Torgatu knew a lie when he heard it. He had spent much time around nobles as well. He drew his sword. "Perhaps we should just kill you now."

"Please," Crispin implored. "We have a connection, you and I. My grandfather, the Grand Magus Prespertin, he fought with the ranks of the Battle Magi in the battle where you won your fame. He presented you with your rank and title. Surely that means something?"

Torgatu was quickly tiring of this. He detested what was to come. Killing children, no matter if that killing prevented them from becoming dark perversions of life, was no easy thing. He did not want to spend any further time hunting out the other child than was necessary. He opted for a change of tactic.

"Perhaps ... Crispin, was it?" he began, as Crispin nodded. "Perhaps, some concession may be reached." Torgatu stilled the questioning stares of Maltia and Selis with a glance. They trusted their leader. "You are, after all, of noble blood."

"Indeed, I am," Crispin sounded relieved. "And know full well that the Clan Claxis will reward well this generosity."

"Yes, well ... that is all good and fine," Torgatu said. How he despised playing these games, but the will of Maars must be carried through. "In order for me to see you returned safely, I must have some prize to present to the Lector Maars. I have no more time to waste. Give us the girl, and you will be spared. Do it not, we will find her regardless and present you both."

Dolthaia blanched as she soaked in the reed filled water. Her every instinct was to stay hidden. Her every memory compelled her to stay put, to seek out an avenue of escape, no matter how improbable that escape might be.

As a small child, she had seen her father cut down in cold blood before her very eyes when he had surrendered himself. He had done so to spare his family pain. Her pain only multiplied when she saw the guardsman's blade drive through her father's chest. She could still see his eyes.

Pulling herself from that horrible memory, she fought for the courage to do what she must. Crispin had not given her up. He did not say a word. Here was this spoiled little noble willing to die for her, yet she sat in that chill water like a child.

"You may do the honorable thing and come out on your own!" Torgatu called out. "At least one of you will be spared."

Crispin was beside himself. Why had he not yet spoken? All he needed to do was turn and point into the reeds, and he would be spared. Why was he hesitating? She was just a commoner. Though her eyes were mesmerizing, even in his memory. That was ridiculous. He could find a dozen women with eyes like hers. There was nothing to be found in the grave. The grave was empty and cold.

Crispin turned toward their hiding spot and began to raise his hand and point when Dolthaia suddenly emerged. Quickly dropping his arm, he felt his heart sink to his feet.

"Wait," she called. "I am here. Take me. He is a noble after all," She came to stand next to him. Her eyes were strong. "I am just of common blood."

She looked at him with sincere admiration. She did not know that he was a split second away from giving her up in order to save himself. Perhaps the grave was not the only place that was empty and cold.

"You held your tongue," she said softly to Crispin. "I will never forget that."

Sheathing his sword, Torgatu dismounted and handed his reins to Selis. He walked over and grabbed Dolthaia and Crispin roughly by their respective arms. The horses whinnied uneasily.

"You may share your gratitude with him in the afterlife," Torgatu said solemnly. "You will join each other there momentarily."

"Wait!" Dolthaia yelled. "You said he would be spared."

"And he will be," Torgatu said. No matter how often he had cleared the world of Necromantic darkness, these moments never grew easier for him. "Spared the detestable life of a Necromantic Magi, just as shall you."

"Liar!" Dolthaia kicked and thrashed about. She had been betrayed yet again by those claiming to be lawful.

"Wait, please," Crispin pleaded as he kicked and twisted. He was not nearly as good at trying to rend himself free of Torgatu's vice-like grip as was Dolthaia, but she seemed to be having no better luck at escaping than he.

Maltia dismounted and took Dolthaia from Torgatu's grasp. She still held her flaming sword whose fire was now virtually extinguished. Her grip was apparently every bit as strong as Torgatu's. Dolthaia could not free herself from it either. Torgatu wrapped Crispin in both hands and walked him toward the thicket of trees.

"Please!" Crispin begged. "Please, don't do this! I will give you anything you want. Please let me go! Lord Torgatu, have mercy!"

"I am a lord no longer," Torgatu said and threw Crispin forcibly to the ground. "I have renounced land and title to follow the truth. You and the darkness you will usher into this world shall be purged."

Torgatu drew his sword once again.

"Yes! Maars wills it!" Selis was emphatic in his cries, now holding Maltia's reins as well as those of Torgatu, "Maars wills it, Necromancer filth!"

Dolthaia bit Maltia's arm and held on with all her might, drawing blood at the unprotected wrist. Maltia winced in pain. A sharp strike with the hilt of her sword on the back of Dolthaia's neck caused her knees to buckle. The little neophyte's tenacity impressed Maltia. Even nearly unconscious, her teeth remained affixed to Maltia's wrist. She was about to strike Dolthaia again.

The horses whinnied and bucked as Torgatu planted his boot on Crispin's back, pinning him down. "It shall be a quick stroke, I promise you that." He said.

"Please ... no ..." Crisping gasped under the weight of Torgatu's heavy boot.

Sudden movement from deeper within the thicket startled everyone. It seemed like a short, thick tree was charging directly at them. The Greel emerged from the trees with the force of an unimpeded avalanche, slamming its fleshy mass into Maltia and Selis's mounts with tremendous power. His sudden presence stayed Maltia's hand from delivering the second blow that would send Dolthaia fully into unconsciousness.

"Greel!" Maltia yelled in surprise.

Torgatu held his killing stroke.

Slammed to her back, Maltia's sword flew out from her grasp. Hands balled into fists, the Greel brought one of the clubbing appendages down on Maltia's head, smashing it open like a ripe melon. Her skull and gore splattered on Selis, who let loose of the reins as he fought to control his own steed.

The Greel turned its massive bulk and slammed itself into the withers of Selis's horse, swinging its arms wide as it did so. The horse bucked back and threw Selis into the water headfirst.

Torgatu easily ducked beneath the Greel's awkward swing, coming up into a defensive crouch. He launched a couple of strikes, each in a downward arc across his body. They found their mark and tore a deep gash in the Greel's massive forearm. Blood of a molasses consistency oozed out like when Crispin plucked out the thorn. This time, however, the Greel moaned in pain. It's strange pseudo-lifeless tone ringing across the flats and streams.

It brought its other huge arm down in a powerful swing, attempting to crush Torgatu between its mighty fists. He, however, was faster and dove out of the way, rolling into a defensive stance at the Greel's side. A quick horizontal slash caught the Greel at the calf, ripping a huge gash in its lower leg.

The Greel moaned again but did not stop swinging arms that resembled tree trunks out and around itself in a vain attempt to crush the speedy man.

Crispin made his way to Dolthaia and clutched her carefully. In truth, he was as much holding himself up against her as he was holding her upright.

Torgatu moved in once again. How he wished his blade was still on fire. The flames would have done actual, severe damage to this minion of undead magics. Moving with a high guard, Torgatu shifted at the last moment and came in low. He spun and slashed a deep wound into the side and lower belly of the Greel.

One of the Greel's untrained swings finally found its mark. Its huge fist connected with Torgatu's shoulder and launched him into the thicket of trees. Torgatu slammed onto the ground with a thud. He landed in a crumpled heap but managed to hold onto his blade and keep his wits. He rose to his feet. Feeling the full effect of the Greel's blow on his shoulder, he switched his sword to his left hand, his right arm now numb. He would not be surprised to find his collarbone broken. There would be time to deal with that later.

After sending Torgatu launching into the trees, the Greel rapidly scooped Crispin and Dolthaia into its massive arms. Hands still balled into fists, it carried them as if they weighed nothing at all.

Seeing the Greel speed off down the stream bank, Torgatu rushed out from the trees, while Selis came out drenched from the stream with sword drawn at the very moment the Greel passed by. He gave a half-hearted swing that missed the massive creature completely.

"Prepare to ride!" Torgatu commanded. He mounted his horse and moved as fast as he could, pushing through the pain in his shoulder. If that hit had landed flush, he might well be lying alongside Maltia in the dirt.

Never one to be called pretty, she would be called a hero for the cause. Torgatu would ensure that. He looked upon her headless corpse, her skull smashed like an adolescent's pimple. That was no way to die. The Necromancer's would pay this butcher's bill heavily.

Regar, Dantin, Odgar, Bojon, and Trav approached.

"The Greel has escaped with the Necromancers!" Torgatu shouted. "To arms. We will run them down and slay them all, I swear it." He looked down at Maltia's corpse. "You will be avenged."

After all, Maars wills it.

11: Viper's Legionnaire

Feeling moisture around his sandaled foot, Crispin looked down the front of the creature to see that the entire lower half of the Greel's body was saturated with the crimson of blood. The Greel held Crispin and Dolthaia firmly in its huge, tree-like arms that engulfed their entire torsos, leaving only their legs dangling like the limbs of a pair of rag dolls. The hulking pseudo-human moved across the landscape with incredible speed, even injured as it was and weighed down with Crispin and Dolthaia. Whether the terrain was rocky and sharp, watery, or a boggy mixture of the two, the huge creature kept its steady pace as it made its way along the Canodrian flats.

"Report," Torgatu ordered.

"I found Molk and Kal further downstream," Regar said, pointing in the direction he came from, opposite from where the battle had taken place. "Their heads were bashed in. Horses gone."

That made no sense. Greel would not attack unless they were cornered and only then in a last ditch effort to prolong their miserable lives. The Necromancers enchanted them to be cooperative and easily controlled, which was a good thing with beasts that powerful. Torgatu only hoped it would expire before his horses did. He would destroy the vile thing for what it did to Maltia. He would destroy the Claxis boy and the girl for the part they played in her death as well.

From behind the massive Greel's shoulder, the shouts of the pursuing, Necromancer-hating followers of Maars the Lector echoed in Crispin's ears. The Greel managed to open up a near half-mile lead on them. It was fast as the horses, but he knew it would not be able to sustain this pace forever due to its injuries. Thankfully, the day was quite overcast; anytime the sun's rays broke through and shown down on the Greel, its pace diminished considerably. It seemed distance and injury did not fatigue the beast as much as did direct sunlight.

The Greel kept close to the edge of the streams as it ran. Ahead lay the churning waters of the Sharp River. That river would eventually feed into the great River Ennin.

"It can't run forever!" Dolthaia shouted. "It is bleeding out."

"Maybe it can outlast the horses!" Crispin yelled.

"Not injured. It may bleed slowly, but it is bleeding to death regardless. They will not stop until we are dead."

"Where is this thing taking us?"

"To Crag Devlin, most likely," Dolthaia said loudly. "It is the place it was charged to go."

Crag Devlin, the dark tower of the Necromancers of the Southern Watch was several days hard ride further south. Excepting Crag Drannon far to the north, Crag Devlin was the largest of the Necromantic strongholds.

Crispin and Dolthaia both looked behind over the Greel's swollen, enormous shoulders. The riders had closed the distance even more. Each of their pursuers now had their weapons drawn, sensing the kill close at hand.

What kind of man is this Maars person, who could incite such rabid devotion in his followers? Crispin thought.

Crispin knew the Greel was exerting what had to be its final energies on this run. He had to admire the strange creature. Upon its death, its soul would be given completely to the Necromancers, yet it seemed unconcerned as to its fate. He twisted in its thick arms to look it in the eyes. Those huge, bulbous black eyes seemed as lifeless as they ever had, staring straight ahead in a mask of gaunt, emotionless expression. It was going to die.

Why had this thing that showed no emotion or even more than a passing awareness at all chosen to return to save them? It must have been ordered to do so. Otherwise, Crispin could not see any reason for it to return. He certainly would not have. Crispin was also going to give up the commoner for a lie. That thought brought the cascade of guilt crashing back down upon him with a force that almost stole his breath. He was saddened to admit to himself that were he given the choice a second time, he might well do it again.

That thought barely had time to register since the Greel completely lost its footing and slammed onto the ground. Rotating as it fell, its shoulder smashed onto the high embankment ledge, sparing the children the crushing death that would have befallen them.

"Crispin!"

"Dolthaia!"

The portion of the ledge the Greel fell atop gave way beneath its mass. The Greel, along with a huge chunk of bank wall, plummeted into the fast moving waters of the Sharp River. They caused an enormous splash that sent water all the way up the 15 feet of embankment wall.

Torgatu and his company closed the distance, stopping where the Greel and the two neophytes had plunged into the river's speedy waters.

"What now?" Dantin asked.

189

Torgatu looked down in frustration at the huge gouge left in the embankment. He was not about to let his prey go so easily.

"The river bends to the south, coming back on itself two miles further west," Torgatu said. "The banks on both sides of the river get very steep just beyond that ridge." He pointed to a tree-covered ridge a quarter mile away. "The water moves too fast and the walls too steep and slick for any purchase to be gained there. If they make it through the rapids, we will be waiting on the other side where the water calms and the banks grow shallow.

"Trav, Selis, follow the river as best you can. If, for whatever reason, they are able to get out of the river before the rapids, one of you, open fire, and the other, come and get us. We will be back posthaste. And light your arrows. Even wet, the filth of the Necromancers will easily light. The Greel will not be a threat. Go! Ride!"

"Yes, sir!" both men answered in unison and galloped off along the riverbank.

"The rest of you, ride with me!" Torgatu heeled his horse forward and led the rest of his men.

Maltia, he thought sadly. "You will be avenged, I swear it." This he spoke aloud. He needed his anger to be heard. He needed the visceral charge of what had happened to her to drive him forward. He rode fast. If the neophytes were able to get out of the river before he set his trap, they would be easy targets, silhouetted against the rocky, clay river walls. Even if the Greel could slow their attack, it would not withstand a volley of arrows in its weakened condition. Perhaps the rapids would finish them off; that would make his work far easier. Either way, they would wash out where the waters grew still, and they would die today. He would make certain of that.

190

The impact of the cold, rapidly moving river stole all of Crispin's breath as he broke the surface of the water with a slap. In his horror, he kicked and flailed about. A passable swimmer at best, his meager robes now threatened to drown him. He fought to clear his arms and legs of their twisted fabrics as he paddled desperately. The Greel and Dolthaia were quickly carried away from him.

He sunk beneath the water; his lungs burned in agony while he fought to free himself from its murderous grasp. It seemed as if the river itself was conspiring with his attackers, trying to pull him to a watery fate. He kicked and lashed, using all his might to break through the surface, which seemed just out of his reach.

He closed his eyes, ready to finally succumb to his fate as his consciousness left him. Drinking in his death, he thought, *thus ends the tale of the young Crispin Claxis.*

His eyes opened suddenly as he felt himself fill with energy, the energy of the magics. Without thinking—for he could hardly have put a clear thought together even if had he wanted to—he reached out, hungrily calling in as much of the magics as he could. The water pulsed around him. Bubbles, huge and buoyant, surrounded his body on all sides. They were so thick that he could see nothing but froth. A bubble of air formed around his face, and he found that he could breathe; no more water was trying to force itself into his nostrils or down his throat.

He exploded from the river's surface on a jet of bubbling water some 30 feet high. It expelled him with such force that he was launched over the remainder of the rapids and splashed back into the water where the river had grown much calmer.

Landing face down, Crispin noticed that the bubble around his face remained. He was beneath the surface, yet he could still breathe.

Amazing. He bobbed along in the much slower current. The bubble also made his vision beneath the water as clear as if he had been on the surface. He saw the underwater scenery clearly. A virtual forest of reeds and tree roots, thick and gnarled, grew in a spider web patchwork beneath the water's surface. The roots extended far into the river bottom on both banks. The water was deep here. Schools of fish, brown and rainbow trout, swam at the lower depths.

What kind of magics were those? Crispin felt the Life's Spark of the energies begin to leave him. He realized that he was not paddling at all, that the effects of the spell had kept him buoyant. With the magics now gone and the spell broken, he had to paddle again. His heart raced with sudden fear.

This cannot be happening! Crispin stopped paddling and sank helplessly. Whatever magics he had tapped into to save him from the rapids were nowhere to be found now. He knew that whatever had happened pulled all the magical energy from the water around him. He was out of time. Just as suddenly, the club-like arm of the Greel hooked Crispin by his waist and brought him to the surface. The water around him, mixing with the Greel's blood, took on a crimson hue.

Crispin faced the Greel and Dolthaia, who the thing held in his other arm.

"We thought you were dead," Dolthaia said, smiling.

"We?" Crispin gasped. He was still trying to catch his breath.

"Well ... I. He still doesn't say much."

"How did you ...?" Crispin began before a fit of coughing took away his breath.

"Corpses float," Dolthaia said flatly. "So do Greel."

Crispin turned to consider the Greel. It slowly turned to consider him as well. The Greel still wore that blank expression with bulbous eyes staring lifelessly. Crispin would never get used to it.

"They also swim like snow bears," Dolthaia continued. "By the way, what happened to you? We got through the rapids and saw you flying on a wave of water 30 feet in the air."

"I told you; I have studied the magics before," Crispin lied. "Do you think we lost them? What do we do now?"

"Now," she said. "We make for land." Dolthaia pointed toward the southern bank. "That way." The Greel began churning its legs. In the slow moving current, the going was quite easy. "I hope we lost them. I really hope so. For our sake and the Greel's."

Dolthaia touched her hand to the Greel's gaunt face. It looked pasty when she first saw it. Now, it looked absolutely dreadful. Apparently, even the dead wore their death masks poorly. She looked upon the thing with the compassionate eyes most would reserve for a small child. It had saved their lives.

The river wound its way around a sharp bend where the water was peaceful and relatively shallow. From here, they could wade across to the other side, though the water would still reach their mid-chest.

Upon reaching the southern bank of the Sharp River, the Greel placed them both down. It still bled in its slow fashion but registered no hint of pain or emotion.

"Thank you again," Dolthaia said softly.

That blank face of the Greel changed in an instant as its enormous back burst into flames.

"No!" Dolthaia yelled.

Arrows filled the air. The Greel let out an unearthly wail and sank to one knee, two flaming arrows protruding from its back. There was no doubt it was in pain.

"Run," it whispered in its deep voice.

"No!" Dolthaia yelled, splashing water on its back.

The Greel, in a last surge of effort, hooked its arms, hands still in fists, around them both and took them farther up the riverbank. It deposited them behind the stump of a large tree. The fire spread across its enormous girth.

"No! Please! No!" Dolthaia cried.

Crispin grabbed her and started to pull her away, but she resisted.

"We have to help it!"

"It is dead already!" Crispin responded. Dolthaia shot him daggers from her eyes. "If we stay, it died for nothing."

Dolthaia considered this for a moment before looking back at the Greel, once more. "I will not forget you!" With that, she and Crispin turned and fled up the riverbank and into the surrounding tree line.

The Greel sank to its knees with a final, horrid roar of agony. It was a yell that chilled the marrow of any who heard. It was as if all the pain that the transformation from human to Greel came flooding into its massive body now at death. It fell forward and extended its right hand. Its fist opened and out fell a small, crushed, yellow wildflower. The flames completely consumed it.

Crispin and Dolthaia moved hastily. Tired as they were, the sight of the burning Greel pushed them forward. And run they did, directly into the waiting arms of Dantin, Odgar, and Regar.

"Time to pay your due," Dantin said coldly.

Odgar and Regar easily caught the tired children in their arms and held them fast. Try though she might to fight her way free, fatigue mixed with sorrow forced tears and uncontrollable sobs from Dolthaia. Her inability to escape only led to more tears. Crispin was not even trying to fight anymore. He just sobbed uncontrollably.

"Quit your racket," Odgar said in his drawling voice. "Torgatu'll be over here with the rest in a minute. Then it's all over."

"Not so brave now, are you, filthy dead lovers," Regar said with distaste.

"Shut up!" Odgar yelled.

He threw Dolthaia to the ground and drew an axe from his belt. Old and nicked, it was primarily used for chopping wood, but it would split a skull open just as easily as it ever had any log. "I will do it myself."

"Wait!" Dantin ordered. "Torgatu said to wait for him."

"Damn Torgatu!" Odgar shouted, his lust for the kill fully consuming him. "Maars wills it."

Raising his axe high, Odgar brought it down on Dolthaia's sobbing form with full force. Halfway through its downward arc, his forearm was sliced clean in half. The axe, along with arm still holding it, flew off into the bushes, spewing a trail of blood in its wake.

"Aaargh!" Odgar yelled in agony, not to mention in complete surprise. He clutched his stump of an arm and fell to the ground.

Dantin and Regar mirrored that surprise, both of whom looked in shock at the man who had so suddenly appeared among them. Blood dripped down the wicked blade of his stout, black falchion. He was in armor as dark as midnight; his helm's visor was shaped into the twisted skeletal face of death. His oblong shield, which came down to a point at its upper and lower tips, was very maneuverable. Sharp all the way around, the shield was employed as much for wide, slashing strokes as it was for defense. It was ridged and dark as the armor with a crown and thorn etched on its surface.

"What kind of Necromancer are you?" Dantin asked in fear as he reached for his sword.

"I am no Necromancer," Reese Pelingril growled. "Nor am I a murderer of children. Stay your weapons, or it shall be you who dances with the Demon Reaper."

Dantin and Regar were beside themselves. This dark man had appeared as if from the shadows, cleaving their comrade easily. Dantin delayed. Regar did not. He had barely pulled his sword halfway from its sheath when Reese struck again. Leaping across the prone, wailing Odgar, Reese twisted and cut a downward slash that met Regar at the crook of the elbow and ripped right through it. Regar howled in pain as he lost his sword and arm.

In the same twisting motion, Reese brought his shield arm up and around, catching the stunned Dantin with a backhanded blow that launched him off of his feet and knocked him to the ground, completely unconscious.

Hearing movement from down the embankment, Reese quickly brought his shield arm up and around, rotating his arm and shoulder to deliver a punishing blow to Regar's skull with the flat, front side of his shield. The thorn and crown delivered an impact that, once again, brought unconsciousness. Regar fell flat on his back, his head bleeding freely.

Reese dove into the cover of the brush behind a large tree stump when Torgatu and Bojon rode up from the river.

Upon seeing his men lying unconscious on the ground, Torgatu immediately drew his blade and found a defensible position. Without wasting a moment, Reese leapt off of the flattened tree stump and launched into the air. He crashed into Bojon and sent him crashing harshly on the other side of his horse. Reese bore himself up quickly from the collision. Like Dantin and Regar before him, Bojon now lay in an unconscious heap at the feet of the deadly warrior.

Torgatu took in the scene before him. The crying Necromancers hid in the bushes, Odgar and Regar both bearing viciously severed limbs that would mean their deaths if they could not soon find a healer, and Dantin and Bojon lying prone, probably dead.

"What is the meaning of this?" Torgatu bellowed. He had the advantage on horseback and was not about to give it up to the stranger. He heeled his mount backwards, unsure as to how many others there were.

"I am a foreigner to your lands, but I am sure that even here, the murder of a child is as grievous a crime as in my kingdom," Reese said flatly.

"These children are Necromancers and none of your concern!" Torgatu spat. "Leave lest you force my hand."

"I care not whether they are Necromancers or spawn of a demon's arse," Reese moved slowly forward. "You will not kill a child so long as I am near. That I vow."

"Your vow means nothing to me, Morilander," Torgatu said. "I recognize your armor and the crest you bear on your shield. Go back to Morilan and take your poisonous filth with you, Viper."

Reese knew he could not hide his identity, covered as he was by the dread armor that marked the soldiers of the Viper's Legion. The armor was a dark green, though it appeared virtually black to all but the most discerning eyes.

It was no ordinary plate, sturdier than steel, yet supple as gossamer, forged by some of the finest smiths in all the kingdoms. The armor was ridged and pointed at every angle, with nicks and gouges torn out of the surfaces of the breast and back plates that appeared to be the results of brutal impacts from battles long bygone. However, they were an intentional result of the armor's construction and lent to its deadly purpose.

Coarse to the touch, the armor had small spikes protruding at the elbow, knee, and shoulder joints, with edges honed to a razor's edge where the plates meshed and came together. Worked greaves, as wickedly gouged and sharp as were the rest of the armor, protected his calves and ankles. Solid plates ringed his thighs.

The breastplate and back plate were fashioned to fit snuggly, worked to appear like dense musculature, a physique of death. Gouged faulds protected the hips and lower back, and those below the breastplate looked like rippling abdominal muscles. The effect was quite intimidating. The gorget covered his neck fully yet allowed for easy rotation.

His gauntlets were as pliable as silken gloves, though just as hard and sharp from knuckle to wrist as the rest. His forearms featured perhaps the most vicious components of his armor: bracers that were worked with razor sharp rings of barbed metal, meant to rip and shred with the slightest impact.

The armor was designed to cut an enemy on contact, unleashing its deadly surprise against anyone foolish enough to get too close. The surprise it held was poison, which lent the armor its color. Only those trained for years in the savagery of the Viper's Legion could don these special suits of battle armor, suits whose poison made them toxic to the touch, save to the Vipers whose tolerance was built over years of training, hardship, and battle.

The look of the armor paled in comparison to the physique it protected underneath. Lean muscles forged by years of brutal training gave Reese the look of a predator always on the verge of explosive movement.

Torgatu had run into the soldiers of Morilan in the past. As a student of war, he was well-versed in their tactics. It was rare, nonetheless to see a member of the Viper's Legion so far from home. It was even more so to see one donning full battle armor. Because of its toxic nature, kingdoms rarely permitted Morilander soldiers to enter their domains while wearing their armor.

"If you know what I am, then know full well that I will not relent," Reese said. "Not for a moment." Reese tugged at the transparent scarf that hung loosely around his neck. Thinner than rice paper, it shimmered with a faint, metallic green hue. It was really the only noticeable color on him.

This warrior would have to die. People died when they crossed Reese's path. Again, such was the way of things. Death always seemed to follow him as well. Reese put his falchion in his left hand. Even though his left hand was strapped into the shield, he could still hold a measurable grip on the stout blade. He then drew a small throwing axe that he had attached at the back of his sword belt.

"You mean to strike me with that axe?" Torgatu asked. "I will run you and your cursed armor through."

With that, Torgatu charged.

"I don't mean to strike you," Reese said, as he threw the axe at the eyes of the charging horse.

The horse bucked and stumbled forward when the axe cut into it just along the ridge of its nose. That was all the time Reese needed. Torgatu, arm weakened as it was, lost hold of the reins. Thrown off, he landed heavily on the ground. With his shoulder already injured from the blow of the Greel, Torgatu was forced to fight through renewed pain as he rapidly rolled to his feet.

Reese was on him in a moment with a controlled fury that Torgatu had rarely seen. Torgatu brought his sword up to parry Reese's downward strike with as much strength as he could manage. Even had he been fully rested and uninjured, he doubted he could have parried the blow all too effectively. For a lean man, this Morilander was gifted with a powerful sword arm.

Torgatu's blade was batted aside with relative ease. He dove out of the way, hoping that the speed of Reese's charge would send him off balance. It did not. Reese stopped with a controlled step and shifted toward Torgatu's new position. Torgatu struck high to pull Reese's defenses up, then pulled his blade in and struck forward with a low stab.

Reese had seen these sorts of feigned strikes before and easily countered with a low block of his shield as he pivoted and spun around Torgatu, bringing his sword up and around.

Torgatu saw the brilliantly executed move as Reese spun to his rear. Had Torgatu met a warrior of this skill at the Battle of the Kerathic Plains, even completely healthy, he would not have lived to be declared a hero.

Maars wills it. Torgatu thought in resignation. It was his last thought before his head was removed from his shoulders. His body stayed standing for another moment or two, blood spurting from the severed arteries, before it fell to the ground.

Reese turned when he heard the movement of the children in the trees and approached them. He sheathed his sword and raised his skeletal visor; he knew what an imposing figure he was when it was down. Little did he understand that he was just as imposing when it was up.

A handsome man, he had gray-green eyes, steeled through years of combat, ever alert and attuned to their surroundings. With a stern jaw and constant scowl, Reese was all hard lines and determination.

The scars crossing his face accentuated his lines. One dropped from his left eye all the way to his jutting, well-pronounced chin, making him look as dangerous as he actually was. Another over the bridge of his nose and trailing down below his right eye, made him appear as if he had a tear, torn permanently from his flesh. The scars gave his face a strong bearing, as opposed to a hideous appearance, as they would have on most. The scars he had sustained in his defense of the Ivory Crown of Morilan accentuated his attractiveness. It seemed to affect all aspects of his life.

"It is alright," he said. "I will not harm you."

Crispin continued blubbering uncontrollably. Dolthaia, however, seemed to have regained some of her composure. Stunned, she stared at Reese with eyes of the most striking green he had ever seen. It was the strength in those young eyes that held his attention though. He knelt before them.

"You are safe now."

Crispin tried to speak but could only suck in gasps of air. Reese knew he would get nothing from the boy anytime soon.

"My name is Reese," he said to Dolthaia in gentle tones. Tones far more gentle than he had used in a very long time. "What is your name?"

"Dol ... Dol ..." Dolthaia began.

"When you find your voice little one, you can tell me then. Follow me. I am camped nearby."

Having seen this black clad warrior dispose of five of their attackers so easily, they were under no false pretense of thinking they had a chance against him. If he wanted to kill them, he would have done it. Dolthaia helped Crispin to his feet, and they made their way behind Reese on shaky legs. After going about 200 feet, Reese led them behind another large rock outcropping. He sat them down next to his fire pit,

201

its embers burning low, and doubled back to ensure they were not being followed.

Dolthaia and Crispin just sat in silence, leaning against each other for support. They were too tired to entertain any further thoughts of escape.

Reese blended with the trees easily. He made his way back to the battle scene. While walking beneath a clouded sky, he pondered over the situation. All he had wanted to do was make it through these southern kingdoms and to the relative obscurity and freedom of the wild north. He wanted to disappear into a frontier that would forgive him his past, blemished as it was. Now, he had two children waiting for him at his campsite. How could he be so foolish?

How could I not have been? he thought. Hearing the screams of children in peril awakened something in him that he feared he had lost long ago. For the first time in a very long while, he had felt compassion.

Compassion, he thought skeptically. It was compassion that drove him to leave Morilan, the home he loved. It was compassion that took from him the people that he loved. He wondered what compassion was preparing to take from him next.

12: Transfer of Souls

Ronulen exited the cold dark of the mausoleum, squinting under the light of the overcast sky. The heavy stone doors creaked closed behind him with an oppressive boom. Unseen forces, fully under his control, sealed that path. Those forces would stand silent guard until his return.

While walking across the cemetery toward the large gray home that served as both chapel and mourning house for the people of the small town of Farmalkin, he contemplated the majesty of his current residence. Where others saw only slate gray slabs of rock, fashioned into tombstones and statues to commemorate lives lost, he saw markers that spoke of true life, life beyond the warmth of this world. Most came here to mourn. Fools all, in his opinion. They did not understand that he walked among active energy. Death was more alive than they could ever comprehend.

Soon enough, they will see. He thought with satisfaction. He pitied those who could not grasp the splendor of the cold beyond. This life was so fleeting. Only in transitioning onto the next life should any accomplishment be celebrated. This life was incomplete. It was imperfect. As such, it was impure. He would change all that. He would baptize this life with death and purify it. Ronulen smiled at that thought in his fashion.

His thick black robes dragged across the hard-packed ground as he passed row after row of tombstones. Walking through the oldest part of the cemetery, he knew full well he was not alone in this dismal place. The wind carried the strained cries of the dead softly to his ears. Those desperate moans he was attuned to hear. Some of the living occasionally heard the speech of the dead. In those sounds, the living felt fear. In those sounds, he felt power.

Tilting his head up toward the cloudy, gray sky, he brushed his black hair from his face with a hand gloved in black satin. It was a chilly northern day, the sort of day that he liked best. He was not pleased that he had to leave his work to go to a meeting. He would much rather spend the entirety of his waking time deep in the catacombs below the surface, surrounded by death's many faces. He knew the importance of this meeting, however, and had to take it. Gascon, that narcissistic, power-hungry, little whelp of a man awaited him in his study.

Brother Terrid, Ronulen's chief assistant, informed him of the Weaver's arrival last night. Ronulen knew full well that the little man would not make the three-mile trek from the town of Farmalkin proper to the cemetery at night. Gascon showed ample courage in traveling to Crag Drannon, that he had to admit. However, that trip was built upon Gascon's lustful pursuit of power. Ronulen knew full well that, had he not needed to be there, the Weaver would not have made the trip to the dark keep at all. Gascon would meet with Ronulen as he always had in the light of day. That was when Gascon thought he held the advantage.

Insufferable little fool, he thought. How Ronulen longed for the day when he and the rest of the Necromancers would no longer need to hide behind the propaganda spun around them by the Weavers. That day was coming. It would be here soon.

Gascon walked up the steps of the gray building, its stone supporting a thatched roof that hung low to shed the winter snows. The stained glass windows showed a fire on the hearth inside. The wooden front doors opened as Ronulen approached. But the force that opened them this time was very much of this world. Brother Terrid stood aside, bowing humbly as the tall figure of Ronulen entered.

"Good day, my Lord," Terrid said, as he lifted from his bow and closed the door behind Ronulen. "The Lord Herrod awaits your presence in the study."

The entry room was sparsely decorated, with old wooden cabinets and dressers along its walls. Several chairs were placed about a long wooden table off to one side of the room. No colors other than the cooler shades of grays and blues accented anything.

This room did not give the feeling of wanting company in the least. Rather, it spoke to getting business quickly done, then leaving just as fast. It was a large room, the lack of furnishings adding to its atmosphere of desolation. At the far end, the hearth bled its yellow light into the room, blending with the light of several lit sconces on the walls. The flames flickered weakly. Even the light seemed to wish itself removed.

"Good," Ronulen said. "I hope to be done with this business quickly. I have far more pressing engagements that require my presence."

"Of course, my Lord," Terrid replied with another bow. "Shall I await you here?"

"No," Ronulen said, as he reached the far door. "You may return to the mausoleum and be about your business. The Greel need to be fed."

"Of course, my Lord."

With a final bow, Terrid left. The hearth fire did nothing to remove the chilly draft that swept through the room when Terrid departed. Ronulen liked that. He paused for a moment, getting into character. He opened the door to the study and entered.

"My good Lord Herrod Gascon," Ronulen said, closing the door behind him. "I do hope your wait was not too uncomfortable.

"My dear Brother Ronulen," Gascon spoke as he arose from a plush chair of deep lavender velvet. "My wait was pleasant if not a tad long. But such is the way of things." Gascon bowed with all the lavishness of the grand performer that he was.

Buffoon. Ronulen thought, as he crossed past Gascon to sit at his desk.

Whereas the outer room was cold and uninviting, Ronulen's study was quite comfortable by comparison. Ronulen's desk was a dark hickory wood, worked in fine gilded carvings around the edges. His chair, along with Gascon's, as well as the other three in the room, were all deep, plush, and high-backed with soft velvet pillows of matching lavender. Two tables of the same wood and gilded design, on one of which sat a flagon of wine and a set of drinking glasses, accented the desk. Ronulen noticed that Gascon had already poured himself a drink.

Both rooms shared the common fireplace, but this one seemed to hold its heat far better than the other. Pictures of ancient Necromantic Magi hung on the walls. Though well-painted, they all seemed rather sinister and gave the impression of being watched. And the room had the musty scent of a space that was seldom used.

"Now, let us get the business at hand?"

"Ah, yes. To it, then," Gascon said. He finished his wine and began pouring himself another. "I have several topics which need to be addressed."

"There is only one topic I need addressed," Ronulen said. His demeanor became much more serious.

The severity of Ronulen's tone was not lost on Gascon; he even paused a little while pouring his wine.

Gascon set the flagon down and cleared his throat. "Yes. Well ..." he began. "I am here to work with you, of course." They were equals. Gascon emphasized the word to reassert that. "To what topic do you refer?" Gascon knew full well what was coming next.

"Let us not play games, you and I," Ronulen said, leaning forward in his chair. Even seated, his height gave him an imposing air. "What word have you received regarding the woman? The Lyndrian?"

"My sources have told me nothing as of yet. I listen to the wind daily for any news."

"We should have heard something by now," Ronulen's cold stare bore deeply into Gascon. "I thought that was why you had come. To inform me of her impending arrival."

"As I said, there are other matters—"

"There are no other matters," Ronulen's voice boomed, cutting Gascon off in mid-sentence. "Your 'sources' were to be contacted when she crossed near the town of Silverton, were they not?"

"Yes."

"According to our last conversation, that contact should have been made by now," Ronulen continued. "Please tell me that we were right to put our trust in you. I thought your network of informants was ... extensive and completely competent. Is that not what you said? Perhaps we should have approached one of the other First Order Herrods?"

"My network is both extensive and competent. As am I," Gascon was quickly losing his footing in this meeting. He needed to reassert himself. "The Nortgard is a vast and dangerous wilderness. Any delay in information could be the result of any number of factors."

"Yes, factors for which you were supposed to have accounted. I cannot have any mistakes made in regards to this most important mission."

"Yes," Gascon countered. "Which is why I took the steps to bolster the number of informants in Silverton. I have secured the best hands in the business for the task. Hands that do their work well and in total secrecy."

Ronulen stared at Gascon for long moments.

"Brother Ronulen, please," Gascon continued. "I have dealt with kings and queens. I have navigated webs of noble gameplay and intrigue at the highest levels. Trust me."

"We have," Ronulen said, his voice growing ominous. "With the most important of tasks. Do not forget, your position of prominence in our new order is not yet assured. You promised us secrecy and success. We do not hold promises made to us lightly."

"Nor do I give them lightly. I contracted the best for the purpose of acquiring this Lyndrian and have masterfully covered our steps. No one can trace anything back to me, to you, or to any Necromancer. She is a ghost."

Ronulen's eyes darkened as he leaned forward further.

"As will you be, should we fail to acquire her."

That threat hung in the air for long moments as the two men stared at each other. Ronulen then stood and carefully smoothed the folds of his robes. "We must have the Lyndrian soon," he said calmly. "Our time grows short."

Gascon stood as well, although his stance was a bit uneasy. It must have been the wine.

"I must leave you now," Ronulen said and made his way to the door. "I will await your word."

"I shall stay in Farmalkin until news comes on the wind."

"Indeed, you will," Ronulen's tone suggested that that point was never in question.

"One more thing if you please?" Gascon asked, as Ronulen was about to open the door. He turned to face Gascon. "What about the disappearance of all the women from around the kingdoms? Surely you can tell me something?"

Ronulen stared at him for a moment. "There is only one woman about whom I am concerned," he said. "Find me the Lyndrian. As for the rest ... you are a Weaver. Spin something."

With that, Ronulen left. Gascon swallowed his wine in one gulp. He was beginning to question the wisdom of working so closely with the dark Magi.

Ronulen went swiftly back to the mausoleum. This time, he barely noticed the grandeur of all the death around him. The huge doors flew open with a wave of his hand. He entered and made his way across the cold tile floor. Rows of marble coffins lay embedded in the walls with three huge sarcophagi in the center. Ronulen continued on and went down a narrow hall where more rows of coffins were embedded. The northland was a rough place. Though the town was small, many had seen their transitions there.

He reached a stone door with carvings of ghoulish faces carved on its exterior in the hopes of frightening away evil spirits.

Fools, he thought as he approached. The living were the evil ones, not the dead. He waved his hand again, and the door swung open, slamming hard against the wall. He descended a long staircase. Halfway down its length, the stone walls gave way to walls of rock and hard-packed earth.

209

At the bottom of the staircase, the ground also became dirt. From this point forward, the tunnels had been dug out of the earth itself. He moved through the catacombs. Wall sconces gave off weak light every several feet. Many offshoot tunnels extended to the left and right of this slowly descending main tunnel. It curved the further he went, twisting around as it deepened. The earthen walls were smooth with perfect rectangular holes fitted with doors.

Every Strand of the Magics had some form of elemental energy at its base. As Necromancers dealt with death and the burial of the dead, it was only natural that they would have developed a skill for working with the earth. These catacombs were far more elaborate than any honed from mere digging. The Necromancers worked the earth well. Ronulen stopped suddenly and looked down a dark offshoot tunnel.

"Come," he commanded.

From the tunnel's depths approached a shadow that vaguely resembled a human. It was a demi-shade, a negative spirit bound to this plane through dark magics. An evil being in life, it bound itself to the Necromancers to protect it from the punishments that awaited it in the planes of existence beyond this one. A full shade could cause all sorts of damage and were harder to control. A demi-shade, however, was a weaker conjuring, only capable of carrying and delivering messages.

"Tell Terrid to make ready," Ronulen ordered. "I wish to speak to Lord Cartigas immediately."

"At once, my Lord," the evil entity hissed. With that, it disappeared into the darkness.

At these lower depths, all manner of sounds greeted Ronulen: shuffling of feet from some rooms, moans and wailing from others, and whispered conversations from others still.

Necromancers were not huge in numbers, but there were several who called these catacombs their home. On occasion, a Necromancer, Greel, or other dark figure would cross Ronulen, all pausing to bow in respect to the powerful Magus. He barely noticed as he approached a room with a heavy, oaken door.

Once he entered, he saw Terrid making ready. The room was large with an arched ceiling carved out of the earth. In the center was a circle of dark red powder on the floor. Within the circle, several designs of stars intersecting each other were ornately drawn as well as various magical runes both outside and inside the circle.

At the very center of the star design was a table of wrought iron. Atop the table was an intricate work of interconnecting steel rings, soldered to hold two thick crystal vases. Each cone-shaped vase, fully two feet tall, had a crystal topper. Between the two vases, at the center of the steel rings, was a small tablet. On the tablet were two small, red marbles. Each marble pulsed with a faint internal glow.

Two smaller circles were drawn within the larger one. Within each circle sat a woman on a chair directly in front of one of the rune carved vases.

Both the women were dressed in rags. Each one was filthy, undernourished and pale. Their bedraggled hair clung in matted clumps from their heads.

"Please," the woman closest to Ronulen whispered. Her voice cracked and strained with effort. "Have mercy. Please … I have a child. A daughter … Pella … Please …"

Her words drifted off into meaningless garbles as Ronulen entered the circle and stood behind her. He removed his silk gloves and placed them in one of the many pockets of his robes. Instantly, the scent of decay filled the room. He held up his hands, inspecting them. He was well-pleased with what he saw.

Ronulen's face was strong, with a commanding air that many would find attractive. He was always chosen to represent the Necromancers at any and all meetings of the Strands of the Magics because of that fact. In a class of Magi who did not prize physical beauty, he was the beautiful one. However, his hands bore the full effect of his dealings in the Necromantic arts. They were rotting and gangrenous. Where the skin was not decaying, it held the gray pallor of death, stretched taut to the bones beneath.

"Beautiful," Ronulen whispered to himself in admiration.

"Indeed, my Lord," Terrid said. "Truly, you have been blessed by the magics."

"Please ..." the woman whispered again. "Have mercy ..."

Ronulen put his rotting hands on the shoulders of the woman. The instant that he touched her flesh, her body tensed in a full spasm, her eyes growing wide as she was filled with a dark, magical power.

"Make the summons," Ronulen commanded Terrid.

From his position outside the circle, Terrid raised his hands in invocation. "*Tellad theroon.*" he whispered.

The red marble in front of the woman with Ronulen began to glow more radiantly. It lifted off of the tablet and floated in the air some six feet above the ground.

"The summons has been issued," Terrid said.

Long moments passed before the other marble began to glow brighter and levitate. As the second marble rose, the runes and symbols drawn on the ground glowed as well. Faintly at first, the dark red powder grew in intensity, changing from a muted reddish glow to a bright burnt orange as the magics in the room gained in intensity and strength. The entire room was lit with the magical glow.

"I welcome the great Lord of our order into this chamber," Ronulen began. As he spoke, the woman, whose body was still stiff from the induction of magical energies, started speaking. Her mouth was forming the very words that Ronulen spoke. As she did so, a change overtook her. Her flesh grew even more pale, becoming ashen and even sicklier than before. Her eyes grew sunken and glazed over with a milky film.

"I invoke the energies and bend them to my will. All hail the great Lord Cartigas," as Ronulen continued to speak, his voice no longer emerged from his mouth, but rather, came out full and clear from the woman's.

She was now a dried husk. Her body was shriveled, with the look of a corpse that had been buried for several weeks. As her body wasted away, the vase in front of her began to glow with a white light.

Suddenly, the woman on the other side of the circle began to spasm. Her body also grew stiff, her eyes and mouth opened wide in a mask of silent pain. She, too, began to decay. The vase in front of her filled with the same sickly light. Her skin became ashened, her cheeks hollowed, and her eyes rolled into her head and shriveled into nothing, leaving only dark, empty pits staring at Ronulen.

Ronulen smiled, but it was the husk of the woman who spoke his words. "Greetings, great Lord," he said, bowing as low as he could while still maintaining contact with the seated corpse. "We bid you welcome."

Terrid dropped to one knee outside the circle. His head he held low.

"What news have you?" Lord Cartigas's voice rumbled like thunder through the chamber, issuing from the other woman's mouth.

"The Pride is, as of yet … unaccounted for, my Lord," Ronulen said, with no small degree of worry. It befell him to secure the Pride, a task issued from Lord Cartigas, himself. Lord Cartigas's disapproval promised a fate far worse than death: eternal damnation at the hands of the great Lord of the Necromancers.

"This news displeases me," Lord Cartigas's avatar responded.

"We have received word from Crag Devlin," Ronulen hoped this next bit of news might alleviate some of his master's concern. "A neophyte of unique potential is being taken there now, potential unlike any we have seen in centuries. The Prophecy speaks of many rare talents emerging around the Pride, talents that could aid us."

"I, too, have been in contact with Crag Devlin," Lord Cartigas growled. "Our soul wagons continue to be attacked by this 'Maars the Lector.' None have arrived. Besides which, there is no talent that can aid us if we have not the Pride. Time is of the essence. I must begin her training soon. She alone can lead us to absolute victory."

"I am prepared to take all measures necessary, great Lord, to see her brought to us."

"What of the Grimward?" Lord Cartigas was growing frustrated. "Are they ready?"

"They will draw more negative attention to our cause. Already, people begin to focus blame on us for the disappearances of the female populace." Ronulen knew to be concerned with any mention of the Grimward.

"The 'people' have always blamed us for every dark happening that has plagued the land." Lord Cartigas said coldly. "Even after we saved the world from the Mourning Night, they still feared us. They do not understand that to follow us is to guarantee dominion over not only this plane but over the planes beyond as well.

"We will issue the world into a new order, where the living and the dead are merged. They cannot comprehend

214

that glory. We will conquer with the sword and rule with the tomb."

"I want nothing more, my Lord," Ronulen said. "But we need the people of the kingdoms to continue to respect us until our armies are at full strength."

"They will never achieve that strength without the Pride!" Lord Cartigas roared.

The corpse shell that his essence now occupied shook with the power of his words. The walls of the room, having been created by the magics, began to crack slightly.

"The merging of living and necrotic flesh can only be completed through the magics of the Pride. So it is foretold. I have worked the great magics and can speak to the truth of this," Lord Cartigas calmed his voice, but it still held displeasure. "It is time to touch the land directly with our power. Have our Weavers blame the ancient evil of the banished Oracle magics for the darkness that begins to spread. Once we have the Pride, we will disappear and grow powerful in the dark."

"As you wish, my Lord. The living do not care about the dead as long as they are unseen."

"That is as it has always been. That is our greatest strength, making the world believe we do not exist."

"Until we strike," Ronulen said. His words quivered with restrained excitement.

"Until we strike," Lord Cartigas repeated. "I give you license to utilize a more pronounced display of our power. Our measures will be fearsome. Find her."

Lord Cartigas's eyeless avatar leaned forward, its gaunt cheeks growing slack.

"It shall be as you ask, great Lord."

"Do not fail in this."

With that, Lord Cartigas's avatar shuddered once, then fell from the chair.

Ronulen released his grip on his avatar as it fell forward as well. He gripped the back of his chair for support, his balance suddenly leaving him.

"My Lord?" Terrid asked, concerned.

Ronulen waved him off weakly.

Letting go of his avatar, Ronulen's release of the magics caused the glowing red dust to immediately fade. The spell had used up most of the dust. Where once all the lines on the floor were filled in completely, now several gaps appeared. The solid lines were now thinning throughout all the designs, some runes having been used up completely.

"The transference of souls is a taxing process to say the least," Ronulen responded. His head hung low as he tried to regain his strength. He kicked the corpse at the foot of the chair aside and sat down. "What of the transients?" he asked, as he continued to catch his breath.

Terrid walked over to the vases and inspected them closely. The vase sitting in front of the avatar that housed the soul of the great Lord Cartigas had what appeared to be a faintly glowing gas at its base, almost like a low hanging fog. The thick gas had a weak pulse, very akin to a heartbeat.

Terrid shook his head in disappointment when inspecting it and moved onto the other vase, the one in front of Ronulen's avatar. It brought Terrid to a thoughtful nod. It had what appeared to be a thick mass of writhing flesh at its base. The glob of flesh rippled and moved as if in pain. It was covered in what appeared to be blood that glowed faintly, smearing the inside of the vase with the glowing gore. After several more minutes of inspection, waving his hands over each vase and muttering incantations that made his hands glow faintly red as he did so, Terrid finally turned to Ronulen.

Ronulen, for his part, slowly regained his strength but was still a far way from his full faculties.

216

"Unfortunately," Terrid began, as he gestured to the vase that held the thick, white mist. "That soul is unsalvageable. Try as I might, I cannot turn it. It is too pure."

"I thought you had been instructed to acquire only the dregs: whores, murderers, and thieves?" Ronulen asked, his eyes closed as he breathed deeply.

"We did, my Lord," Terrid countered. "Who would have imagined that there existed a lady of the night with a pure soul?"

"Far more exists in this world than a kind-hearted wench," Ronulen said, as he opened his eyes. "Her soul is useless to us. Her transition does not serve the greater good. The women we take must be viable. Her disappearance now gains us nothing more than further rumor." Ronulen's disappointment was clear, even in his taxed state.

"Of course, my Lord," Terrid said, apologetically. "I will ensure it does not happen again. I beg your forgiveness."

"You are an apt pupil, Terrid. I know you will see to it. Now, what of the other?"

"Ah," Terrid said, with a smile. He walked over and lifted the vase that held the disgusting glob that oozed with the faintly glowing blood. When he lifted it, the bloody flesh lashed out at the side of the vase as though the movement caused it pain. "This one ... is perfect. Completely corrupt. Apparently, motherhood could not salvage her soul."

"Giving birth does not redeem one's soul," Ronulen said, as he arose. "It is only a path to redemption. A path this one obviously chose not to take." He kicked the corpse casually as he spoke. "Take the soul receptacle and load it onto the next wagon headed to Crag Drannon. It will be fed to the great womb." Ronulen inspected the crystal soul receptacle carefully. "Yes, several warriors can be spawned from the vileness contained within this tainted existence." Ronulen tapped the vase hard, which caused the remnants of the damned soul within to lash out again. Ronulen smiled as he put his black silk gloves back on. "I must take my rest." As he headed for the door, he looked at the cracks that were clearly visible on the walls of the room. "The energies we utilized have completely taxed this room of its magics."

"My Lord?"

Ronulen turned.

"What of the pure soul?"

"Hold it for now. Perhaps we will one day discover the magics necessary to pervert it."

"Yes, my Lord."

"And what of the Pride?" Ronulen asked. "Any news?"

"None, my Lord."

Turning to leave, Ronulen smiled ominously. "Unleash the Grimward."

13: Banderghal

Terrid neared the one chamber in the catacombs that actually filled him with dread. In this deepest part of the tunnels, no one other than the most skilled Magi dared to wander. Even the dark spirits and otherworldly beasts summoned to the Necromancers' aid avoided this dark place.

An orb of soft, blue light floated in front of Terrid, illuminating his path. When he reached the opening of the chamber, he drew in a deep breath. He left the orb outside; the faint light would do little to brighten the darkness within. The chamber was huge, with a defensive gate that wound around the entire oval space. Terrid walked to the edge of the wall and looked down. Some hundred feet below, he heard their breathing. Harsh rasps of huge lungs filling with the vile, rotted air of their soggy dwelling. Claws scraped along rock, and fangs clicked in the darkness. If any light could have cut into the darkness, it would have shown dozens of caves feeding into the main chamber. They were holes of the darkest black, opening like hungry mouths ready to spew forth their hateful offspring.

Terrid could feel their anger, their revulsion for all things living. The scrapes and clicks grew louder. He could see a dozen plus sets of glowing red orbs, staring up at him. Terrid raised his hands up into the air. They glowed faintly red. "Grimward!" he called down, his voice magically enhanced. "Arise!"

Howls of vile fury echoed out from the deep hole that was the home of the Grimward. They filled Terrid with fear. He was most sincerely glad that it was not him at whom that awful spearhead was aimed. The howls grew in a frightening pitch, filling all the catacombs with their rage. In the

219

darkness of the night, deep within the belly of the earth, hate had been awakened.

Corwyn, Velladriana, and Harper had ridden long into the afternoon. That night, Corwyn found an isolated clearing and started a fire. The tall, soft grass allowed him to set the horses very near to graze. They settled in beneath the stars, hardly saying a word.

Harper sat near the fire, staring into the flames. She did not respond when Corwyn asked if she was hungry, nor did she accept any of the rations he offered. In the space of an afternoon, everything that she knew was right and safe in the world had been turned upside down.

Her uncle was a fur trapper in his younger years; he gave that up when presented the opportunity to run the saddlery. He had forsaken taking a wife, that he might give her more of his time. Tears started rolling down her cheeks again as she thought of all the good times she had experienced with her uncle.

He would often disappear into the deep woods for long stretches at a time. Being one of the last people to interact with Mama Weaver, he convinced the old lady to take charge of Harper in his absence. It did not take much convincing, as Harper was as loveable and charismatic as a child as she was now as an adult.

Harper grew up wild and free-spirited. Her knack for mischief often got her into trouble. She had lost her parents during an attack on a northern settlement when she was just a small child. Never did she think that she would encounter the kind of trouble that had befallen her now. Even the fond memories of her childhood were not enough to stem the pain that she now faced. That pain had turned to anger. It had turned to rage.

The rage grew in Harper anew as she thought about all that her uncle had sacrificed for her. He was a good man. He was taken from her by filth. She could still feel the hot iron poker in her hand, plunging deep into the murderer's chest. She could see the blood issuing from his mouth. Given the choice, she would have done it again. She would cry a great deal all night. She would cry a great deal for many nights to come.

Velladriana wanted to be there for Harper. She did not, however, go to Harper, feeling ill-equipped to help her deal with the devastating loss of her uncle. She had enough to worry about without trying to come up with hollow words of comfort.

Every moment that they had been on the run, the haunting fear that she could be given to another strange attack like while they were with Mama Weaver troubled her. Mama Weaver said it was the magics, dark, Necromantic magics at that. Strange things had happened to Velladriana in the past but never with the overwhelming force of that night. The worst of it was that she could not remember the incident. People had died for her, and now here she was, in a foreign land, led by a power she could not even remember possessing. Velladriana lay back and stared helplessly at the canopy of trees.

Corwyn kept careful watch as he scouted the perimeter of their camp. He would not allow anything, human or otherwise, to surprise them in the night. He moved through the forest, ensuring that they had not been followed by retracing their steps and covered any sign of their passing.

His Heart's Eye would alert him to danger sooner than anyone else would even notice something was amiss, but that is not why he focused on it. Reaching out with his Heart's Eye calmed him. He was searching for serenity. Corwyn needed tranquility now more than ever. He felt every crisp motion in the air and fully breathed in the smells. He took in the sounds with a clarity that few could understand. Even though his senses were sharpened, he did not find the answers he sought.

Corwyn could not help but wonder why it was that his life had now become so chaotic. The very thing he was trained for years to see clearly through now clouded everything around him.

His first time out of the Glass Tower and he did not feel anything like one of the most highly trained warriors on the planet. He felt like a beginner holding a wooden training sword for the first time. Nothing made sense to him now.

He touched the bark of a large birch tree, feeling its strength beneath his fingers. He wished that its strength and its stability could somehow transfer to him. Nothing at all made sense.

Corwyn had the added weight of a destiny that he felt was unjustly thrust upon him. He had learned in the Glass Tower how to fight, how to control unruly crowds and how to establish order. He had never been taught how to deal with a situation such as this. He had to keep the savior of the world from falling into the hands of evil.

Corwyn needed to get Velladriana, the 'Pride' as Mama Weaver called her, to a place deep within the Nortgard

Mountains, far to the north. The Nortgard Mountains were a difficult place to trek when surrounded by capable companions. To add to his concern, there was the strange pull Velladriana exerted on his Heart's Eye. Even now, he could sense her. That was what kept him from swearing that Mama Weaver was crazy. She was right. There was a reason he was pulled toward Velladriana. Could she really be this mythical 'Pride'? It was quite a dilemma, one of many he now faced. Not to mention, he now had the added responsibility of caring for a girl who had just seen her uncle killed. Harper was another in the growing list of chaotic factors appearing in his life.

She was not really a girl. In point of fact, Corwyn put her age at somewhere near Velladriana's, perhaps around 19 or 20 winters. That would make her only one or two winters his junior. Still, the youthful exuberance she displayed and how quickly it had been ripped away made her seem younger than she was. As an Oslyn, he had been trained to find clarity in chaos. Unfortunately, Harper was dealing with that chaos now.

Once Corwyn got closer to the campsite, he released his Heart's Eye. One could not maintain concentration through the Heart's Eye indefinitely. The focus required was too great. Meditation and rest were required to keep that focus. Corwyn feared he would not get the chance to do either for a very long time.

Stepping back into the camp, Corwyn found Velladriana and Harper in much the same positions, though Velladriana was a bit closer to Harper than when he had left. They both looked up with a start when he approached.

He appeared like a ghost from the shadows. His form loomed large and intimidating as he emerged from the trees. The two women visibly relaxed when they saw it was he, settling back down into their previous thoughts. They both soon lay down in an effort to sleep. Corwyn doubted they would find much rest. At one point, he knew that he heard Harper's soft weeping blending with the sounds of the forest night.

The loss of the pack that Mama Weaver had given him definitely set them back. They would need to be well-provisioned for a push deeper into the Nortgard. That night, Corwyn studied the map he was given with great care. It would take a long time to reach this Mount Elderstone if it even existed. Getting more provisions, however, would have to wait until the morning. Corwyn settled himself away from the fire and more into the shadows, which was the best place to keep watch. For Corwyn, there would be no sleep tonight.

When Harper had awakened, earlier that morning, before dawn, she had not seen Corwyn in their camp. That did not surprise her though. She had heard him moving often throughout the night, keeping watch. She assumed that he was making another patrol early. That thought brought her a great measure of comfort.

She had gotten up, not that she had actually slept, and was careful not to disturb the still form of Velladriana as she walked off. She found the clearing where she now stood a short distance away. It was an isolated, rocky, raised area, just like Mama Weaver had instructed her to find. It was a good place to sing to the wind.

She removed the dradar from her pouch and began spinning it over her head, calling the wind to her. Her notes quickly formed the wind walls, and she called out to Mama Weaver. She and Mama Weaver spoke at this time on most mornings. Within moments, Mama Weaver had returned her call, and the wind song connection had been made.

"I am so sorry, child. I loved Tornvil as if he were my own. As I do you. I did not intend for this to happen." Mama Weaver's image in the wind wall shimmered. Her sorrow for Harper's loss was very sincere.

"I miss him so much," Harper cried. "All I do is think of him holding me, his beard tickling my cheeks. His arms holding me tightly ... he was so strong ..."

Harper began to weep inconsolably. She lost focus and slowed the spin of the dradar. The entire wind song room began to shimmer and dissipate into smoke.

"No child!" Mama Weaver called. "You must keep your focus. If you stop spinning the dradar without finishing the wind song properly, it could lash out violently and rip you apart. You must focus, child!"

Harper caught herself and increased the dradar's momentum. Instantly, the wind walls grew more solid as did Mama Weaver's image.

"I am sorry, Mama," Harper cried. "I will stay strong."

"You must," Mama Weaver said in as comforting a voice as she could. "We all must. We will all be tested in the days and months to come. You must remain strong."

"What do I do now?" Harper asked between sobs. "I want to come home to you."

"That is impossible, child. Death has already visited my door once. I am afraid it may come to find me again before all is done."

"But what do I do?"

"Be strong," Mama Weaver's voice took on an air of strength. "Fate has moved you into this position. Rightly or wrongly, you are there now. I wish more than anything that Tornvil were still here, but wishing will not make it so. You must carry on, lest he died for nothing. And know this, if

Velladriana falls into the hands of the Necromancers, all will suffer worse fates than death."

Harper stared at Mama Weaver's shimmering image for some time. Having only had the training Mama Weaver had given her, she was not as proficient in the ways of a Weaver as she would have been had she studied consistently at a theater. Blessed as she was with tremendous natural talent, she was able to hold her focus.

"I will be strong," Harper said, stifling her tears. "I promise."

"Good," Mama Weaver responded with a smile. "Remember, you are traveling with an Oslyn. The road is dangerous, but you are under the most capable of protections. Now, we must speak of your trek into the deep Nortgard."

"Mama, we lost what supplies you gave. We would have needed more, surely. But with the loss, we need to resupply now. There is only one outpost for provisions near enough to give us what we need."

"The Skinner's Outpost," Mama Weaver said with total understanding. "I was hoping that all I packed would have seen them past that place. To the garrison at least. I had not counted on you joining them either. Well, fate does what it must. Corwyn must stay focused on the task at hand. It seems fate will play some powerful cards soon. Over fate, as you have seen, we have no control. Just move quickly."

"We will. I promise."

"Be done with me now," Mama Weaver said, with a smile. "I cannot eavesdrop on the wind song of others when I am caught up talking with you, no matter how much I enjoy it." Mama Weaver looked at Harper lovingly for several long moments. "I love you child. Be strong. Be well."

"I love you too, Mama," Harper said, beginning to cry again.

"No, no, child. What did I say?"

"Be strong," Harper said, stifling her tears once more.

"Be strong," Mama Weaver repeated, as her image dissolved into smoke and faded away on the wind.

How Harper loved her time with Mama Weaver. She had a brilliance few could understand. That thought made Harper smile as she longingly watched Mama Weaver go. How she wished she could be in the familiar confines of Mama's cluttered tent once again. Alas, that happy place seemed forever removed from her now. Harper silenced her song and brought the dradar to a rest.

The wind settled in the clearing immediately.

She carefully wound her rope around its dradar and placed it into her soft brown, tasseled pouch. She slung the pouch over her shoulder and took a deep, calming breath. The forest was beautiful, and yet, something seemed strangely wrong. No birds chirped in the tall evergreens, no small animals rustled in the brush below. Harper froze. Her eyes widened in fear. Something was definitely wrong.

Damn me for a fool. Harper thought. *I should have been more careful.* She had lived long enough in the forest to know when she was being stalked.

The beast exploded from the cover of the outlying trees and raced across the clearing in three easy bounds, roaring loudly as it launched its bulk directly at Harper.

Harper screamed in panic. It was a *banderghal*, a huge, apelike creature with the face of a baboon. Its open mouth snarled with huge canine teeth that protruded like eight-inch daggers from its upper and lower jaws. It extended its long arms wide as it came crashing down upon her, its claws preparing to rip her limbs apart.

Harper fell to the ground and covered her head—for what little good that would do—when Corwyn suddenly appeared, springing over her with Taryn in his hands.

227

Corwyn yelled with a roar almost as loud and primal as that of the banderghal as he met the creature in the air, bringing his sword down in a diagonal slash that ripped through its chest. Bloody pulp and fur spilled to the ground.

Corwyn landed lightly and dove into a roll and coming up to the banderghal's side. Slightly taller than Corwyn, the injured beast rose to its full height and spun on him, only to be met with a horizontal slash that struck low at its hip. The beast howled when Taryn bit into it tough hide, ripping open another deep gash.

Corwyn faced the creature, spinning Taryn in defensive arcs to fend off a sudden rush. The banderghal was not a stupid creature, nor did it attack mindlessly. Seeking out an easier target than this dangerous foe, its huge head turned toward Harper. It's elongated, bright red nostrils flared as it took in her scent. Corwyn struck again and slashed high across the creature's muscular shoulders. He reversed the momentum of the blade back along its arc, cutting its lower back.

Enraged and injured, the beast lashed out wildly at Corwyn. He ducked beneath the large swinging arms and swung his sword out as he crossed the creature's path, taking a huge chunk of its arm in the process. Without missing a beat, Corwyn leapt into the air, bringing the full force of his strength and momentum down across its skull. Taryn bit deeply. Blood and gore spewed out when Corwyn ripped his sword free. The huge creature fell forward and twitched in its death throes. Corwyn spun Taryn around and drove it into the creatures exposed back, ensuring it a quick death. It stopped moving, and blood pooled beneath it.

Corwyn pulled Taryn free and ran over to Harper. Though he had been impressive in handling their attackers at the saddlery, Harper was really too shocked to have actually taken account of what he had done. This, however, was a display the likes of which she had never before seen.

"Are you all right?" Corwyn asked, as he kneeled beside her. "Are you hurt?"

"No ... no, I'm fine," She said, as he helped her to her feet. "Thank you."

"I was just fortunate," Corwyn said. "The creature had his focus set on you. Something is not right here. I have never heard of a greater banderghal being this far south before. They normally only inhabit the colder mountainous regions." He looked around warily. He noticed, much to his dismay, that Velladriana had not listened to his order to stay at the camp and was staring at them from the tree line, some 30 feet away. "You should not wander off alone. Our strength is in numbers. The Nortgard is a dangerous place."

"I know how dangerous the Nortgard is," Harper began. "I have lived near and around it all of my life."

"I just meant," Corwyn began, quickly backing off of the sternness that she obviously misconstrued as condescension. "The Nortgard is no place for a ..."

"A what?" Harper said. "A woman?"

"No, of course not." Corwyn was quick to reply. "I know many very capable women who could handle themselves perfectly well here. This is no place for a ..."

"A girl?" Harper finished his sentence for him. "A girl! You listen to me. I can handle myself just fine here! I am not some girl you need to rescue! Do you understand that? And if it weren't for you, I wouldn't be here in the first place! If it weren't for you, I'd be back at the saddlery and my uncle would be just fine!"

Corwyn just stood there, completely stunned by the truth and the weight of her words. Harper spun and walked off toward Velladriana. She remembered Mama Weaver's advice and did her best to control her tears. But at the moment, it was not working as well as she would have hoped. Harper passed by Velladriana.

Hood pulled over her head, Velladriana followed Harper back to the campsite. She did not leave without giving Corwyn a very cold glare, however.

Corwyn stood there for some time before carefully wiping Taryn's blade free of blood in some thick grass. He sheathed it and headed back to the campsite. He had not meant to insult or demean Harper. His words just never seemed to come out quite right when dealing with women. Even so, he could not deny the truth of her words. Death had followed him to her door.

14: No Loose Ends

D olver walked the streets of Silverton, fuming in suppressed anger as he recounted the blow that Corwyn had landed flush to his chest. It still ached painfully. Much of the previous day and night he spent in the common room of The Leaning Oak, one of the two taverns in the town. He had wanted to give immediate chase to the two women and warrior who had cost him so much. However, the commotion had brought out the fire brigade and the city guard in force. He had no choice but to hide out until things settled. In the rougher southern portion of Silverton, The Leaning Oak was very close to the Weaver's Theater and provided drink and relaxation for most of the entertainers and travelers who were passing through.

Dolver walked passed all the shops and residences, all but the various butcher's shops and bakeries dark with inactivity. In these small hours before dawn, activity was limited to only those services that provided meals or rest. As such, the smell of fresh baked bread wafted down the street, a subtle invitation to the residents to awaken and begin their daily activities.

The town's tall, defensive walls on its outskirts hemmed in the narrow streets of this quarter as well as buildings that rose two and three stories high, taking full advantage of the hilly terrain.

Taylors, butchers, tinkers, smiths, and cobblers, to name a few, were but a small sum of the businesses that made a town prosperous. Most had their storefronts at the bases of the structures with residences built above. The narrow, winding streets meandered up and down the landscape, giving the town an undulating feel. Many of the wooden buildings were being fortified by stone and brick masonry. It was a sure sign that the town was growing. Dolver headed toward the Weaver's Theater. The fact that this frontier town even had one surprised him to no end.

As he made his way along the narrow street, his anger resurfaced when he thought back on the previous day's encounter. He had her. He had a Lyndrian—a *Lyndrian*—in his grasp. It had to be the Lyndrian Gascon told him to look out for. How could it not be? Seeing a Lyndrian on this side of the Great Rift was rarer than seeing a griffox.

Dolver rubbed unconsciously at the spot where Corwyn had kicked him. A human had never hit him with that much force in all his life. An oarkman could pack that kind of power, to be sure; they were known for it, but a man? It was unheard of.

Were it not for that warrior ... child—he could not have been more than 20 winters—I would have had a fine catch. Dolver thought. *Corwyn, I'm sure that's what the woman yell out, cost me a winter's worth of gold that a Lyndrian could fetch.*

Dolver did not like being kept from his due and proper. This Corwyn would have to pay for that ... dearly. The boy owed him much. First, the Lyndrian. Next, he had killed Brenner and Worrick, two solid murderers. Those were two more deaths that the boy owed. Thinking on it honestly, Dolver probably would have wound up killing Worrick himself, but that was far from the point. Finally, and most infuriating of all, the boy had landed a humbling blow on Dolver, quickly dispatching him. That infuriated the assassin. The boy owed him a life for that as well.

Dolver turned down a smaller side street and walked up its inclining grade. He kicked over a small can of rubbish in disgust. He pulled his dark green cloak tighter around himself as he approached The Lonely Wanderer Inn at the top of the hill, just across from the theater. He was not trying to stave off the chill of the morning; his night of excessive drinking was working wonders for that. He did not want to be seen.

The Lonely Wanderer was not a large establishment, but it was maintained, with gilded framing and large, inviting double doors, whitewashed to match the window panes and latticework that adorned the front. This was the inn that held the Weaver's most important guests and performers when the Theater itself ran low on accommodations.

Dolver did not enter through the inviting front of the inn, but rather, made his way to a staircase that ran along the side of the building near the alley. When he reached the second floor landing, he checked to make sure no one had seen him before entering. Content to find that no one had been following him, he entered the inn.

He made his way rapidly down the dark hall. In these last hours before dawn, the wicks burned low in the sconces on the walls, providing more shadow than light. That was the perfect environment for a killer such as he.

He went around a corner and saw his destination, a set of large, double doors with bronze handles, at the end of the hall. It was one of the inn's suites, and a quite lavish one by the standards of the northerners. The corner suite was rather isolated and gave those who stayed there an abundance of privacy. He would expect nothing less from a Weaver. Merid Loa was a Herrod of the Third Order and was the chief liaison between Gascon and people like Dolver, who had seedy reputations. Dolver needed to communicate with Gascon now. Merid Loa was his key.

Dolver removed a pouch with small, lock-picking tools from his coat and quickly got the door open. The interior was very comfortable, with large couches of soft browns and greens in the room. Beautiful tables were in the room's center, and fine cabinets adorned the walls. A rug of golden-brown pulled all the décor together, while the room's two tapestries blew slightly in the morning breeze coming in through the open windows.

Moving silently past the slightly open bedroom door, Dolver peeked in and saw the sensuous form of a naked woman on the bed, half-covered with a thin sheet. Her steady, heavy breathing let him know that she was in a deep sleep. Hearing soft footsteps approaching from a third room, he moved back and positioned himself just off of the door beside a tall, decorative plant. He drew his dagger from his belt. Merid Loa, dressed in only a loose fitting nightshirt, walked past Dolver, completely unaware of his presence.

Dolver stalked like silent death, moving behind Merid and placing the sharpened edge of his dagger up against the Weaver's neck. Merid's breath caught in his throat upon feeling the blade. Dolver grabbed the scruff of Merid's silken nightshirt and pulled him close.

"Outside, on the balcony. Move," Dolver ordered, in a whisper.

Weavers would always get rooms with balconies, if possible. That way, they would have an open space to sing to the wind as necessary. When the door had shut, Dolver spun the concerned Weaver around to face him.

"What is the meaning of this?" Merid asked, with all the bravado he dared muster. "What do you want?"

"Merid … you disappoint me," Dolver said. "You know I am currently in the employ of your master. Yet I have heard nothing from you in such a long time."

"Dolver," Merid began. "We Weavers do not consider ourselves masters or servants, but that is beside the point. The Herrod for whom I work—"

"Gascon," Dolver interrupted "Let's not play games."

"Yes, well, he … will have me reach you when he has something to say," Merid smiled weakly. "I meant you no insult."

"Sing to him now," Dolver demanded. "Right now. I have news for him, and it will not wait for you to roll in the bed again with that woman. As much as I respect that."

Merid seemed taken aback and insulted by the request.

"Surely, you do not mean for me to dance the dradar myself?" he asked. "I am a Herrod after all."

Dolver was growing tired of this nonsense. He looked away for a moment before snapping a solid uppercut into Merid's side. Merid dropped to the floor, his wind taken completely from him. Dolver kneeled beside him, again putting his dagger to Merid's neck.

"Now, hear me and mark my words well," Dolver whispered. "You will dance the dradar and reach out to Gascon now. If you do not, I will flay what I am sure is the very pretty little thing sleeping in your bed. That is, before I flay you. Do you understand?"

Merid lifted his head and gasped for air. He fully believed this assassin would do as he said. Merid had worked with Dolver before. Never had Dolver acted in such a manner. This was highly irregular. He was an assassin, but assassins could be easily manipulated with the right amount of coin. In this instance, Merid knew no amount of coin would stave off the killer.

"Alright," Merid huffed. "But just know that Gascon is too busy to be listening to the wind, himself."

"Don't play me for a fool," Dolver said. "Gascon will have someone listening. Especially now. I know that dawn and dusk are the best times to send your messages. Why do you think I am here now? Get to it."

Merid rose and walked to a corner of the balcony. There he opened an ornate cabinet and pulled out his dradar. The long rope to which it was attached dragged on the floor.

"Tell him," Dolver said. "That I have found his package. Then we will see how long it takes him to respond."

Merid nodded. He had no choice. It was true. Gascon would have one of his underlings listening now. Merid cringed at the thought of spinning the wind himself. That was just not something that Herrods of any Order did. It was beneath his rank and station.

"I might need more room," Merid said, in a final attempt to get out of it.

"Perhaps your pet's screams will motivate you to get it done," Dolver said with a snarl.

Merid extended his dradar, the bone whistle hanging by the end of the rope, and spun it. Dolver stood nearby. The wind closed in around them. Merid's voice joined with the whistle of the dradar. The wind surrounded them both, growing solid. Merid changed the notes he sang and the ceiling of wind above them extended into the heavens, becoming a wind tunnel visible only to them.

"I sing to my lord, the Herrod of the First Order, Gascon, Herrod of the North," Merid sang. "It is Merid, Herrod of the Third Order, calling from the northland town of Silverton, who wishes his counsel."

Dolver did have to admit that the man did have a beautiful voice. Even though his voice resonated within the walls of wind, Dolver knew that anyone outside their shield of solid air would hear nothing other than the soft whistle of the dradar. It was quite a talent these Weavers had.

In a few moments, a voice descended from the wind funnel, this one was a woman's.

"This is Ceiran, chief scribe to the Herrod of the North. I shall pass along a message to him," the woman's voice melodically responded. "What message do you bring him?"

Merid hesitated for a moment, looking at Dolver before he responded. Dolver ran his finger along the edge of his dagger; he knew what effect it would have.

"Please tell my lord Herrod that … his package has been found," Merid sang those words with a bit of a nervous waver to his voice.

"Remain in the wind," Ceiran's voice sang in response.

Merid kept the dradar spinning. The wind funnel spun in a continuous cyclone, Merid's earlier notes ringing softly in the air. The song would be answered. Of that he had no doubt.

After several long minutes, another voiced descended from the wind funnel. This voice was far richer and more melodic than that of Merid. Dolver recognized it at once. Gascon had arrived.

As Gascon's song merged with that of Merid, an image began to take form in the wind across from them. There, in a silken nightshirt of purple with lace ruffles along the wrists—Weavers were gaudy even when they slept, Dolver noted—was the image of Gascon. He did not look pleased to have been awakened with this news so early in the day. Dolver nonchalantly sheathed his dagger back behind him.

"Merid," Gascon huffed, clearly not pleased. "What do you mean, my package has been …" Gascon then noticed Dolver in the room of wind. "You," Gascon said. "Explain yourself."

Dolver cast a sidelong glance at Merid.

"Of course," Dolver said, very politely. "But what I have to say is for your ears alone."

Merid looked quite insulted by that. It was bad enough that Gascon had to see him spinning the dradar like some first-year understudy. Now he was being asked to leave the discussion that he himself spun? This was insulting to Merid at the utmost.

"Do it now," was all that Gascon said.

With that, along with an insulted huff, Merid raised his hand that held the lower end of the length of rope and aimed it at Dolver. With a high-pitched vibrato shift in his song, a wall of rigid wind spun up between Dolver and Merid, effectively cutting Merid off completely from the conversation.

"Well?" Gascon demanded, impatiently.

"You are sure he cannot hear us?" Dolver said.

"Do not play the fool with my time, assassin. The wind walls of the song are more rigid than stone. Where is my package?"

"She is gone," Dolver said, with finality. "I saw a Lyndrian on my way to drop off other cargo."

Gascon's image in the wind shimmered for a moment. Whoever this woman was must have been important indeed to get him to lose his focus in such a manner.

"Did this have anything to do with the fire yesterday?" Gascon said, after he had composed himself.

News did travel quickly among the Weavers. Their ability to communicate over the miles always impressed Dolver. He often wondered how much more effective his Guild would be if they could do the same without the aid of the Weavers.

"It did. You hired me to keep an eye out for a Lyndrian woman. Well, I saw her, along with a warrior who killed two of my men yesterday. I even had to dispose of my … cargo, as the fire brought multiple patrols out into the woods. Sure enough, I got word last night that they found and confiscated my wagon. I am owed greatly now."

"Enough!" Gascon yelled. He seemed both furious and nervous at once. "You are owed nothing. Whatever other 'cargo' you have is not my concern. You were supposed to alert me when you saw any sign of a Lyndrian slave, not report to me that she is gone."

"I can find them," Dolver said, with all seriousness. "That is what I do. They are prey. I am a hunter. Also, I understand your need for discretion. Do you mean to say you can employ, inform, and place another man or men with my skillset in position here in the north in the time needed to hunt them down?"

Gascon knew Dolver was right. Say what people might about the man, he was good at his job. Also, Gascon had worked with him often in the past. Ascending the ranks of the Weavers was as much about talent as it was about deceit. Gascon knew that Dolver would keep his mouth shut; his career depended upon silence. It seemed Gascon's career now depended on it, as well as did his very life.

"Find my package," Gascon said. "I will always have a Weaver listening to the wind for you. Whatever you need, I will provide. Say nothing to anyone of this. Mark my words. If you do, you will wish for the quick death of your suicide sigil."

"Of course. I am at your service. I just want you to know that, to do this silently, I will need to clear up some loose ends in Silverton."

"Do what needs be done," Gascon said, with growing impatience. "Disappear and get me the girl. Do whatever it takes, and tell no one else."

"I will find your package," he hissed.

"See it done."

With that, Gascon's image wavered and dissolved into the mist. As he vanished into smoke, so did the wall between Dolver and Merid.

Merid looked absolutely irate at Dolver as the wind wall vanished.

"We are done here," Dolver said.

Merid sung the wind room closed. The stiffness of the wind dissipated into nothingness, as Merid grew silent and brought the dradar's whistling spin to a halt. He walked away to place the dradar back into the cabinet.

"Now, if you and I are quite finished?" Merid said. "I have business elsewhere."

Merid turned into the point of a sharp knife that stabbed up through his ribs and into his heart. His eyes grew wide in pain and horror. His life was bleeding out of his body.

"Now," Dolver said, the rapture of the kill glowing in his eyes. "We are quite finished."

Merid's lips moved as if to say something in protest, but he uttered no sound. His strong voice was now forever silent. He slumped forward into Dolver's arms, who gently set the Weaver to the floor.

"No loose ends," Dolver said to Merid's corpse. "No one saw me enter, and no one will see me leave. And … never play games with my time."

Dolver smiled and walked to the balcony door. He turned to address Merid's corpse one more time. "Don't worry about your business in the bedroom, either." Dolver's smile grew malicious, never reaching his eyes. "I will take care of that, myself."

Dolver deftly spun his knife in his hand. He opened the door and slipped silently into the suite. He smiled the entire time.

15: Skinner's Outpost

Corwyn, Velladriana, and Harper had ridden east for several hours, covering many miles of sloping terrain. With luck, they would soon reach the Skinner's Outpost, resupply, and quickly get back on the road. Velladriana rode by Harper's side, staring at Corwyn, who rode several paces ahead. Neither Velladriana nor Harper had spoken to him since the banderghal attack earlier that morning.

"We'll have a chance to eat when we reach the Skinner's Outpost. The plates may be dirty, but the food is hot," Harper said.

"That sounds ... nice," Velladriana responded. She liked this Harper, and as they talked a bit, she was working on lowering her guard.

"Were you," Harper began, unsure quite how to proceed, "were you born a ... you know, a slave?"

Velladriana self-consciously tugged her hood lower over her slave loop. It was a movement not lost on Harper.

"I'm sorry," Harper stated quickly. "I overstepped. I do that a lot."

"It is alright," Velladriana answered. "No. I was not born a slave, not ... precisely. You see, to try and keep our people from breeding, the Therak'onian Lords who rule over Lyndria imposed the Law of the Second. Every second child is born a slave, pulled from their mother's breast shortly after birth."

"How horrible," Harper whispered.

"It is hoped that the prospect of losing the second will keep parents from wanting a third. But ..." Velladriana trailed off sadly.

"I am so sorry," Harper finished, her tone also deeply saddened.

"The Therak'onian may only hold some of us as property, but their oppression of all of us extends far beyond the slave caravans. At 10, most slaves are lashed together, ropes tied to our loops, to begin the long trek to Therak'on. They are luckiest, I think, taken far to the east to be whipped and defiled. Those of us who remain in Lyndria tend to the Lords who have strongholds there. We are forced to work the lands closest to the Great Rift, to live in the shadow of its horror. We are never allowed to see the families from which we were taken. That is the worst torture. To know they exist just outside of our reach." A single tear rolled down Velladriana's pale cheek.

"I am so sorry that you did not know your parents," Harper whispered.

"I did." She turned to Harper, anguish pouring forth from her eyes. "I was a twin ... I was the second. My brother was stillborn. The midwife who helped birth me quickly disposed of my brother's body. My mother never recovered from the pain of his loss. Her grief slowly consumed her. I lived as my parent's only child until I was 14. I lived free until the Therak'onian found the truth."

"How?"

"My father was chieftain of our clan. We were warriors once ... proud, strong. The Therak'onian sought his downfall. But to remove him without cause, even in a newly conquered territory under rule of martial law, would have been to incite rebellion.

"My mother's slow descent to madness gave them their solution. Her grief grew, and she would ramble about her lost son. It did not take long for them to find the midwife," Velladriana paused for a moment. "She suffered greatly before confessing. I was taken, but not before being forced to see my father torn apart by Lyndrian hounds for breaking the Law of the Second. With him died the strength of my people. With him died my freedom." Velladriana's ice-blue eyes burned with a cold intensity that matched their striking hue. "I know not what is worse: to know freedom and lose it or to never have known it at all." She took a deep breath. "And now, I am here, on a journey I do not understand. Led by a power I do not understand. In a land I do not know. I would run, but ... where would I go? For me, home no longer exists."

They rode in silence for a time.

"Thank you," Velladriana said after some time.

"For what?"

"For listening." It had been so long since she had a woman in whom to confide.

Harper's eyes welled with tears. "You're welcome."

They rode on. The sun was halfway through its decent in the western sky behind them. Corwyn would occasionally reach through his Heart's Eye, sending his senses out into the forest, feeling for the slightest hint of danger. Harper came forward and brought her horse beside his large stallion. He shot her quick glances from the corner of his eyes.

"I want to apologize," she said, her hazel eyes sincere, searching his. "You saved my life. I had no reason to lose my temper."

"No, no. I am sorry for this morning," Corwyn replied. "I had no reason to talk to you that way. You have lost much in aiding us. I am sorry for your loss. Your uncle seemed ... a good man."

"He was a great one," she replied.

Corwyn looked back at Velladriana. "How are you doing?"

"I am well," Velladriana responded distantly, her thoughts still on her previous conversation.

Corwyn turned back to Harper. "What of this Skinner's Outpost, then? If I remember correctly, are we not near the settlement of Northbriar?"

"You're correct," Harper said. "Be there in a few miles. The small town was completely deserted about two years ago. This far into the forest, it just seemed too remote for any families to be able to take hold and defend. Most of the people relocated to Silverton. Just because families couldn't flourish here didn't mean trappers and traders couldn't." She pointed toward some northern hills. "The Gale River passes nearby. The 'Post,' as the locals call it, is built on the swampy banks between the river and the old town. The Post is the sort of place where people who don't really want to be found bring their business if you catch my meaning?"

"Yes, I catch it well. We will be alert. Perhaps you should let Velladriana know to be cautious as well."

Smiling, she fell back with Velladriana. Corwyn was instantly on alert. People who didn't want to be found were just the sort of people with whom he was trained to deal. He hoped they could be about their business quickly.

It was just as Harper said. Within 20 minutes, they approached what looked to be a ragtag shantytown. Tents were set up with no random order throughout the trees. The people who camped there had clotheslines strung from one tent to the other, with latrine trenches and poorly constructed wooden outhouses on the outskirts of the tents. Various campfires burned, being tended by men who looked rough on their best days and downright scandalous on all others. This did not appear to be their best day, Corwyn noted.

The sounds of lutes and pipes filled the air, along with the scents of cooking mutton, venison, and a variety of smoke weeds. As they rode quietly by, the three of them were happy for the different smells since they masked the earlier stench of the latrine trenches and outhouses.

Everyone they passed turned a watchful eye on the trio. They did not stare too directly, however, as Corwyn's stern demeanor spoke of someone with whom no one would want to hassle. Besides, people like these would rather stab someone in the back than engage them in a battle of skills.

They rode now along a small dirt road past the ruins of the town once known as Northbriar. All the wood framed buildings were in various crumbling states of disrepair, having been destroyed either by fire or abandonment to the elements.

Just past the broken down homes, they passed the town's cemetery. Wooden grave markers had been worn down to nubs in most places, although there were several marble tombstones that dotted the dreary place. A rickety metal gate ran around the cemetery grounds, though it too was as ruined as everything else. Meant at one time to keep grave robbers out, it was no longer in any condition to keep anything at bay. It was not like there was anything there for anyone to take. These dead were of no interest to the living.

Corwyn could not help but notice how many grave markers there were. Many people had lived their last moments in this empty shell of a town. Sadly, the town was destined to share their fate and died along with them.

Just past the cemetery, the ground grew thick with tall grass, which marked rising moisture in the soil. Ahead, they were treated to the sounds of music, loud carousing, and the scents of burnt meats. Three haphazardly repaired buildings stood on the banks of a slow moving river. Large willow trees hung their listless branches around the buildings, obscuring them from a clear line of sight.

Each of the three buildings was worn down and ramshackle, though they seemed to be teaming with life. The central building had a wide, weatherworn porch wrapping around the exterior, which was missing several planks of wood throughout. Five steps led from the front entrance down to the ground level. All the buildings' roofs had several apparent holes, the shingles and thatch that remained appeared to be barely hanging on.

Many horses were lined up in front of each. There were three covered wagons in front, spread about the grounds. The grass here had been trampled to nothing more than mud from constant use. Strange, dirty looking men and women stood next to each wagon, hocking their various wares.

"Here love," an ugly, hawk-nosed woman with the beginnings of a mustache called to Velladriana. She held up one of the many jars she had set on a table in front of her wagon. "This unction is guaranteed to put some lead into the pencil of any man." She then looked Corwyn over hungrily. "Though by the looks of him, this one's got no need for that. Do you pretty?" She cackled loudly at that comment.

A fat woman in a dress that was far too small for her suddenly stuck her head out of the wagon's open rear door. Her black hair hung greasily around her face and four chins. She looked at Corwyn with the same hunger. "Oh! He is a pretty, isn't he? Like mine uglier though," she laughed. "The ugly ones last longer!" The two woman laughed all the louder. Along with several other people who heard the discussion.

"I've got something for that too!" cackled the first woman. They all laughed again.

The closer the three of them got to the Skinner's Outpost, the louder the sounds of laughter and roughhousing became. Harper and Velladriana rode to either side of Corwyn. Velladriana did not look the least bit frightened, while Harper actually seemed to be enjoying the surroundings. Her large smile was back on her face.

Corwyn led them to a small birch tree off to the side of the buildings and tied their mounts to it. Horse theft was frowned upon, even among thieves. Nonetheless, Corwyn tied the horses' reins to each other with intricate knots.

"Let us be about our business quickly," he said to the women. "The sun will be setting soon, and I want our business finished."

Harper pointed to the building in the center.

"That middle one is the Post."

It was the only one of the three that was two stories. Closer inspection revealed the word 'POST' written sloppily in white paint along the side of the establishment.

"That makes sense," Velladriana said, under her breath.

"We'll find who we need to talk to there," Harper concluded.

"This looks more like a tavern than a trading post," Corwyn said. He subconsciously checked the tightness of the bracers on his forearms.

"It is," Harper said. "Last place you can get provisions for a couple hundred miles if you plan on heading into the deep woods. Last place for a drink and a bed too. Though by the looks of all the trappers we passed, a bed probably won't be possible. I think they have all come out of the deep woods before the heavy fall weather sets in."

"That's fine," Corwyn said. "I trust sleeping in the forest far more than I do sleeping here. Come on."

With that, the three moved up to the Skinner's Post's swinging, saloon style front doors. They were attached by rickety hinges and hung slightly lopsided. The hearty noise of lute, song, and rowdy conversation poured out. In the waning light of day, the warm glow of the interior also spilled out. That warm orange light made the place look almost inviting.

Corwyn was about to swing the rickety doors open when a huge man launched through the entrance from the inside, ripping the doors off of their hinges. He crashed on the muddy ground outside. Corwyn, Harper, and Velladriana jumped back on the porch, just off to the side of the door. The huge man had been knocked completely unconscious and was lying face up, snorting in the mud.

An even larger man suddenly walked out. He wore dirty, grease-stained breaches, and a loose, dingy yellow shirt that strained to cover his massive frame. He was thick with rounded muscles. This large man's frame was workmanlike. He towered over Corwyn who himself was just slightly over six feet. He had long, dirty blonde hair that he wore down his back in a braid and a braided beard to match. The scars on his face spoke of more than one late-night bar tussle.

Corwyn and the ladies stepped forward, raucous laughter and talk spilling out loudly from within. The huge man turned and looked him over suspiciously.

"Here now," the huge man said. "We don't allow no weapons in the Post." He pointed a long, grubby finger at Taryn, strapped to Corwyn's back.

At that moment, two other men walked up the steps past the big man to enter the Post. Each of the men had an axe on his belt. One actually had a sword on his back.

"They carry arms," Corwyn said, referring to the two who had just entered.

"Them I know," the large man said, looking down as he stepped forward to loom over Corwyn. "You I don't. Go home, boy." He poked Corwyn hard in the chest once to emphasize his point.

Corwyn kept his composure. He understood that, to this large ruffian, he must truly appear like child who had snuck his father's sword from the house.

"You hear me, boy? Go home." He poked Corwyn again for good measure.

"You're new here," Harper said, stepping forward. Her large smile lit her face. "We've never met. Name's Harper. My uncle, Tornvil of Silverton, knows the owner, Old Sten. I used to play here some. From time to time."

"I don't know your uncle," the man said, his scarred face turning into a lusty smile. "But I wouldn't mind knowing you better." He then looked at Velladriana, who was still standing two steps behind Corwyn and Harper.

Velladriana kept her hood low over her head and looked at the ground.

"I wouldn't mind knowing you either," the man said, slightly licking his lips. He stroked his beard with his hand. He took a step toward Velladriana. "Here, let's have a look at you."

Velladriana became instantly guarded, her hands balling into fists. This was the sort of treatment she was used to from men. This was all she ever expected from them. Corwyn stepped between them, cutting the big man from getting to her. Corwyn looked at him, eyes simmering.

"We want no trouble," Corwyn said, trying his best to keep his tone even. "But I will not allow you to insult these ladies further."

"Allow?" the huge man asked. He erupted in laughter, throwing his head back. "Little boy, don't get between a man and his meat."

The man grabbed Corwyn's shirt at the shoulder with his enormous hand and shoved him aside. Corwyn was surprised by just how powerful the large man was, but he used that power to his advantage.

Corwyn stepped with the push, reaching his hand over to grab the man's wrist and thumb with his right hand. Putting downward pressure on the thumb, Corwyn simultaneously shot his left hand into the man's elbow, fully extending it. He used the momentum of the man's push against him, twisting with continued pressure on the man's thumb and elbow.

"Aargh!" the huge man exclaimed. He was genuinely shocked as Corwyn's pressure dropped him to one knee, his right arm completely extended.

Without stopping his momentum, Corwyn stepped through, removing the man's hand from his shoulder and twisted his arm further, putting tremendous pressure on the man's shoulder joint to the point of almost dislocating it.

"Let the little she-thing sleep in the mud!" someone yelled from inside. "I'll buy it a pint when it wakes!" A roar of laughter erupted from the interior.

Corwyn paused suddenly, thinking he had heard what sounded like a familiar voice. He slightly relaxed his grip on the huge man's wrist.

That distraction cost him dearly. The large man pulled his hand free and sprang up, launching a sloppy front kick that slammed into Corwyn's back. The impact sent him flying across the front opening and landed him face down on the far side of the porch.

More laughter erupted from the inside. "Looks like another she-thing will be sleeping soon!" the man from within yelled again. "Big Rogen's got another one."

The huge man, Rogen, was on Corwyn quickly. Spinning him over, Rogen clamped his hand around Corwyn's neck. Corwyn grabbed Rogen's hand, keeping it to his neck as he fired a kick with his right leg that caught Rogen on the side of the head. He swung his left leg up as well, hooking his legs together behind Rogen's neck.

Straightening his body, Corwyn used all of his body weight to hyperextend Rogen's powerful arm. Corwyn sunk this hold in deeply.

The powerful man grunted in pain but was still able to lift Corwyn from the ground, slamming him back onto the porch. The rotted planks cracked under the impact.

Corwyn changed his tactics, slightly dazed from the powerful drop. He released his hold and brought his legs in, firing his heels into Rogen's bearded chin. Rogen released the hold and fell hard onto his back. The porch rocked.

Corwyn got up and shook out the cobwebs, staggering through the doorway and into the common room of the Post. Harper ran up next to him and offered her support.

"Are you all right?" she asked.

"I am fine," he said, looking down. He was regaining his balance.

"Looks like the she-thing got the better of big Rogen!" the man said.

Several men suddenly stood, pulling out various weapons and turning to address Corwyn as he slightly raised his head.

"No worries, boys!" the man yelled, continuing his running commentary. "Rogen's back!"

Corwyn sensed the huge man behind him as Rogen stormed into the Post.

"You're mine, boy!" Rogen yelled, his blonde beard now saturated red from the blood spewing from his torn lower lip. Corwyn shoved Harper aside.

"AAARGH!" Rogen yelled, a shout that everyone in the room collectively took part in.

Corwyn turned to see Rogen fall to his knees, holding his crotch in his hands. He fell forward, hands still on crotch, and his head thumped to the floor. Behind him, Velladriana was retracting her leg, having firmly planted her foot into the huge man's tenders.

"Well, looks like my break's over," the other man said with a hearty chuckle. "I've got it handled, boys!"

The men who had drawn their weapons all smiled and lowered them. They shoved each other knowingly. Obviously, the man who spoke was good at dealing with disruptive presences in the bar.

Corwyn turned, seeking out who the person was. The room was smoky from all of the various pipes of smoke weed. The large fireplace was not well-ventilated and added to the haze. It was a large room, with many round wooden tables, each of a different make, set throughout. The bar along the back wall was old and battered, with bottles of spirits lining the rear wall and several people standing in front of it.

The room was full of people. From the rear of the room near the bar, a man with a goatee was approaching. He playfully patted an attractive serving wench in a low-cut dress on the rear as he passed. She smiled and gave a little laugh.

"Don't hurt him much," she said to the man, as he walked by. "He's a pretty one."

Corwyn moved forward, all expression draining from his face.

"Is he now?" the man asked, as he stepped up. Suddenly he stopped, looking as if he had seen a ghost. Slowly, he and Corwyn moved toward each other, stopping no more than a foot apart.

Corwyn looked the other man in the eyes. He had a young face, though it seemed weathered and wizened by hardship. His eyes were brown, with clear intelligence behind them. He was tall, at least as tall as Corwyn, himself, with a more densely built frame. The man was all muscle, a fact that his sleeveless black undershirt clearly displayed. He had tan skin and short, black, curly hair. He was wearing weathered, brown breeches with tall, black, leather boots of the northern style. They were very similar to Corwyn's.

"Eryk?" Corwyn asked, slightly hesitant.

"Corwyn." Eryk stated. He did not need to ask.

Corwyn was stunned, suddenly flooded with emotions. He had not seen his old friend, his closest of friends, since leaving for the Glass Tower. Hearing Rogen starting to stir, Corwyn looked over his shoulder.

Corwyn turned back to see his old friend's fist the moment before it smashed into his cheek. It was a powerful punch. Corwyn buckled and dropped to one knee, his eyes watering from the impact.

"Welcome home, old friend," Eryk said.

Rogen, now up on all fours, was looking on keenly as Eryk headed for the front door.

"Been a couple of years, Harper," Eryk said in passing. "Interesting company you keep." He walked out into the night.

Corwyn rose to his feet. He could taste blood in his mouth. He looked back at the door. His face would heal soon enough. His less than warm reception, though, would stay with him for quite a while.

16: The Beckoning

Corwyn and Velladriana sat at a table in the corner of the Post that Old Sten had cleared for them. The tall, round proprietor of the Skinner's Outpost had indeed known Harper and her uncle, and when she had found him in the building next door, he was happy to cast out some dregs that she and her companions might sit.

Harper was currently at the bar, talking with the loud, burly man about days gone by. Old Sten was extremely saddened to hear of her loss and told her that they could stay in his rooms in the liquor distillery next door.

The Post was a profitable, albeit illegal, business for Old Sten. It was far enough removed from the North Road, more than 35 miles, to keep any but those who knew about it away. The Aldaran soldiers at the garrison could not be bothered with policing trappers and hunters whose only real crimes were killing more creatures than were mandated by the king's laws. As such, the Skinner's Outpost became a welcome refuge for those who did their business just outside the scope of the law.

With the deserted town of Northbriar there to be stripped for wood and building material, Old Sten and the trappers had made a fairly nice community for themselves. It was a community of drifters and wanderers, not usually as busy as it was now. With the colder months steadily approaching, the men and women who made their livelihoods off of the forest were all gathered for one final meeting. Here, they could barter and trade, sell what they could, and get information on the comings and goings of the peoples to the south.

She and Old Sten spoke for quite a while. He kept laughing his wheezing laugh and rubbing his bald head with a dirty dish rag. His eyes were small, almost beady, but they shone with mirth and a lifetime's worth of experience. He looked quite old to Harper now, yet she could never recall when he looked all that young. Old Sten was definitely a well-deserved moniker.

After a long while, Harper returned to the table at the far corner of the Post's common room and took a seat next to Corwyn and Velladriana. They each had a flagon of mead in front of them, though neither looked like they had taken a drink. Thankfully, the plates of three-day-old mutton and stale bread had been eaten. That was something at least. Harper looked over at Velladriana, who was positioned in the far corner. Corwyn had placed her there so that, should anyone wish to harm her, they would have to go through him. After seeing Rogen's bloody lip and the way Corwyn was able to take Eryk's punch, no one in the Post had any desire to go through, around, or anywhere near him.

Corwyn merely sat and stared blankly at his drink, strumming his fingers slowly on the table. He was obviously replaying the earlier events of the evening in his mind. He seemed oblivious to all else other than his own thoughts. The reappearance of Eryk brought all his fears and remorse back to the forefront of his mind. He had left Eryk, so long ago, as he had his brother, Alek. He had also left Wren and Terridous to die.

"Here now," Harper said, pushing his flagon of mead closer to him. "The flagon may be dirty, but the mead they brew here is quite good." She gave a warm smile that Corwyn did not seem to see. She looked at Velladriana who only raised her eyebrows slightly. "Old Sten says we can stay here tonight." Harper was trying her best to change the mood. "I know you wanted to be off quickly, but he thinks it best if we stay. He says that there have been large packs of banshee wolves seen in the area. Can you believe that? This low in the Nortgard? Good sport for groups of hunters though. That is why they are staying. They go out in groups of eight or more, seeing what they can find. Dangerous work, but banshee fur is prized down south."

Corwyn looked up at Harper.

"Very well. We leave at first light," was all he said.

Harper put a gentle hand on his. He looked up at her. His cheek would heal quite well. Though it was a bit bruised now, it was not as bad as she had thought it would be. Harper had to admit Corwyn had a soft face. It was as if his expressions belonged to some tender poet, as opposed to a highly trained warrior. His brown eyes held a distant saddness.

"I am sorry I did not tell you about Eryk," she said. "I met him a few years ago when my uncle would bring me here. Eryk mentioned you, once or twice, his best friend who left to become a mighty Oslyn. I think he was just jealous that you left and he remained behind."

"I did not know that jealousy could hurt so much," Corwyn said, touching his bruised cheek carefully.

"It will heal," she said, her smile bright.

"Harper," Corwyn began, changing the subject. "The road ahead will be difficult, I fear. Perhaps ..." Corwyn paused, unsure as to how to continue.

"Perhaps, what? Perhaps I should stay here. Let's see, give up the protection of an Oslyn, one who singlehandedly killed a banderghal, by the way, for the protection of trappers and thieves. Yes, that is a splendid idea."

"You killed a banderghal on your own?" the deep voice asked as a tray of flagons, filled to overflowing with mead, was set down on the table. "Really?"

Looking up, the three of them stared at Rogen's huge frame. He was so large, the room seemed a bit darker for the shadow he cast.

"Really," Harper said, pointedly. "Killed him with that great sword on his back. Good thing he didn't pull it on you, or you might have been the second ugly ape he killed today."

Velladriana let out a little chuckle that seemed to surprise even her. She put her hand to her mouth, but her shoulders still moved in silent laughter.

Rogen seemed to be getting upset by the slight.

"We want no more trouble with you," Corwyn said, as he casually slid his chair back in preparation for an impending attack. He would have to put the huge man down swiftly. The force he would have to use to take down this powerhouse would border on fatality. He truly hoped it did not come to that. "You struck me harder than just about any man I have ever faced. I do not wish to feel your force again."

"Really?"

"Definitely," Corwyn continued, lacing his words with honey. "I see Old Sten is well-protected with you nearby." Flies to honey, as the old saying went. It was best to keep the big man calm, and flattery worked wonders in that regard.

"Yeah, well …" Rogan began. "That's right, he is." He cleared his throat. "Anyway, I am supposed to bring you these drinks and say …"

"Yes …" Harper said, playfully.

Rogen took another deep, steadying breath. "I am supposed to say sorry."

"We accept your apology, mighty Rogen, and honored we are for it." Corwyn gave him a very appreciative bow from his seat.

"I must thank Sten for bringing us these drinks," Harper said. She looked over at the bar at the far end of the room and waved at him. He returned her wave with one of his own before resuming wiping down the bar with the same rag that he used on his head.

"Wasn't Sten," Rogen stated.

"Who was it then?" Harper pressed.

"It was me," Eryk said, brushing Rogen aside and taking a seat next to Corwyn.

Corwyn's demeanor suddenly grew tense, as did that of Harper and Velladriana. He had no unease at preparing to put 300 plus pounds of muscle like Rogen in his place, but his best boyhood friend, that was obviously another matter entirely.

Corwyn and Eryk stared at each other in silence for some time. Finally, Eryk grabbed one of the flagons of mead. "Excuse me." He said, before downing the contents in one gulp. The belch that he released after he finished was loud and smelled of old meat, drawing a smattering of applause from some of the nearby patrons.

"Most people would say excuse me after belching, Eryk," Harper chided, though she had a wide smile on her face too.

"Really?" Eryk said. "After? Why in the great heavens would they do something like that?" Eryk grabbed another flagon and was about to drink when he noticed Rogen was still standing over them. "Is there something you have to add to this conversation other than your musky scent of armpit?"

Velladriana laughed again. She covered her mouth as she had done before, but she did not keep her laughter quietly reserved.

Harper laughed outright, pinching her nostrils closed as she did so. "So that is where it's coming from, aye?" She shook her head at Rogan in mock disapproval.

Even Corwyn smiled at that remark. He did not want to fully laugh though, for fear of making the large man angry. He did not want to undo all the work he had just put into calming Rogen down.

Rogen, for his part, merely laughed the comment away. He went on as if Eryk had not insulted him at all.

"She says he killed a banderghal all on his own," he pointed from Harper to Corwyn. "I seen one kill three men, once."

"I am sure he did," Eryk said, taking another drink. "He is an Oslyn, after all."

"Oslyn!" someone shouted from a nearby table. The word spread quickly about the loud common room. Like a wave of silence, table after table grew quiet until even Old Sten glanced over disapprovingly from the end of the now silent bar. The man who was playing the lute, and doing so quite badly, stopped with an off-tone twang. Several people got up hurriedly and made their way out the door.

"Here now," Harper said, standing. She produced two pieces of a white oak flute from her tasseled bag, screwing them together to make one long, delicate instrument. "Let's have a real lively tune to welcome the night. Come on, big man," she said to Rogen. "Clear me a space."

Grabbing Rogen by the hand, she led him by to the fire. Rogen merely glanced at four nasty looking individuals, who quickly rose and moved away without so much as a word, taking their drinks with them. He shoved the heavy table aside to make more room for Harper. She patted him sweetly on the arm.

"Many thanks, Rogen," she said. "This one's for you." Apparently, Corwyn was not the only one who knew how to use honey to attract the flies.

Rogen sat down on one of the now vacant chairs as she started to play. Immediately, her skill was apparent. She made the notes of the swift jig sound snappy and vibrant. Within moments, the low din of conversation began to pick up again. Some people even started clapping and stomping their feet. The sad lute player did not even try to keep up. He knew full well that he could not match her skill; so instead, he drank and clapped with the rest.

At the end of the bar, Old Sten smiled appreciatively. One thing that could get people's minds off of something as heinous as the law around these parts was a good song. Harper was definitely delivering that.

As the song played, Eryk turned to face Corwyn and Velladriana. He took another long sip, finishing his second flagon.

"I heard how Rogen treated you, lady," Eryk said, followed by another, albeit smaller, burp. "I apologize for that. He means well. You just have to keep his mind on the job at hand.

"And you," he turned, addressing Corwyn. "I never expected to see you around here. I'd call you ugly, but I already bruised your face. No need to bruise your ego too." He laughed at his own joke. Eryk found himself quite amusing.

"It has been … a long time," Corwyn said, once Eryk stopped laughing. "I cried every night I was away from home."

"You cried!" Eryk bellowed. "Ha! What a she-thing they made out of you at that tower."

It had been years, yet this was the same Eryk that Corwyn remembered.

"How have you been?" Corwyn asked.

"Well, that is a story that should take about a fortnight," Eryk said. "I got taken to Tanner's Landing. I got beaten up in Tanner's Landing. Just about every single day until I learned I had a wicked nasty one-two combination. I floated around from house to house, eventually ending up on the street."

"I thought you went to live with your grandparents? Why did you leave them?"

"I don't know how it works down south in the Glass Tower, but people die up here in the northland," Eryk said. "I didn't do the leaving. They left me … just like everybody else."

That cutting comment was not lost on Corwyn, but he was willing to let his friend vent his years of disappointment in any manner he so chose. He was just happy they were speaking.

"I am … I am sorry I left."

"Me too," Eryk said with total honesty. "I am too. But," he raised another glass. "Now you are back. In any matter, I know you didn't want to go, you just didn't stop it, either."

"I did not want to go; you are right."

"Anyway," Eryk continued, finishing another flagon and grabbing the fourth. Apparently, he had meant for these drinks to be brought solely for him. "Floated around till Old Sten found me. I snuck into the back of his trapper's wagon. Been with him ever since. But that is a whole other can of bait. Now, what are you about? And how is it you know Harper?"

"I am on my Testing. I came back because this is home," Corwyn said. "Then, well, things happened."

"Isn't that always the way? Well, I know about that. Things happen all the time, aye?"

"Have you seen Alek?" Corwyn asked. "Do you know where he is, or how life finds him?"

"I can't say that I do anymore," Eryk replied. "He got taken to Tanner's Landing too. That much I know. But I lost track of him pretty quick. Hard to keep track of people when you don't have a clue where you're going to sleep at night."

"I am sorry things have been so difficult," Corwyn said.

"Bah! Things are fine. I'm still around," Eryk said, taking another drink. "So where are these things that are happening taking you now? Or have you come back to grace us with your presence for good?" Eryk's sarcasm dripped with every word.

Corwyn honestly did not know what to say. He had to take Velladriana into dangerous territory, searching for something that may not even exist. He was about to speak when a loud yawn from Velladriana shifted Eryk's attention.

"Oh, sorry, lovely," Eryk said. "Corwyn's company obviously has this effect on women." He turned to look back to Corwyn. "You need to learn how to show a lady a better time."

Eryk stood up and offered Velladriana his hand. She reflexively pulled away.

"No worries, I don't bite … much," he laughed again. "Come on, you all can stay in my room. It's next door in the distillery."

"Really, we do not want to impose," Corwyn said.

"Look, I know Old Sten said you could stay," Eryk continued. "We already had your horses stocked. You have as many supplies as your horses can hold while still holding you. Don't worry; no one would dare touch them. I have seen to that. Besides which, I have two beds in my space. The ladies can have one. I'll take the other. You can sleep on the floor."

"I ... I ..." Corwyn stammered.

"You mean to tell me you plan to take two women, no offense," Eryk bowed slightly to Velladriana. "You mean to tell me you plan to take two women out into the Nortgard in the middle of the night with banshee wolves running around? I thought the Glass Tower was also a school?"

Corwyn inherently knew Eryk was right. He could not deny how incredibly tired he was. One night under a roof would do him well. Perhaps tonight he could get some much-needed rest.

"You have my thanks, Eryk," Corwyn said, with a small nod of his head.

"Let's be off then," Eryk quickly finished the last drink. Corwyn was amazed by the amount he had consumed. He barely seemed drunk at all. "I'll come back for Harper."

Corwyn and Velladriana followed Eryk out the front door. Before leaving, Corwyn glanced back and saw Harper playing merrily. Her music seemed to shield her from her loss. She nodded slightly when they made eye contact. With large Rogen enraptured by her playing, she was every bit as well-protected as if Corwyn had remained by her side.

Eryk led them around to the back of the distillery. The smell of sharp spirits and heart mead being brewed filled the cool night air. Eryk had their horses moved and retied by the river bank, that they could enjoy the water, murky as it was. Corwyn wondered how Eryk was able to untie his knot until he remembered that he, Eryk, and Alek had all learned how to tie intricate knots from his father. That long forgotten memory brought a smile to his face.

Eryk led them into a dingy room lit by an oil lamp on a small, beaten-up dresser. Surprisingly, though the room's furnishings were old and worn, Eryk kept the space very clean. What few clothes he had hung in an exposed closet, an extra pair of boots on the floor to their side. He had some weapons and loose chain armor set neatly in the corner. It looked like it was ready for him to jump into at a moment's notice.

Eryk removed the mace that he wore at his side and placed it carefully by his long bow and other weaponry. Corwyn saw the care he took with his items. It reminded him of the way he himself handled Taryn.

Eryk turned to face them. "It isn't much, but it is home. I am sure you Oslyn are used to much finer accommodations at the Glass Tower."

"Actually, this reminds me very much of the accommodations at the Tower. We did not have much more than a cot and a small nightstand."

"Well, then you should do just fine here. I'll go back and let Harper know where we are." He walked to the door, turning briefly. "Whatever the reason you are here … it is good to see you again." With that and a hearty belch, Eryk stepped out into the night.

"Your friend is … quite outgoing," Velladriana said.

"Yes. Yes, he is."

Velladriana lay down on the bed closest to her without removing her cape or hood. She stared up at the cracked ceiling, her eyes darting with her racing thoughts.

Corwyn removed Taryn and set it on the ground. Eryk said the floor, so Corwyn was not about to take liberties undue him and lie on the bed. Instead, he grabbed a small pillow; certainly Eryk would not begrudge him one of those and propped himself up near the entrance, with Taryn by his side. His position ensured that anyone entering the room would have to cross him prior to reaching Velladriana. He sat up for a time, trying to fend off his drowsiness. Soon enough, his fatigue proved too much, and his eyes closed, his chin slumping to his chest. His breathing was deep and even.

Velladriana did not fall immediately asleep, however. She sat up in the bed, looking over at Corwyn. Here was a man who had risked so much for her. He did not know her, and yet, he was willing to risk his very life to keep her from harm. She got up and sat near him on the floor. His presence comforted her.

Corwyn's heavy breathing informed her he was sleeping soundly. The thin walls did not keep out any noise. Along with some very heavy breathing and moaning going on in some distant room, she heard the commotion of the common room quite clearly. She also heard Harper's flute whistling into the night.

Harper was excellent at playing that instrument. Velladriana had even wanted to tap her feet a time or two when she heard it. That sort of blatant display of joy was unacceptable for her as a slave in her homeland, so she only entertained the thought for a few moments. Still, Harper was quite good.

Velladriana began to feel very removed; it was as if she were looking out of her eyes, yet her senses were drifting, sliding farther and farther away. Harper's music seemed to echo from a great distance. Energy, cold and powerful, started to fill her. She recognized this. A part of her was wrought with fright, wanting to fight this feeling off with all her strength. Yet another part of her welcomed it, embracing the sensation of attachment to such amazing power. She tried to push back the part of her that welcomed the feeling. When last this happened, she had apparently tried to pull out the souls of the two people who had shown her any kindness at all. She did not want to imagine what she could be capable of if she gave into this force now. She fought against it, but its grip was too powerful. She wanted to scream out, but she could not find her voice.

As if struck by a splash of ice-cold water, Corwyn awoke from his sleep. His Heart's Eye alerting him to some sort of danger, it was as if he heard Velladriana screaming in his mind.

"Velladriana!" He yelled. Taryn was in his hand in an instant.

Corwyn reached her just as a blast of blinding red light filled the room. He had to turn away from its intensity. When his eyes adjusted, he saw that Velladriana's body was completely tensed. She stared up to the ceiling with eyes that glowed with the same red energy that blinded him only moments before.

"The Pride has awakened. All that was shall be no more. All that is will be washed away. The time of the prophecy is at hand!" Velladriana spoke, but it was not her voice that Corwyn heard. It was the same ancient voice with which she had spoken at Mama Weaver's, speaking in a language that Corwyn did not know. Yet this time, he understood the words perfectly.

"Velladriana!" he yelled as he tried to shake her free. The moment he touched her, a tremendous rush of energy charged through him. It propelled him from her, sending him crashing into the far wall, knocking a hole clean through it.

Velladriana screamed. It was a loud, piercing scream that rang out with shrill vibrancy. Its ear-splitting resonance carried out across the water, through the deserted town, and out into the mighty forest. Velladriana convulsed once and collapsed onto the bed. The silence that followed her scream was as deafening as the scream itself had been.

A gray bearded man cautiously looked through the hole in the wall.

"Are you all right in there, Eryk?" he asked, greatly concerned.

Corwyn shook the cobwebs away from the power of the impact, forcing himself to focus. He stumbled back to Velladriana, checking her condition. She was unconscious but otherwise unharmed. This was the second time he had witnessed her power. In the darkness of the night, he knew the Necromancers were reaching out to claim her as their own. That he would not allow.

17: The Pride Lives

Terrid was about to leave the scrying room to get Ronulen at the very moment his master entered, bursting in with a wild energy in his eyes.

"My Lord," Terrid began.

"I know," Ronulen growled. "I felt it. The Pride lives. We have found her!"

Around the room, various Necromancers, all in their telltale thick, black robes, were at work on various devices. Two held pendants over a map of the realms that was 10 feet long. The surface of the magical map seemed to move as if showing the real world as opposed to a drawing. Both the pointed crystal pendants' sharp tips came to rest at exactly the same spot. It was east of their location, somewhere in the Nortgard.

An old crone of a witch, her face horribly scarred by some dark magics, lifted her gaze from a large crystal ball. The ball contained the wavering image of a deserted town near a river.

Other dark Magi, all with their own devices, from bones thrown into a metal cauldron to a Necromancer who was apparently speaking with an old, ivory skull, all turned to face Ronulen. Each bowed in respect.

"She is near, relatively," the old crone cackled. "In the northland, the Pride awakens. Just as prophesy foretold."

"How did you know, my Lord?" Terrid asked. Even here, in a room devoted to seeking her out, some of their greatest magical tools amounted to nothing.

"I have dealt in magics and made deals with beings the likes of which you could hardly imagine," Ronulen said. He walked over to the giant map. Images of the countryside, perfect in detail, shifted and moved, as if viewing the world from a great distance.

"She will be ours," he said to Terrid. "We will have her soon. How many of the Grimward did you release?"

"All, my Lord," Terrid said. "Their hunger drives them. They are eager for flesh."

"They will soon have that flesh and more."

Terrid walked over to the map and pointed at the section where the scrying crystals landed. "Even at the pace with which they move, it will still take several days for the Grimward to reach her."

"Then we shall assist them," Ronulen said, matter-of-factly. "She is there," he said, pointing. "In Northbriar. There is a cemetery there, is that not correct?"

"It is, my Lord," Terrid said.

"Prepare the room of summoning," Ronulen ordered.

"Immediately, my Lord."

"And prepare another avatar for soul transfer, I wish to speak to the great Lord this very evening. Surely, he has felt the Pride as well."

"My Lord, you are still weak, recovering from the last conversation," Terrid stated.

Ronulen suddenly turned on Terrid and extended his hand. A spray of black mist sprang from his fingers and shot to Terrid's throat. The mist formed a spectral hand of pitch-black energy that choked Terrid. It spread and entered his mouth and nostrils, choking him from the inside out.

"Leave us!" Ronulen ordered.

Without delay, all the other Necromancers in the room hurriedly left, none dared make eye contact with Ronulen. Terrid was convulsing now, his eyes had gone almost completely black. It was as if the entirety of his body had been filled with the dark energy. Just when Terrid was about to slip from the world of the living, Ronulen released the spell. The black energy dissipated into mist.

Terrid fell to his knees, grasping his throat with his hands and coughing so hard that he began to vomit and spit blood. Known as the *black soul*, very few Necromancers now living had mastered the spell Ronulen had just employed. Indeed, perhaps only one or two others, aside from the great Lord Cartigas, of course, were powerful enough to utilize the spell.

Ronulen approached and towered over Terrid who had crumpled into a fetal position. The spell tore apart his body and soul from within. Ronulen looked down with no remorse.

"Know this, if you ever comment on my weakened condition in front of anyone else, I will hand you over to the Grimward, and tell them to 'play' with you, slowly."

"Yes, my Lord. My apologies," Terrid rasped. He had seen firsthand what the Grimward did to their victims. Their 'play' was the stuff of nightmares. Indeed, they were the spawn of nightmares themselves.

"Now," Ronulen said, his deep voice rumbling. "Make ready an avatar for my communication with the dark Lord. I will speak to him at once."

"As you say, my Lord," Terrid replied, rising on shaky legs.

"We must move with haste," Ronulen said, turning to leave. "The time of the Great Reawakening is at hand. I will have her if I must find her myself. I am destined for it. I will be the sword that cuts this world apart."

Ronulen left the room. Terrid had never heard his master like this before. It seemed that the search for the Pride and the constant threat of the wrath of Lord Cartigas were pushing Ronulen to a fevered pitch. To be the sword, that was talk reserved for Lord Cartigas himself. Terrid wondered if the strain of finding the Pride was becoming too much for Ronulen.

Whatever the case, Terrid's job was to prepare another woman for the communication. Since women carried life within them, they were vessels powerful enough to carry death as well. They were far more suited to death magics as a result of their ability to make life.

Terrid left in a hurry to prepare one of the captured female slaves. He had no desire to do anything more to upset his master. Every glory that awaited them now rested on the retrieval of the Pride.

Their heavy footfalls thundering throughout the forest, the beasts moved like a force of nature. Their only purpose was to fulfill the whims of their masters.

Standing well over eight feet and easily weighing 350 plus pounds of sheer muscle, the beasts invoked fear at a glance. The magics that created them granted them unbelievable strength. It came at a cost however. They always hungered. They always craved. Torture was their pleasure. To inflict pain and misery upon any creature was the intoxicant that drew them comfort. The more they destroyed, the more they yearned to.

Their skin ranged from ashen gray to almost black where it had not been flayed away to reveal the tissue underneath. Skin that remained was stretched taut over their huge frames, attached by hooks that dug deeply into their underlying tissue. Their faces, once human in form, were now grotesquely exaggerated. Their foreheads were pulled far back and their eyes set wide apart, almost too wide. It gave their glowing red orbs, sunk deeply below a pronounced brow, extended peripheral vision. They were designed to

272

hunt. Their noses, such as they were, had been virtually ripped away, leaving just two holes. Their upper and lower jaws were lined with teeth filed to razor sharp points. Their faces were locked in a perpetual sneer of skeletal rage.

Continuing at their tireless pace, the beauty of the forest was lost to these huge beasts. They ran barefoot, where once they had the feet of men, they now stomped with cloven hooves, and hairy fetlocks grew at their hugely deformed calves. Bone spurs like sharpened daggers protruded from their shins and knees as well as their forearms and elbows. Long and curved, they extended well beyond their clawed hands, forming natural weapons that could tear through bone and metal with equal ease. Sickly yellow puss constantly oozed out. It gave off a suffocating stench of decay and would cause immense pain if it entered the bloodstream. Every facet of their beings was designed to enhance their ability to inflict punishment. Each wore heavy armor, breast and back plates of black metal, along with ridged armor to cover their legs. They were designed to be instruments of death.

They suddenly all caught the scent in the distance, still several miles away, of flesh. They smelled human flesh. Looking around the darkened forest, its vision perfectly clear at night, the leader changed direction, angling them more toward the southeast. They were on the path to their prey. Nothing or no one would stand in their way. Over a crest in the terrain, they saw the lights of the small farm and shouted with a killing lust. Their dark calls carried deep into the night.

At the farm, perhaps seven or eight separate scents of man awaited them, not to mention the beasts in the barn and fields. It was in their path, so they would feed. To keep their otherworldly pace, they had to feed. The leader roared again, picking up their pace. Each of the others answered. Their cloven hooves moving with renewed fervor at the anticipation of the impending kill.

For these humans, there was no hope, not against them. Theirs was a destiny of destruction. These snarling beasts were the image of how hideous and painful death could be. They were the messengers of terror, the bringers of pain. Beneath a darkened sky, they prepared to slaughter the innocent and feast on their remains. They were the Grimward.

He sat on his mount in silence; the darkness of the forest suited his mood and his purpose. He needed to retrieve the Lyndrian. He kept reminding himself that that was his only goal. Get the Lyndrian and all the gold her capture promised. To do that, he knew he would have to face the boy again, the one who took so much from him, including his pride. It was that encounter for which Dolver secretly hoped. He had picked up their trail skillfully. Assassins were master trackers. One could not kill if one could not find the prey. As poorly provisioned as they had been on their escape, he knew of only one place where they could restock while keeping the Lyndrian relatively hidden: The Skinner's Outpost.

Dolver had talked with some trappers earlier that night, along the encampment near the ghost town of Northbriar. They told him that they were in the Post when a boy bested some giant of a man, a sword arm they called Rogen or some such. Word was that the boy was an Oslyn. That explained much.

So, there Dolver sat on his dark steed, quietly hidden amongst the trees, staring at the light pouring out of the Skinner's Outpost. He had heard the scream earlier in the night. An almost otherworldly cry. It was as if its shrill tone had torn the very night air.

A strange quiet had descended over the Post after that. There was still activity, to be sure. A place such as the Post never got completely quiet, but there was a subdued restraint that seemed to exist now. He rubbed his hands together, warming them from the chill in the air. He would have to be cautious, but he would strike soon. He hoped the next shrill cry that filled the night would be the one that he forced from the boy.

Velladriana lay sleeping, exhausted by what had happened two hours before. Sleep eluded the others though, after Corwyn had recounted the tale. Corwyn, Harper, Eryk, and Rogen sat across from each other in Eryk's room. Eryk and Harper sat on the other bed, while Corwyn and Rogen sat on two rickety chairs that were brought in.

"So," Eryk said, after a time. "This is what you are doing here?"

"Yes," Corwyn answered. "This is it. Have you even heard of Mount Elderstone?"

"I have," Old Sten said, entering the room. "It is an old trapper's legend. It is a mountain you have to fly to get to. Supposedly, it is unreachable otherwise. Unless you can climb sheer granite walls, they say."

"Do you know where it is?" Corwyn asked.

"North of here, deep in the mountains," Old Sten replied. "Supposedly. Like I said, it's just a legend."

Corwyn produced the map he was given by Mama Weaver and handed it to Old Sten. "Does anything there look familiar?"

Old Sten scooted Eryk and Harper aside and stretched the map out on the bed. He wiped his brow with his mead soaked washrag. Everyone gathered, looking intently.

"Interesting," Old Sten poured over the map. "I recognize most of the landmarks. Here's the Gale River ... over there the Triple Lakes. But this," he pointed to the trails leading to the mountain marked Mount Elderstone, "this I've never seen." He looked up at everyone, wiping his forehead again. "I've skinned, poached, trapped, and hunted these woods and mountains for most of my life, young and old. I've been all about the area. It is the deep woods, sure, but I can't ever recall any of those markers or trails this map shows."

"Thank you," Corwyn said, defeated. He rolled the map up and tucked it away in his belt.

"What do we do now?" Harper asked, confused and deflated.

"Well," Old Sten remarked. "You can stay here, as long as you need. I can always use another good sword arm."

"We go on," Corwyn said, with finality. "I believe Mama Weaver. I believe in what I have felt. It is time for me to see more. We go on." The words Mama Weaver spoke suddenly rung clearly in his thoughts. He did indeed think too much. He was certainly seeing too little.

Harper gave him a knowing smile. It would appear that she had heard much the same things during her years with Mama Weaver as well.

"Your horses are set," Old Sten said. "You've got enough dried foods to last you a couple weeks in the wood if you know how to ration them. You won't feast, but you won't starve. You can be sure of that."

"It'll be dawn in a few hours," Eryk commented.

"We will leave at first light." Like it or not, Corwyn knew there was nothing for them but to continue.

Velladriana suddenly awoke. She was shaking with fear. Looking around, her eyes shone with panic. Immediately, Harper went over and put her arms around Velladriana.

"Shhh, it's alright. Everything is alright," Harper said, as she tenderly stroked Velladriana's head. Velladriana was so frightened that she did not even notice that her head was exposed.

"They have come," she whispered. "They are here."

Someone screamed in the distance.

Corwyn immediately reached out through his Heart's Eye, feeling into the surroundings. Everywhere, he felt death. Instinctively, he strapped Taryn to his back and drew the sword out of its sheath.

"We've got trouble!" he declared. No longer was there any confusion in his voice. He was now the Oslyn warrior, trained for combat.

Eryk immediately grabbed his chain mail and threw it on, also grabbing his long sword and mace. His sword had a pommel that covered his knuckles, with three wicked spikes protruding from it. A brawler's weapon, it seemed well-suited for him.

Rogen reached under the bed and pulled out a huge, two-handed sword. Easily five feet long, it would have dwarfed any of the others but fit the giant man to perfection.

"What is going on?" Old Sten asked, concerned.

Another scream echoed in the night, followed by a third. Suddenly, a skeletal torso smashed into the window, its empty eye sockets glowing with an angry redness. Another skeletal form smashed the other small window, trying to gain access by climbing through. A third and fourth smashed through the door, charging fearlessly ahead, glowing eyes locked onto Velladriana.

In an instant, Corwyn had slashed the first undead creature in half, reversing his strike and ripping the second one apart with his return swing.

Eryk yelled, as he smashed the skull of one of the skeletons trying to gain entry through a window. The undead creature went limp, the red glow in its eyes evaporating into mist around the smashed skull. With a roar, Rogen swung his huge blade down on the other skeleton, its head and torso virtually exploding with the impact.

The first two skeletal creatures were still moving and pulled their torn torsos toward Velladriana. Harper screamed, pulling her legs up onto the bed, next to Velladriana who looked on in fear. To her credit, she did not scream whatsoever.

Corwyn smashed one of the skulls of the crawling undead, while Eryk smashed the other, which made the torsos returned to their lifeless state. Before they could take account of what happened, more creatures stormed into the room. Undead at different levels of decay all tried to gain entry. They all were reaching their skeletal hands for Velladriana, trying to get to her at any cost.

"Crush the heads!" Corwyn yelled, as he tore Taryn through another skull, dropping it to the floor. "That is the only way to stop the enchantment!"

Old Sten grabbed a chair and smashed it over the skull of another. Two more came to take the first one's place. In the darkness outside, the sounds of shouting, screaming, and battle filled the night. One thing about the people who frequented the Skinner's Outpost, none would shy from a fight. Even if that fight was against the undead.

"Clear a path outside!" Old Sten yelled. "I'll be damned if I'm going to let them destroy the Post!"

"They are here for us!" Corwyn shouted, as he kicked one in the head, it still had some flesh and hair tufts on its skull. "We can lead them away if we get to the horses!"

With a roar louder and angrier than the first, Rogen dropped his shoulder and bull rushed the door, clearing five skeletal creatures from his path.

"There go the boney she-things!" Eryk yelled, with a laugh. He charged out into the night. "Follow me Sten. No ghoully beasties are taking the Post! Or my mead!"

"Come on!" Corwyn yelled, grabbing Velladriana.

Harper smashed a moving skull with her dradar and was quick to follow.

Battle had erupted everywhere. It was indeed a ghoulish sight. The dead, their burial clothes hanging on them in tatters, moved about in uneven strides. Off balance but strengthened by death magics, their glowing eyes hunted for their prey. Upon seeing Velladriana, all of them turned their attention squarely toward her.

"Get to the horses!" Corwyn yelled to her and Harper. He cut a path through the undead. His blade danced with practiced skill, every stroke taking a head with it.

Eryk fought with equal determination, though his style was markedly different. He was athletic and quick, but he used his dual weapons in much more of a rowdy, bludgeoning way. He would jump at anything that moved close, swiping his right-handed sword low while his left hand would smash high with his mace.

"Let's make the dead she-things dance!" he roared. Even these surreal ghouls did not seem to dampen his spirits.

Rogen was a bestial force all on his own. Whatever undead his sword did not crush, he would simply trample under his bulk. He had a portion of a skeletal torso, one arm, a sternum, and skull hanging on his back. The skull was biting deeply into his thick muscles, but he apparently was not aware it was there. He just kept slashing and stomping.

Two other walking corpses surrounded Corwyn as they neared the horses, the strength of their attack driving him away from Harper and Velladriana. Harper shouted in fear. She, too, was being attacked. She fended her skeletal attacker off with wide swings of her dradar. Velladriana picked up a large piece of wood and was swinging it as powerfully as she could.

Then, out of the darkness, rode a figure clad in black leathers. He rode directly for them, crushing any undead that got in his path under the weight of his dark horse.

Corwyn thought for a moment that another ally had arrived when he suddenly recognized the face. It was the man from the saddlery!

Dolver covered the distance quickly, having caught sight of Velladriana. He had hoped to sneak in and kill the boy in his sleep, stealing away with the Lyndrian in the stillness of the night, but this Necromantic diversion worked just as well, bringing his target out into the open. He reared up near Harper and Velladriana, his mount's hooves knocking the undead away and knocking Harper to the ground.

"Velladriana!" Corwyn yelled, as he made his way towards her.

Velladriana recognized the dark rider as well, swinging her makeshift wooden club now at him for all she was worth. Dolver easily batted the wild swing aside and clubbed Velladriana on the side of the head. In a swift motion, he grabbed her and hoisted her easily up and across the pommel of his saddle.

"NO!" Corwyn shouted. He tore through the undead in his path with desperate energy.

All the creatures had their sights set on Velladriana, so Corwyn's anger-fueled charge only cleared Dolver's path.

Dolver heeled his mount into a full gallop, launching a dagger at Corwyn as he did so. Corwyn managed to deflect the dagger with Taryn, but the blade still bit into his chest and knocked him to the ground. Dolver sped off into the night. He was sure that would be the last of the boy warrior. He rode with abandon, trampling anything, living or dead, that got in his way.

With their prey speeding off, the undead turned and began their shambling, stiff march toward the direction in which Dolver had taken Velladriana. They were interested in only her.

Eryk had reached Corwyn in moments. Seeing the dagger strike true, he thought it certain he would find a new corpse to join all the ones that had arisen from the ground. When Corwyn got up, Eryk's laugh was one of both relief and sincere admiration. Corwyn had only a slash where there should have been a protruding dagger. That dagger was lying off to the side.

"So it seems you take a dagger to the chest as well as you do a punch to the head!" Eryk yelled. "Means I'll have to hit you all the harder next time!"

Corwyn completely disregarded Eryk as he quickly mounted his stallion. "Ha!" His horse erupted and took off into the night after Dolver and Velladriana.

Corwyn gained on them quickly. Even with a head start, Dolver's mount was no match for the speed and quality of Corwyn's horse. Looking back over his shoulder, Dolver was shocked to see the boy closing on them. That dagger should have been the end of him.

Dolver rode as hard as he could in the moonlight, but Corwyn rode harder. Dolver drew a short sword he held in his left hand.

Corwyn closed the gap and swung Taryn for Dolver's back, which caused him to slow greatly. Dolver blocked the swing easily. The two combatants exchanged several more strikes at one another, the sound of steel on steel ringing loudly into the night. Their pace was still brisk but far from a gallop.

Velladriana stirred from unconsciousness. Corwyn suddenly did the last thing Dolver had expected. Leaping from his horse, Corwyn crashed into Dolver and toppled both of them to the ground. Dolver grabbed hold of Velladriana, yanking her down with them. She regained consciousness just in time to feel the impact of being slammed to the ground. She groaned, but she was coherent.

Corwyn got to his feet as quickly as he could. It was never an easy thing, being knocked from horseback. The two steeds cantered a bit further but with no rider pressing them, they stopped a short distance away.

Corwyn stood and brought Taryn forward. Dolver got up and armed himself with a short sword in one hand and one of his knives in the other.

With that, he struck out, slashing his sword high while bringing his knife in a lower strike. Corwyn dodged the attacks and reset himself, but he felt … odd.

"You are good, boy, I'll give you that," Dolver said. "But the woman is mine."

Corwyn steadied himself.

"Matter of fact," Dolver smiled wickedly. "You're mine, too."

Dolver swung his short sword in two very skillful high attacks. Corwyn blocked both and deflected a follow-up stab, but he was a step sluggish. Corwyn seemed to be slowing a bit.

"You will not have her," Corwyn said, his breath becoming labored. He could feel himself sweating profusely.

Dolver laughed, striking out again. Again, Corwyn blocked the attacks and kept his guard, but he was weakening. Dolver's first series of attacks would have felled any lesser fighter.

"You obviously have some strength to you, lest my dagger would have stopped you back at the Post." Dolver slashed, and Corwyn deflected the strike but stumbled a bit with the effort.

"I wonder," Dolver continued, sizing Corwyn up. "How long that strength will help you against poison?"

Corwyn knew the truth of it. He glanced quickly down to where the dagger had struck. The slash the dagger had left burned intensely.

Velladriana, still shaken, had managed to get to her knees. She was still working to bring herself back to clarity.

"I heard a rumor that you were an Oslyn, is that true?" Dolver asked. "Never killed one of those before. I'm sure it feels quite nice. Though I'll know that in a minute."

Dolver struck again. Corwyn blocked and backed away. He could feel the poison taking hold. Immediately, he calmed himself, extending his senses through his Heart's Eye, slowing his breathing and pulse.

Corwyn got very still, his shoulders slumping slightly. He let Taryn fall from his grasp, its hilt landing atop his right foot.

"I think after I am done with you, I'll have myself a little taste of the Lyndrian. It is the least you owe me." Dolver moved forward to deliver the killing stroke.

"You will not harm her," Corwyn whispered, as Dolver brought his blade high.

"Corwyn, no!" Velladriana managed to yell, as she saw Dolver swing at the defenseless Oslyn.

As the blade came down, Corwyn kicked up his foot, caught Taryn's hilt in his hand, and blocked Dolver's

283

incoming strike. With all the strength he could muster, Corwyn brought Taryn around and drove its razor sharp tip into the chest of a completely surprised Dolver. Corwyn pushed the blade into Dolver until he drove it to the very crosspiece that guarded his hand. He stood and held the assassin up an inch from his face. Dolver's eyes were wide with shock in their final moments of seeing.

"You will not harm her," Corwyn whispered again. "Under the sight of the gods, this I swear."

Corwyn pulled Taryn free from Dolver's chest. The assassin fell to the ground.

Corwyn dropped to one knee. Velladriana was by his side in an instant, laying him in her lap. Corwyn looked to her with profound sadness.

"I ... am sorry," his breathing became very labored. "I fear ... I will not see you to Elderstone." He spoke softly. "My road with you, I am afraid, is at an end."

"No," Velladriana said, tears welling in her eyes. "No, it is not."

She produced the small vial of magical elixir that Mama Weaver had given them. Without another word, she uncorked it and poured it into Corwyn's mouth.

The elixir was sweet, almost like liquid chocolate. It was also powerful, causing him to splutter. Corwyn took a deep breath, letting his lungs take in the cool air of the night. His eyes brightened a bit, and he looked on Velladriana with extreme gratitude. "I thought we had lost that elixir at the saddlery."

"I removed it from the pack when I dressed your wounds at Jundin's Pass," she said, smiling. "I thought it best to keep it close at hand, just in case."

She had a beautiful smile. Corwyn liked to see it. He started rising to his feet, feeling reminiscent of how he felt when he awoke at Mama Weaver's hut.

"That is indeed a powerful elixir," Corwyn stated. "It is a shame it had to be used on me."

"There is no shame in that," Velladriana said. Noticing that her hood had fallen back, she covered her head.

Velladriana no longer looked down, choosing instead to stare straight into his eyes. They looked at each other for long moments, faces bathed in the pale glow of the moon. Corwyn's senses reached out into the night, feeling the dread death magics and the creatures they animated. He looked away, bringing them back to the situation at hand.

"We are still in the thick of things," he said. "Even now, I sense the undead homing in on our location. They will be on us quickly."

It was true. Velladriana was still being hunted. The speed of their horses did not carry them far enough to be safe from their pursuers.

"Can you ride?" Corwyn asked.

"Yes."

They moved quickly and retrieved his horse. He placed Velladriana in his saddle, climbing on behind her. They would move more swiftly if he controlled the stallion than if he would have placed her on the assassin's foreign mount. "Hold tight, and fear not."

Velladriana held the reins tightly as they rode back to the Post. Corwyn's arms around her made her feel safe, indeed. They rode hard, once again riding past the dozens of undead that moved through the forest after them. The stallion outpaced any pursuer, and they found themselves quickly back at the Post.

Harper was on her horse, riding forward when they arrived.

"We were about to send out a search," she said, smiling as they approached.

285

"We are not out of it yet," Corwyn said, as he helped Velladriana from his steed and onto her own mare. "We need to ride."

The dead were returning. Velladriana's presence was a beacon to them. From all around the dark woods, the sounds of movement could again be heard. Corwyn heeled his stallion around and faced Eryk.

"Eryk," he began.

"Go!" Eryk called. "We'll hold them off here."

Corwyn wanted to say more but knew they had to move. Many people had died when the town once existed. Each of their corpses seemed to have risen now, all with the intention of reaching Velladriana.

"Ha!" he yelled, launching into the night, Velladriana and Harper close on his heels.

Behind them, the undead continued to follow.

"Ha! Time to die again!" Corwyn heard Eryk yell in the distance.

As they rode off, Corwyn wondered if he would ever see his friend again.

18: The Road Ahead

Mama Weaver sat in her hut, delving deeply into a tome of magic. She had several glass containers on the table in front of her. Each one contained a liquid of varying thickness and color.

She would occasionally look at them and mumble a spell, making one of them bubble and then settle quickly down. She poured over the tome, searching for something, anything, that she could use to help Corwyn, Velladriana, and now, sadly, Harper, complete their task.

She glanced up again at the liquid containers, and her jaw dropped. She could feel the blood drain from her face. One container that was formerly clear was now blood red.

She lifted her hand, waved it over the container, and whispered a small spell. A soft fan of white light extended from her hand to the glass. The liquid bubbled but remained red. The fan of light faded, and she dropped her hand. She had enchanted the liquids to warn her of impending danger, of evil drawing near. She knew full well what the redness meant. It was far worse than she had feared.

"Heaven help us all. The Grimward are unleashed."

"Nooo!" Dolthaia awoke in a cold sweat. She breathed heavily, regaining her composure in the sobering moments that follow a nightmare.

Reese looked at her from across their small campsite, his armor making him appear as nothing more than a shadow cloaked in the darkness of night. He was concerned about her, yet he made no move to get close.

Crispin, for his part, rolled onto his side, barely registering a shudder at the loud cry. The weight of their journey had fatigued him into exhausted unconsciousness.

"Are you all right, little one?" Reese asked.

Dolthaia seemed embarrassed. "I am ... fine. I should not have yelled. It was just a dream after all."

"Dreams reveal truths that are very real. There is no shame in acknowledging them."

"There is no use in giving in to them either," She readjusted the roll she used as a pillow and gazed at the stars.

Reese smiled in spite of himself. *Too true,* he thought. "Do you wish to speak on your dreams? It helps ... sometimes."

"Lately, it is always the same dream. Dark hands, Necromancers' hands, reaching out for me, pulling me toward them. I don't know how I know they are Necromancers. I just do," she shuddered, clearing the image from her mind. "As I said, just a dream."

"Rest now. No hands will find purchase on you tonight. That I can assure you. It will be dawn soon, and we will have to ride."

Dolthaia closed her eyes. A short time later, she was breathing as heavily as was Crispin. The fear of returning to that nightmare could not overcome the aching exhaustion in her very bones.

Since rescuing them from those child killers, they had ridden hard for a few days, just barely missing being captured several times. Their pursuers were relentless, giving chase at every turn. So there Reese sat in the starlit night, not daring to light even a small fire. He looked long at these unique children, wondering why fate had dealt them into his hands. As if on cue, Crispin farted and startled himself awake just long enough to roll over.

"Bloody hard ground ..." Crispin mumbled his complaint, falling quickly back to sleep.

Reese closed his eyes, knowing full well he would be hard pressed to get any rest. The dawn would be upon them soon, and with the rising sun, their pursuers would come once more.

Corwyn, Velladriana, and Harper raced as rapidly across the forested terrain as was safe under the moonlight. The patchy clouds often obscured the moon, forcing them to slow their pace. From behind, the distant moans of the walking dead were constantly hounding them. The Necromancers were very powerful to have extended their reach to that degree.

As they rode, Velladriana thought on the unimaginable power that apparently resided in her. Having lain dormant most of her life, she now felt it coursing through her soul, erupting more and more frequently. It was awakening, and it was taking greater hold. Somehow, though, this all felt right.

The dawn was almost upon them. It would arrive in less than an hour. The little that Corwyn knew of death magic told him they would have a measure of safety but only a small amount. Their pursuers were relentless and powerful. He had to get Velladriana to safety. That was all that mattered.

He thought back on his most recent encounter. He was unaware of taking Merril's life, but he was fully aware when he ran Dolver through. He looked down at his hands. They still carried the stain of the assassin's blood. He thought somberly. *This is what it means to live the life of an Oslyn.*

289

He had already learned much, and his Testing had only just begun. Was he truly ready to live the life of an Oslyn? He hoped so. Only time would tell if he could wear the weight of his duty with the conviction he knew he needed. To be an Oslyn meant to be true to one's duty. His duty was to Velladriana. In that capacity, he knew he would have to take more lives.

They rode on at as quick a pace as they could for a long while. Soon, the first rays of light brightened the distant sky. Corwyn reached out with his Heart's Eye, searching the surroundings. The feel of the dead was growing weaker. However, in the distance, some riders were gaining ground quickly and nearing them.

"Harper, Velladriana, someone approaches," he said, calm but concerned. He pointed up ahead. "You two, move into that copse of trees. If they continue to follow, I will engage them here."

They went into the trees and sat in wait. In a short time, they saw two riders. Corwyn could not believe his eyes, a smile coming across his lips. Riding hard were Eryk and Rogen.

Corwyn came out from his hiding spot and went to them.

"Ho!" Eryk yelled when he saw him. "It was a hard pace you set. Impressive in the dark of night."

"How did you find us?" Corwyn asked.

"We saw the direction you were headed, then just followed the dead bodies," Eryk said with a laugh. "The beasties took off right after you, leaving all of us behind. So we packed up and followed," he laughed again. "You should have seen the little dead she-things collapse at first light. They just froze and dropped. A blind man could follow that trail."

"Easy enough to find, that is sure," Rogen added.

Velladriana and Harper emerged from the trees and joined them.

"What about Old Sten?" Harper asked.

"He is salty as ever. I told him I would be damned if I was about to let the Oslyn here ride off and leave me to clean up bloody dead bodies," Eryk spat for good measure. "Besides, a nice vacation in the deep woods would do us some good. Aye, Rogen?"

"Good it would ... in the wood," Rogen laughed aloud. Eryk joined him.

"The road will be dangerous. I don't want to put you in that kind of trouble," Corwyn stated. Though he was more than happy at seeing his friend.

"I don't see how you can stop us," Eryk spat, again for good measure.

"Neither do I," Rogen stated.

"Besides, now we can have a chance to catch up. If I find you boring, we'll just leave you behind. Aye, Rogen?" Eryk gave a sly wink.

"Anyway, looks to me like you could use an extra sword or two with the company you keep," Rogen added.

He was right. Corwyn knew they would need all the help they could get in the weeks to come. He really had nothing else to say that would prove reason enough for them to go back. Eryk and Rogen could make up their own minds and had clearly done just that. Corwyn smiled. "Then you are both most welcome."

Riding forward, Corwyn shook both of their hands.

"Welcome, indeed," Harper added, with a smile.

Velladriana gave a nod of acceptance.

"Excellent!" Eryk yelled. "So where are we headed?"

Everyone looked at Corwyn, who was now the leader of this band of travelers.

"North," he said, with all the confidence he could muster. "We journey north."

As the first light of dawn illuminated the road ahead, the five companions set off in search for answers and the mystical Mount Elderstone.

Thank You For Your Purchase

If you enjoyed this tale of adventure with Corywn, Velladriana and the other characters from the Shield of Destiny series, please recommend it to your friends and family. Also, please take moment and go to Amazon.com and write a review. Great reviews mean everything to the modern writer. Once again, thank you for your purchase and see you for book 2, *TIDES OF WAR*!

Social Media

Visit Shieldofdestiny.com to learn more about this mystical tale of Adventure, Magic and Heroes.

Like me on Instagram @CharlesDCarpenter
Like me on Instagram @Ski.terJones
Like us on Instagram – @Shieldofdestiny

Made in the USA
Middletown, DE
11 July 2020

12453071R00166